THE IMMORTALITY OF DISCIPLINE

I0614987

E.L Discipline

Andrea Johnson Books Publishing

Check Out Other Books by E.L Discipline

The Seduction of Discipline
(Book #1 in The Seduction
of Discipline Series)

The Importance of Discipline
(Self-help, inspirational)
(motivational guide through life)

Discipline's World
(Book #2 in The Seduction
of Discipline Series)

To see more of E.L Discipline books, visit the publishing website at:
www.AJBPublishing.com

<u>Acknowledgements</u>

Would love to thank Marissa Jade from VH1's reality tv show 'Mob Wives' season 6, also appeared on VH1's 'Celebrity Big Brother', hit tv show 'Law & Order,' 'Gossip Girl,' and 'The Good Wife.' In addition, she's been in films such as Will Ferrell's 'Elf,' and Modeling internationally as well.

Would love to thank the photographer Michael Zinn for the shots. His website is www.photozinnthesis.com. Would love to thank him regarding these phenomenal photos he shot.

Would love to thank the fans of E.L Discipline, whom have been patiently waiting for this juicy horror thriller to drop.

Would love to thank Andrea Johnson Books Publishing, www.ajbpublishing.com. They have an absolutely amazing team. My motto for 2018, "let's fucking win!" Those whom haven't read any of my projects prior, be ready to be blown away. This book here is mouth opening and eye popping. Once you open this book and begin to read chapter by chapter, page by page, you will never be able to put the book down. You will say to yourself, "what happens next?" There will be more projects in the works, for the near future. Keep a look out for more works from E. L Discipline, coming soon....

The Immortality of Discipline

Cover art designed by Andrea Johnson Books Publishing.

First published by Andrea Johnson Books Publishing. 05/22/2018
6565 N. MacArthur Blvd, Suite 225 Dallas, TX. 75039
www.Ajbpublishing.com

ISBN-13: 978-0692113486

ISBN-10: 0692113487

Contents

Look deep into my eyes and witness the possibilities.
- E.L Discipline

Prologue

(Previously, in Discipline's World....)

I felt a change in the air. It was a warm summer night and all of a sudden, the air changed. I stopped moving, Precious looked at me frantically. "Daddy, what's wrong?" I started looking around. "Something is not right. I feel off balance tonight. You feel that?" She looked around. "What do you mean?" She asked. I stared at her. "There's a change in the air."

   Precious never questioned my instincts. She never called me crazy. She knew if I said something was off, then something was off.

   "Look, forget it. Let's keep moving baby girl." I grab her hand and we begin walking a little faster. Suddenly, I hear a noise, like a branch fall or something. "You heard that?" She looked confused and scared. "No Daddy, I didn't hear anything," she said. Damn, was I going nuts? I mean was I just hearing things that were not actually there to be heard? Fuck! What the fuck? "Let's keep moving baby."

   Suddenly, something jumped from behind us and bit the side of my neck. I don't know what it was, but there was a major struggle with some sort of being. Precious got involved, and I began feeling weak. She was struggling with this thing, this creature, as it threw her to the ground and stood over her. I found the strength to run over to them and fight this being off. It was a woman! Such strength and speed. I yelled out for her.

"Precious!!! Get away from her!" I lunged towards the woman and she ran off. We were in an area where people could hear us from afar, but no one was around. I grabbed Precious' limp body. The damage that was done! She was motionless and not responding to my calls for her.

"Precious!! Wake up baby!!" I lifted her body and held her in my arms. I walked with her for not even a mile when I collapsed and dropped to the ground with her. The bite on my neck got worse and I was extremely weak. I yelled out, "help!!" We were in an open area now. I reached for my cell to dial 911 and the operator answered.

"911, what's your emergency?" I lost consciousness, but my phone remained on.

Someone found us and brought us to the hospital. They were saying Precious didn't make it. As for myself, the doctors were asking themselves, "how can this man's body be so cold, but his heart remains so warm?" They couldn't figure it out. "What's this bite mark on his neck? There are two deep bite marks. I know this sounds weird but, it looks like fangs." The other doctor said, "no, it has to be something else. You're talking about fangs, like vampire? Supernatural or something?" The third doctor said, "let's figure this out."

All three of them went into the other room to discuss the situation and how they were going to move forward. The woman or creature that attacked myself and Precious in the park, came back. Shit, I thought she was coming to finish the job but instead, she helped me out of there.

"These mortals are not about to work on you." She said insidiously. I looked at her with mixed emotions. "Who are you? What are you? How do you know Precious or myself? Where is Precious? Where the fuck is Precious??!" I said, as I demanded an immediate response. This woman was some supernatural shit! We teleported out of there. She took me to her lair.

"I'm going to teach you how to do that one day." She said to me. I thought, 'what the fuck is going on here?' I then said, "fuck that, where is Precious?" Then I attempted to swing at her, but she was too fast, and I was too weak still. I managed to catch her by the throat, but she just shrugged it off, smiled and tossed me across the room.

She said, "silly mortal! You can't overpower a vampire! A supernatural," she assured me of this, that a mortal was no match for her. "Ugh," I brushed myself off, I then asked her. "So that's what you are?" She raised her hand and I was lifted up off the ground. She brought me to her with just her eyes and hands. "Have you ever been handled so violently by a woman before? Perhaps not, but I am not a woman. I am a God. I chose you because you have such extraordinary powers for a mortal. Precious didn't seem to possess what you have. She didn't seem to be the way you were. This is what I saw, and what was left of her." She opened her hand, and it was the jewelry I gave Precious to wear at all times. She handed it to me. "In all of my two thousand plus years of life, I have never witnessed a human like yourself. You impressed me. I am going to mold you into the most elite supernatural to ever exist. You will stand by my side and we will take over this world......"

Chapter 1- Do You Not Want Immortality?

(Present Day)

"Like I was saying to you before, do you want mediocrity, or do you want immortality? I think it's a rhetorical question, you and I both know exactly what you want to be, and what you want to become. We both know what you want to possess. The type of man that you are already, would never settle for less than great." She said all these things to me as if she was reading my mind.

I was extremely confused and all I could think of, was that I wanted Precious by my side. Where was she? As I remembered, we were attacked by this bitch in the park. I carried her, and then I attempted to get us some help. But, I was very weak and began to lose consciousness. The doctors said to me, that someone found us. All I wanted was Precious by my side, not this bitch, this weird bitch that sounds like she is talking such non-sense that if non-sense slapped her in the fucking face, she still wouldn't know what she was preaching. I spoke forcefully....

"I demand some answers, now!" She smirked at me, "what would you like to know, Mr. Discipline?" I shook my head at her and stared at her flatly. "Like that, that's what I mean. How the fuck do you know me, and my name? How do you know us? How do you know Precious and I? Where is Precious? How and why did you attack us? How did you know where and when to find us? Why did you find us in the first place? Is there something you wanted from us in particular?"

She said to me very candidly, "I will answer all your questions in due time." She paused for effect than continued. "I was Precious' slave."

I cut her off. "What the fuck? What the fuuucck! The whole time? This must be a dream, right? No, it is a damn, fucking nightmare!" She quieted me, "shhhh, look, I was Precious' slave and I knew it was because of you why I was dismissed, okay? I was intrigued about your entire lifestyle in BDSM. I wanted to be a part of it, and when I was dismissed, I had plans to kill you both, feast upon you. Yes, I took the form of a human, you pathetic humans, and your weird emotions. However, I was intrigued more by you, sir Discipline. You were someone that was magical in my eye. Someone I believed to be extremely gifted. How can a mortal have so much power? Power over people, power over a woman? Power of women in general? Powers so strong, you can feel it. Feel that power a mile away?

Look, in all my 2256 years of life on earth, I have never witnessed a mortal man do the things you do, or possess the power over such people, without mere threats, physicality, money or damn near magic. I had to know more, that is why I asked your beloved Precious so many things about you. But, who the fuck were the two of you to think you both could dismiss me? Not me, not Alexandria!!"

I thought to myself, 'who the fuck is Alexandria though?' I didn't know her for shit. Who knew who she was, from a hole in the fucking wall? So, who the fuck was she? She then continued.

"I traveled the world, I have been in all these different eras. I have traveled through the past, present and future. I've seen things, that would make mortals cry, fear and run from. I have seen wars, hurricanes, earthquakes, the hate. I have seen how mortals have hate and joy for one another. But, the hate is stronger than the love, and the love has diminished. I have seen the eras change with the women, how they speak, dress, behave towards men, compared to the earlier years. I have seen the jealousy with humans. Jealousy, how they take each other for granted. They cut each other's throats and step on each other's shoes, just to move to the top of the mountain. They call me a monster. No, your humans are the monsters. The loyalty, the honor is non-existent with mortals. They speak loyalty, but they do not practice it. They speak love, but, they know hate is in their hearts.

I see through their souls. I read their eyes. I read their minds. They think with their flesh, they are slaves to their own pathetic desires. They are weak, and they enjoy being weak. I despise mortals, but the irony is, I took a form of one. I took the form of a mortal as I have the ability to shape shift, and I learned your lifestyle from your sub, Precious. I wanted to see and witness how this woman serves you. Why she serves you? A powerful man. Hahaha." She laughed ferociously. I asked her…

"You really count all the years you are on this earth? I mean, you are immortal, correct? At some point don't you just say, 'fuck it,' and you lose count?" She laughed at me. "Hahaha..." I don't know if she was laughing at me, or laughing with me, because I should be the one laughing at her. I then continued….

"Plus, you speak of all this, and I believe you are merely a hypocrite." I said to her, forcefully. She grabbed me by my throat and lifted me off the ground. My feet dangled about five inches off the floor.

"You have such balls to speak to me like this, I can kill you at any given time. I can snap your neck with one hand. You are not a complete vampire yet. Yes, I changed you, but your transformation is not complete. You are still weak."

I struggled and gasped for air. "I'm not afraid to die, and if that was your intension, you would have done it on many occasions. In the park, and instead of rescuing me out of the hospital, you had your chance there as well. You could have finished the job you started. You must need me, that's why you won't kill me. But, you are a hypocrite, you talk about all this and, yet you take life."

She dropped me, and I grasped my neck and began to cough a few times. Damn she had a tight grip. She then said...

"I picked the right person. Most people would not speak to me as you speak to me. You do have some balls, Discipline. Big balls. But, if you may know, and I will elaborate on your concept of you thinking I am a hypocrite, I do not take life. You see, I merely give life. I eat what is weak to survive. Your mortals eat chicken, and all of those are meats and animals. Your mortals are the worst kind." Shit, she had a point here, I could not argue with this woman mentally. I could not beat her physically either, well at least, not yet. And for the time being, perhaps I must comply until I can come up with an adequate plan to get out of here, or better yet, take her out indefinitely. For the first time in my entire life, I feel as if I must comply to a woman's ways, well for now. Just until I learn what I can learn to possibly destroy her. Come on, even though she is supernatural, she is still a woman. She must have a weakness, right? I will expose that weakness to my advantage and that will be her downfall, she will make a mistake, and I will capitalize when time permits. I was feeling faint, she said to me...

"You must feast. That is the only key to your survival, and with that said, you require blood!" I looked at her as if she possessed two heads. "Oh hell no, I am not doing what you do." She stared at me like I had no choice. You can either hunt, or be hunted. This is survival of the fittest. If you cannot feast for yourself, I will provide you with blood."

She grabbed a hold of me, and we teleported out of there. We ended up in the woods somewhere, she then ordered me to remain where I was. "Stay here!" She swiftly attacked this deer she saw, I didn't even see it, that shit was so fast. She came back to me. "Here, drink this."

I drank the blood of the deer. This shit was fucking crazy. "Ugh!" I almost gagged. She laughed, "you will get used to it." It tasted like adamantium, a hard metal or some sorts. It was like I was licking a silver spoon or a silver knife or something. It was terrible. My stomach began to hurt. "You fucking do this shit every day?" I asked her.

16

"What a terrible life to live, what a terrible way to live."
She didn't allow me to drink anymore….

"Shut up!!" She said to me sharply. However, I did feel
a little bit stronger, as if I was gaining my strength back.
She said, I would get used to it, but will I really? Perhaps
it's not a conscious thing, you get used to it because it's
easy to get used to, and you require it for your survival?
Like the difference between eating healthy and eating
foods that are not so healthy. I mean broccoli didn't taste
well as a child, but prior to this transformation it did, yet
again broccoli never changed its taste. Hmmmm?? She
brought us back to her dark lair. She said to me...

"That will hold you for now. However, in order for you
to be full immortal, in order for your transformation to be
complete, you must feast upon real human blood. And
quiet frankly, I don't believe you are ready for that yet."

I said to her, "no, I am not ready to do what you do, but
if you had to throw me to the wolves, I would probably
come back leading the damn pack!" She smiled, "oh,
you're so confident. What if you expose yourself, and you
are taken out?" I stared at her confused, "how would I be
taken out by a mortal? Aren't we physically quicker, more
alert and stronger than they are?" I questioned her. She
then said to me in response to my question...

"You must know how to attack. You must know how to
feed. You must know the human body, in order to attack it
efficiently, and adequately. Three ways to kill someone
(which are certainly interrelated): take out their nervous
system, take out their circulation, or take out their
breathing. The larger the vessel, the more you bleed out.

The faster you die. If a killer wanted to kill someone by blood loss, they would need to go for the carotid arteries in the neck. The carotids would be most effective, so long as the killer cut both of them — the brain would be most rapidly deprived of its blood supply (and ability to get rid of CO_2), causing the victim to pass out, and without immediate care, the brainstem will die. If you lose oxygen more than 4 minutes, the brain is damaged to the point that it cannot recover, but other body organs can be revived even hours later. Eventually, all body organ systems fail, and that is officially when you are dead, but it all depends on how you define death. Now, you see if you break your neck, your brain has no way to tell your heart to keep beating, or your lungs to keep breathing, etc. It has been known for people with a broken neck to survive, if they had immediate attention. They basically fix your skull still with a screw-like device in the hope that the break may heal. This is why you are told to never move someone with a head injury. You can make things worse." She continued with her dark and descriptive education.

"It also depends on the cut. If the jugular vein is cut through , the blood will gush out. It's not the size of the fangs, it's how you bite. It depends on the cut. If the trachea is cut but the arteries are not, cause of death would be from lack of oxygen and aspiration of blood. There are a number of small vessels in that area which would begin to bleed, and the blood could end up flowing through the hole in the trachea and into the lungs, where the effect would be similar to drowning. This is actually a much more survivable scenario than the other possibility.

The most likely cause of death from a cut throat is blood loss. The carotid arteries run up the sides of the neck, before splitting to supply structures outside the skull as well as the brain."

She painted a very vivid picture for me.

"You can feel where the arteries are, by palpating the pulse in your neck. These are high pressure, large vessels. If they are severed, the person will bleed profusely. Blood flow to the brain is compromised and unconsciousness quickly follows. As the blood loss continues, eventually so much is lost that the heart stops."

This is what she explained to me. I was highly intrigued. I then began to pick her brain and proceeded to change the subject.

"So, you were trailing Precious and I the entire time?" She answered my question with a smirk. "Yes. You see, I can shape shift, therefore I was everywhere you both were. Whether I was a fly on the wall, a dog in the street, an innocent looking mortal slave woman, I was there. I was keeping track of you both. I didn't know you had that many tattoos; legs, full back, stomach, chest, arms. Wow!! I find that very sexy for a mortal man. I have traveled through different centuries, and I have never encountered a man like you. Such pain you must have endured." Her eyes seemed to glow with heat, at the thought of my torture.

"You've probably seen plenty of vampire movies, and possibly read books, those are all myths. I don't know what you've heard or may have seen about us. But, I am one of the most elite supernatural you will ever encounter or hear about. First, I cannot be killed with a stake to my heart. Sunlight doesn't affect me, as I can shape shift and blend in the day time as well, if I choose to. I can be beheaded. Burned to a stake. We are cold blooded; a vampire's body essentially dies. It no longer conducts heat the way a mortal person's body does. The body temperature rises or falls to match its surrounding environment. The reason they seem so cold is, in comparison to what you would expect from a normal human being."

She slid a pale slender finger along my skin, to illustrate this.

"A normal human has an internal body temperature of about 98.6 degrees Fahrenheit. When you touch the human skin, it doesn't feel that hot because the heat dissipates as it extends out. The limbs lose a lot of heat along the pathway, which is why people often get cold hands and feet first. With a vampire, there is no internal warming of the body, so their skin will feel cold in comparison to a normal person's skin. Plus, more vampires are active at night, when it is considerably colder out, and have no way of warming their bodies the way that humans do.

As for the pale skin, this follows as a similar logic. The skin is only warm and flush with color because of the blood circulating through it. If you were to cut off the blood flow to a part of your body, say an arm or a leg, you would see it turn pale and possibly blue-ish within a matter of a minute or two."

I stared at her and nodded my head. "That's pretty accurate." She then continued. "The fresh blood supply, having recently been oxygenated, will be warm and red, but that will quickly cease without the heart and lungs pumping fresh blood to the skin. A human turned into a vampire would become pale within minutes of turning. This would only intensify over years with no sunlight. You have had blood; however, I didn't give you a human being's blood. That will make you stronger.

Vampires are magically reanimated human corpses, which are inhabited by the spirits of the deceased person, and who closely resemble the living human they once were before their transformation. Vampires feed and survive on the blood of the living, typically on that of humans, and they can also transform other humans into more of their kind by sharing their own blood with them. Vampires are one of the many known supernatural species."

She was spitting so much knowledge to me, and I was like a sponge. I just absorbed everything that I could, because I know that it would one day come in use to me, all I needed to do was be patient.

We went out and it was very late, the night was extremely beautiful. We saw a couple sitting down. She was ready to swarm in, when I suddenly grabbed her by her hair. Her fangs came out at me, and she hissed.

"Why are you stopping me?!" She questioned me. I stared at her in her eyes. "Not them, let's go for someone else, that's a couple for goodness sakes, having a night out." She shook her head. "So, what's the issue here? We need to feast, and you need your strength. I want you to complete your transformation, so you can be King. Stand by me and rule. I understand you have feelings, and you still have your human feelings that play a factor here. But, that was in the past. You're a savage now. More than you ever were. You are a cold-blooded killing machine. You just don't realize that yet. And at the end of the fucking day, it's either you or it's them. You let dinner get away, you don't survive."

She tried to leave my side, and I walked in front of her. "I said, let's look for someone else. This couple is young, and they have their entire lives ahead of them." She laughed. "You are a cold-blooded killer now, as I will reiterate, fuck your feelings, check those feelings, the younger the better. Your integrity one day, could get you killed, Discipline. Plus, young blood, taste the best. And the more you feast, the more alive and young you appear. You absorb their blood and energy. But as you wish, future King, we will find another candidate to devour."

We found a man walking alone, and she said, "there you go, go get him!!" I hesitated, "what the fuck you mean, 'go get him?' I have never done this before and I can't just go and feast on a man. What if he's strapped?"

She looked at me confused. "Strapped? He doesn't have on a backpack, or strap around his waist." I then had to elaborate, she didn't understand the lingo. "I mean, what if he has protection, a pistol, a knife, etc?" She smiled in response. "Those things can't kill you. They might sting, tickle or itch, but they won't kill you, so don't worry." She shook her head, "you just want me to do all the work, huh?

Okay, that is fine." She swiftly attacks the man, left him injured, then turned towards me. "Here, now bite him and suck. Go for the side of his neck."

I did as she instructed, it was weird. I must admit, at first it felt strange, the metallic taste, but then it was like electricity coursing through my entire body. A million stars exploding in my mind all at once. It's like nothing I have ever felt before. It was fucking amazing, wrong, but so fucking amazing. All I can think about now is……I want to do it again.

Alexandria said to me, "now, your transformation will be completed." We left from there in a flash, like literally in a flash, teleporting out of there. She then continued to educate me. "A vampire in transition is neither truly living nor truly dead, until they make their choice to either complete their transition, or to abstain from feeding and ultimately die. Every regular vampire who has ever existed, is descended from those of their kind known as the original vampires. Who unlike the real majority of vampires, where they were turned not by dying with vampire blood in their system, but who were instead transformed using a spell that was cast performing dark magic. However, the ritual that resulted in their transformation does have similarities to how normal vampires are turned, in that they had to consume blood, before being killed while that blood was in their system.

After the original vampires awakened in transition, they fed on the blood of another human from their village and were officially transformed into the world's first true vampires, from which all other vampires were created. Their blood possessed mystical properties. People have been dreaming up horrible monsters and malicious spirits for centuries. The vampires, seductive, 'undead' predators, are one of the most inventive and alluring creatures of the bunch. It's also one of the most enduring: vampire-like creature's date back thousands of years, and pop up in dozens of different cultures. Every vampire was once a human, who, after being bitten by a vampire, died and rose from the grave as a monster. Vampires crave the blood of the living. The living whom they hunt during the night. They use their protruding fangs to puncture their victim's necks, as you've seen me perform this a few times. And I did it to you, in order to change you. We as vampires, can still walk among the living as undetected. We can be very attractive, highly sexual beings, seducing our prey before we feed. Some of us can shape shift as I have demonstrated to you prior, as a bat, or wolf, in order to sneak up on a victim.

Vampires are potentially immortal but have a few weaknesses. Holy water, garlic, fire, stake through a heart. But, you and I would not die like this. Beheaded, yes, fire, yes."

I am listening to Alexandria very closely, and she fucked up already, she made a mistake. She has told me way too much information, especially what our weaknesses are and ways we can be killed. I then asked her a question, "so, what have you done to Precious?" She shook her head, "you're still concerned with the one whom was holding you back? And your other subs whom were holding you back from your full potential? You were destined for greatness, and your submissive, Precious was holding you back."

I disagreed. "You're wrong, she's made me a better man!" Alexandria laughed. "Was that what you were trying to be? Regular? Have a family? Get married? That's not in your cards. You were born to be great. And you don't have time to be around regular people. Do you not know what you have and who you are now?"

I was extremely persistent, "I want to know where she is, and what happened to her." She just stared at me squarely and then said, "I'll make you a deal. If you can feast five times a day, for a week, on the seventh day you and I will have a race. If you beat me, I'll allow you to see her. If you can accomplish this, you can see her."

I didn't believe her, I don't trust many people, therefore I asked, "so, what's the catch?" She smirked, "no catch, I am a woman of my word, this is a challenge for you, since you hate to feast, and it will test your abilities in the end to see what you have, and if you have what it takes. What are you willing to give up to actually see her? What are you willing to become to see her?"

I mean, this was a win-win situation for her anyways, she wants me to strive, she wants me to be molded into this vampire king that she desires me to be. So I can rule by her side. But, if I can't beat the odds, I will not get what I want. Fuck it, I will deal. Yes, I will deal, for now, I then agreed to her terms.

"Okay, we have a deal."

I was training every day. Just as she wanted, I feasted every day; five, sometimes six times a day. She taught me, "in order for you to kill a body, you must understand and know the body. How it operates. How to kill it. Not just with your fangs. With everything of you." She taught me, "lions don't go after buffalo, or zebra and bite right away. They use their strong build. They wrestle them down, paralyze them if need be, then they feast." This woman made great sense. I impressed even her. I was fucking swift, powerful and stronger after each feast. Stronger than I have ever been. It was exhilarating. It was invigorating. The seventh day had arrived, and it was time to put all my hard work to the test.

"Congratulations," she said to me, "now when we race, we will race for eight miles. The finish line is at that end." She pointed with her index finger, and when I gazed, my vision was enhanced, that I saw down eight miles, where the finish line actually was.

Chapter 2- When Hunger Takes Over

"I'm going to make this fair and square as well." She said. "I will not be teleported either. When I say, 'on your mark, get set and go,' we will both be taking off and may the best woman, or man win." I interjected, "I will." She laughed, "I like your confidence, but, I don't think so."

She put her hand out, so I could shake it, but I just kept staring straight ahead.

"Okay then," she said, and she put her hand down, as I left her hanging. "So, on your mark.......get set......" and before she could even say, 'go,' she took off. Left me in a pile of dust, literally. I looked to my left and she was gone. I started to run as well. Faster than a Lamborghini, faster than a jet, faster than a silver speeding bullet. I have never felt this type of speed before. It was amazing. But I needed to remain focused. I have a goal at hand, and I must accomplish that shit.

Damn, that bitch was fast, nowhere in sight either. I was so frustrated, thinking perhaps she crossed the finish line already. "Think, think, think, Discipline, where is she? Find Alexandria, find Alexandria," I kept saying to myself. I focused so intensely on her, as I ran and was shutting my eyes as I raced, and suddenly she appeared in my head exactly where she was. Instantly, I teleported right behind her, she was steps away from the finish line. I grabbed her by her hair, and tossed her behind me, and firmly swung her through a tree, and crossed the finish line. Thus, winning our fucking little bet. She came back and met up with me furious, some leaves from the tree were still in her hair.

"You cheated!" She yelled out with such ferocity. I smirked, and then said, "first of all, you said we would take off after 'go,' and you didn't say, 'go,' you just took the fuck off. Then, second, there were no rules to this, because you didn't make, nor mention any damn rules."

She was even more furious. "You teleported." She sneered. I began to laugh. "Like I said, you said the things you were not going to do, you never said they didn't apply to me. Plus, I should be given a pass, I don't even know how I did that. I don't know how to even teleport. It just fucking happened."

Suddenly, she smiled. "I'm proud of you, because you learned a few things today without me actually teaching them to you. And you are a cut-throat beast and will do whatever it takes to win. I'm mad, I hate losing, but I am a woman of my word. We will go see your Precious one.

She grabbed me, and we teleported out of the woods, we went to go see Precious. We were suddenly outside of a funeral home. "What the fuck are we doing here?" I asked her.

"You wanted to see your Precious, here she is." She said to me. I was confused as to what was going on here. It was a bunch of people dressed in black, and a huge coffin, being lowered in the ground into a big hole. "Precious can't be here, I don't see her. You are a woman of your word, you said we would go see her." She pointed, "look harder, think harder, she's there." I looked harder, deep inside my mind, and I saw her. She was in the coffin. I yelled out for her.

"Precious, open your eyes, Precious!!!" Alexandria stopped me swiftly. "She cannot hear you, I made it that we are unseen and unheard here, we are in a different form of creatures to everyone else around us."

I then placed my hands on her throat, I got a major boost of adrenaline. And now she was gasping for air. "What the fuck is this? What the fuck is going on here? Is this a fucking joke or nightmare?!" I asked her.

She placed her hands on my shoulder and we teleported out of there. I looked around to see where we were, my eyes wandered up and down, left and right, and because of the distraction, she was able to get my hands off of her throat and breathe. She exhaled.

"You're definitely stronger than ever now, a lot stronger than I ever expected you to become so quickly." She said, as she was short of breath after saying this. "I can see the hunger in your eyes, the anger in your tone, the power in your hands. Precious is gone and you must understand this. In this moment, now your life has changed for the better. You are not what you used to be. Sometimes, when you strive for greatness, you will lose people in that journey. Because, they are not on the same level as you. And when you are not on the same level as those few, it makes them very uncomfortable. Look, I realize you hate me right now.

29

But perhaps one day, you will thank me, because I've taught you plenty."

She gasped for air once again. "You had a major adrenaline boost." I moved closer to her, I was furious, I didn't think about what she was, nor what she could do to me, and quite frankly, I didn't give a fuck….

"So, what the fuck happened to her, you killed her? You killed Precious, didn't you?" I accused her viciously. She stared into the ceiling and said, "I mean, if you want to say it like that, fine, but I like to put it, 'I set her free.' She was not built for this."

I ran towards her swiftly, and she put out her hand and her palm was facing me. I stopped immediately in my damn tracks. I looked all around me, as I had no idea what was going on in this moment. Suddenly, with a slight gesture, she lifted me up off the ground as her hand raised up. Her movements controlled where my body went, and my limbs contorted to her hand directions. She waved her hand forward and I went flying into the wall. Fuck, that hurt, I definitely needed to learn that shit from her. Damn, that was painful, but I admit, that was also cool.

I needed to learn all her powers and then some. I needed to be the fucking best. I needed to be great, not just good, not just better than her, I needed to be the most dominant and elite there ever was. In the meantime, I need to play nice, until I can master my powers to the fullest, and maximize my potential to its most optimal level. She became angry.

"You fool! Are you forgetting whom you are dealing with? Must I remind you of this?" I was compliant with her ways. "No need to remind me." I said to her. She insisted that we leave, and we move forward. "Come, there is more I must teach you if you will stand by my side as king and rule this world."

Oh, I had every intention of being the fucking King, but I had no intentions of being her King. We headed out of there and went back to her dark lair.

"There is so much I must teach you, and you must learn. I mean, you were a beast prior to me, and now I am going to make you into a monstrous and unstoppable force to be reckoned with, believe me. First and foremost, you must understand that you cannot be seen as a vampire, you cannot be exposed as a vampire. Understand, you must not let your guard down at all to the living. You must constantly transform so you are not what is expected. People fear what they do not understand, they hate what they fear. And when they hate what they fear, they will kill what they hate.

You are stronger than any mortal, however, you do not know if there is another supernatural in your mist. But you will learn how to sniff them out, how to feel their energy level, and how to scan your surroundings well. You must learn to adapt to your surroundings, and that will always give you an advantage over your victims. Learn your victim's weakness quickly, and you will always have the upper hand, whenever you feed."

This was some major information I was keeping mental documentation of, as she was speaking. There is much she is saying that I feel will be useful down the line. Then she went on to tell me…. "There are hidden powers of an immortal, and I will tell you and show you them now….."

Chapter 3- The Hidden Powers Of An Immortal

"Okay, so there are things an immortal can do that human beings cannot, and we have gone over that. There are some hidden super powers that I possess that regular vampires do not." She said. And then I was intrigued.

I said... "So, like what type of powers are you speaking of? What type of these hidden powers that you possess that others do not?" I was fucking persistent. Remember, I wanted to soak up as much information and ability as I could, to be the most Dominant and powerful supernatural, even more powerful than she. I had plans to find out her weakness, kill her, then find out where Precious really was. She still hasn't told me what she has done to Precious.

She gazed at me squarely, she paused then she went and continued to tell me more. "Well, there's a lot I do, and I will teach you little by little. I want you to be so great, and rule by my side as King, so we can take over this pathetic planet, and these mortals."

I laughed in my head, this bitch was crazy, I will let her believe that, but, I had no desire to rule by her side. However, I will be patient, I will play the game, until time permits me. And then I will take her out. She then continued.

"First, what you did in the woods, that allowed you to catch up to me, is called telekinesis and telepathy. Teleporting your body or an object to a desired location. I can move objects with my mind, or myself to a place, if I can think of it hard enough, it will happen. Anything you put your mind to, you can accomplish. Allow me to demonstrate."

She lifted her hand upward, and the table lifted from the ground. That shit was amazing. Then she shut her eyes, and then lifted herself off the ground, like she was flying. "My goodness," I said, astonished. "How can I learn this?" She fucking levitated. Then I told her, "I must learn this, I want to know this immediately!"

She laughed, and then she said to me, "you have all of this in you already, which is why I chose you. The only thing is, you need to be able to master them. If you don't know what type of power you have, you can never practice them. And if you can't practice, you'll never master shit. Just like a muscle, it's all about the repetition. Think of the object like a woman, you crave to control her, you need to control her. Now, move the object with your mind, and every fiber in your body will move and levitate that object…."

I squinted my eyes and was focusing on the table, I made it rattle, but I didn't lift it up. "Not bad." She said to me, raising an eyebrow as she was impressed. "You will get it, practice will make you perfect. And perfection will come with repetition. When you do levitate the table, learn how to control, balance and maintain its elevation. It will require discipline and I believe you can do it. Another thing is reading people, their mannerisms, their little tendencies, and their characteristics. Every supernatural is unique. They all have their own hidden and special gifts.

You probably have plenty, but you just haven't seemed to reach beneath the surface yet and dug them up. I bet you have plenty."

I was persistent to know, therefore I asked her, "what are my hidden talents? What are my hidden gifts as a supernatural?" She placed her palm out, and it was facing me. It was an obvious command for silence.

"You will learn when the time is right. Look at you when we were in the woods, you wanted to win so bad, you dug deep, and you fucking discovered one. All by yourself, without my assistance. This is how I know I chose the right man. You will be more powerful than a God, if you play your cards right, Discipline. It will happen in your time of need, it will happen. Be patient, it will occur when you least expect it. You possess unknown powers. Great powers, use them to your advantage. Your energy is so strong, it is so potent, it is so magnetic. I can feel it."

I gave out a sarcastic laugh. "Ha-ha, how am I going to use these great powers to my advantage, if I have no idea how to obtain them from within me?" She then began to educate me. "You can do anything you want with patience and discipline, Mr. Discipline!" She assured me. I knew she was right on the fucking money, I just wanted it right now, at this moment. Working on someone else's time, I was not fond of that. And patience? Yes, I needed to work on having more of that. And I'm always used to being able to obtain things when I wanted them, therefore it was a tad bit frustrating. She then said to me, "*The true measure of a man is what he does with power.* You can also obtain energy and some powers from the human living beings that you feed upon." I asked one last question. "What about another supernatural? Can I absorb her or his abilities if I am physically engaging with them? Can you feast on another vampire?"

She didn't answer me, she actually did gymnastics around the question. "Why are you asking me this? Why do you want to know?" She replied stoically. That right there gave me the answers I needed, and I made sure I kept a mental documentation of that as well, for myself. Perhaps, this could be useful down the line. I then stroked her ego a little bit....

"Well, you're the teacher, I am just the student, and I ask these questions because obviously, I want to learn, and you want me to thrive. Am I right?"

She then said to me, "yes, Discipline, you are correct. You see, we of the 21th century are confident that vampires could not really exist. But then, most of us are never forced to think otherwise. For a number of people, the concept of vampires becomes a critical and often lifelong concern. To live with, love, or befriend a real vampire is to encounter a set of problems which may demand expanding the boundaries of one's accepted reality. To come to terms with being a real vampire, oneself is to face a lifetime's karmic challenge. You're probably thinking, before all this, 'give me a break, real vampires?!" I nodded my head in agreement to her. She then continued....

"Sure, there are some pretty weird people out there, but all they need is a good therapist. Yes, there are people who take on all the trappings of a gothic novel: dressing in black, claiming or pretending to be "vampires" in the supernatural sense, wearing capes, sleeping in boxes, even getting their teeth capped. There are more frightening people who seek to torture or kill animals or human beings in order to gain power, emotional release or sexual thrill, and who sometimes call themselves, or are called, 'vampires.' But most of these individuals are troubled people who have been attracted by the cultural myths about the vampire: supernatural powers, because they feel powerless. Overwhelming sexuality, because most of them have sexual issues and no true relationships. Immortality, because they fear aging and death.

Individuals like these are the most recent 'explanation' for humanity's persistent belief in vampires. But beyond and behind all the folklore, the psychological theories, the role playing, even the traditional spiritual assumptions, lies the real truth about vampires. There are many aspects to the vampire phenomenon, and they would require several books to fully explore. One aspect of vampirism which frequently troubles magical, spiritual and other small groups, the most common form of vampire, is found among living people who share with us the benefits and disadvantages of physical existence on this plane, yet are not quite human."

She paused deliberately at this, then continued.

"These people appear on the surface to be somewhat eccentric members of society, yet their outward idiosyncrasies only hint at how different they are from those around them. Each of us incarnates for a lifetime with a certain way of relating to the physical world through the vehicle of our physical body. A vampire is a

person born with an extraordinary capacity to absorb, channel, transform, and manipulate "pranic energy" or life force. And also has a critical energy imbalance which reels wildly from deficit to overload and back again. This capacity for handling energy is a gift, but the constant imbalance of one's own system is the cause of the negative behavior patterns and characteristics which may be notable about a vampiric person."

Chapter 4- Sexual Desires Enhanced

Alexandra patiently commenced in the breakdown of my education. "Real vampires do not necessarily drink blood, in fact, most of them do not. Blood-drinking and vampirism have been confused to the extent that for the average person, a vampire is defined as something that drinks blood, such as a 'vampire bat.' But when we look beyond casual assumptions to the details of common beliefs, we find something quite different. Throughout both folklore and literature, there is an understanding that vampires require energy or life force.

Many old folktales accept that vampires suck blood, yet never describe this actually happening. The victims slowly decline and waste away, and the survivors assume that some evil fiend is draining them of blood. They know that the Bible says, 'the blood is the life', and anyone who was losing their life force must be losing blood. Yet, in many instances the vampire's 'attack' does not even involve physical contact. In others, it is clearly sexual energy which is exchanged.

Yes, I said you need blood, but it's really the energy you absorb. That's what fuels you and keeps you looking younger and stronger. Fresh blood is the highest known source of pranic energy, life force. Human beings have practiced blood-drinking for many reasons throughout history but drinking blood alone does not indicate that a person is a vampire. Only real vampires can directly absorb the pranic energy in fresh blood, and for this reason, some real vampires are attracted to blood and find different means of obtaining it. However, it is a rare vampire who cannot absorb energy in much more subtle ways. This is the mechanism that causes real vampires to inflict harm on others, and themselves, if they fail to recognize what is happening and do conscious work on transforming their inner natures."

Her gaze focused on mine, and watched me intently as she spoke.

"Vampires are no more likely to be either malicious or spiritually aware than the general population, but without awareness, they can spend their lives making themselves and others unhappy and will continue to incarnate in this pattern until they take some serious action to change it. There are a number of external symptoms of vampirism, but it is important to realize that some of them are found in ordinary human behavior.

Real vampires are identifiable partly because they have a majority of the symptoms, not just one or two. But more significantly, real vampires are distinguished by a certain quality to the energy. While anyone reading a description of the symptoms and behavior patterns might find a few that apply to people he or she knows, or even to himself or herself, real vampires have a way of standing out vividly to everyone who interacts with them. It is like, their energy is so strong, it Dominates everyone else's. They step into a room, and all of a sudden you take notice. You begin to fix your hair a little bit, a woman can check her make up. A male may straighten up his tie. There are few people who do not know at least one vampire. Physically, vampires are usually 'night people,' on a biochemical level. They have inverted circadian rhythms, with body cycles such as temperature peaks, menstrual onset, and the production of sleep hormones in the brain occurring at the opposite time of day from most people. They have difficulty adjusting to daytime schedules and frequently work nights. They tend to be photosensitive, avoiding sunlight, sun burning easily, and having excellent night vision."

She smirked a little at this, and continued.

"But as for myself, Alexandria, I am a vampire whom can walk during the day. I am a day walker and a night walker. Most vampires, their vitality ranges widely, and they can be vigorous and active one day, depressed and languorous the next. They frequently have digestive trouble. Even those with cast-iron stomachs have many issues with food that are rooted in their constant hunger for energy. Contrary to the image of the vampire as thin, many real vampires are troubled by obesity because of a hunger that makes them food addicts, and a system that is sluggish in processing physical food. They are also sometimes troubled by other substance addictions for the same reasons, but since their systems are tuned to pranic energy more than to processing physical substance, they may not be as sensitive to drugs and alcohol as an ordinary person would be."

She shrugged this off in a nonchalant manner.

"Emotionally and physically, vampires are unpredictable, moody, temperamental and overwhelming. The major distinguishing characteristic of real vampires as opposed to ordinary people who share those qualities, is the vampire's intensity. Vampires are extremely intense people. They are frequently given nicknames such as 'the black hole.' When others talk about them, usually to complain about them, vampires are often described by such terms as 'needy,' 'attention-seeking,' 'grandstanding,' 'manipulative,' 'exhausting,' 'draining,' 'monopolizes the conversation,' 'jealous,' 'huge ego,' and so on.

A vampire's emotions are deep, fervent, and powerful, and they usually display great psychic ability and has uncontrolled magical and psychic experiences. Vampires are also empaths, and while they remain unconscious of their natures, they are frequently 'psychic sponges' who simply absorb vibrations from everywhere, with the expected emotional instability resulting. A 'hungry' vampire — one whose energy level is imbalanced to the deficit side — becomes an involuntary psychic vortex, drawing all pranic energy in the area towards them. When the energy does not flow in fast enough — and it is typical of vampires that the energy never flows fast enough for them — they will begin manifesting behavior patterns to increase the amount of conscious attention they get from others.

For this reason, some vampires develop a pattern of being aggressively confrontational, or of constantly antagonizing people with whom they have relationships. Nearly all vampires, whatever ploys they use, have a talent for attracting, or distracting, the attention of everyone present. Once a vampire overloads on energy, it reverses their behavior patterns. They may become morose, silent, withdrawn and introverted. Some vampires become maniacally cheerful when they are satiated, but even their good moods seem to annoy others, and it is more typical for vampires to be infamous as wet blankets. 'Hungry' and 'overload' phases can occur within a few minutes or last for days at a time."

Alexandria momentarily ceased from her dictation like overview, and tilted her head towards me. It was apparent she wanted to know if she still had my attention. My gaze remained fixed on her. Satisfied with this, she continued.

"Vampires are commonly loners, in part because they feel so different from those around them, but also because they have a need to control the degree of contact they have with sources of energy. Real vampires are not the demonic fiends of Christianized folklore, but as long as they refuse to accept their inner nature, their bad reputation is not undeserved. Unconscious vampires have a tendency to reach adulthood with less than the average level of social skill and general finesse, and tend to be selfish and self-centered. The demands of their own energy systems are so distracting to them that it is difficult for them to pay attention to the needs of others. Their relationships tend to be disasters.

Different vampires develop different patterns according to what works best for them in their life situation, but several patterns are common. The 'femme fatale' or 'lady-killer' vampire forms a continuous series of sexual connections with one partner at a time, dropping each unfortunate lover as they become too exhausted, or

defensive, to support the vampire's energy needs. Other vampires form a long-term relationship with a single person: either another vampire whose energy cycle complements their own, or a person who derives satisfaction from being a psychic servant or martyr. You know, a person who is killed for their religion or their own beliefs.

A common pattern, especially in young adults, is to continuously join social, religious, political and magical groups and either blow them apart or end up being thrown out. Vampires may go through roommates, housing situations, magical groups, jobs and lovers like so much Kleenex. Many people find that they feel 'creepy' or 'weird' around a vampire. This is usually due to the effects of one's own life force being drawn towards the vampire's vortex. Most people feel uncomfortable and distracted when their energy is pulled away from themselves. In addition to this, a common result of such an energy drain is for the aura to pull in tightly towards the body, and this causes a prickling sensation on the skin — the 'creepy-crawlies.'

It is no more common for vampires to be psychopaths or killers than it is for any random person on the street. However, a prolonged, or very involved, relationship with a vampire can put a severe strain on the emotional and psychic energy systems of an ordinary person. Folklore suggests that victims of a vampire become vampires themselves. In reality, people who have been seriously 'drained' — that is, have had their own energy pulled off balance into a deficit — also become psychic vortices which pull life force away from other living things. However, they are never as powerful as a true vampire, and unlike vampires, quickly recover and stabilize. True vampires are born the way they are — no one can be 'turned into a vampire.' However, years of energy depletion can lead to health problems ranging from depression and malaise to a suppressed immune system and susceptibility to serious illnesses. Most people will break off the relationship before it gets that far. Many vampires are attracted to magical paths. In a magical working group, their ability to wreak havoc is increased because of the psychic openness and trust that exist there. But there can be a benefit, as well. Some vampires become aware of their true natures and choose to undertake serious work to transform themselves. As soon as they begin doing so, they become more acceptable working partners and companions.

Once in control of their capacity for handling energy, they become extraordinary magicians and healers. Their ability to hold the attention of others gives them the potential to be fine leaders and teachers. Ultimately, the purpose of vampires is not to plague the universe but to facilitate its healing. Vampirism is the dark, or unfocused, side of a certain kind of psychic talent, one which has been developing for many lifetimes. It is destructive only when a vampire either refuses to face the truth about themselves and work with their abilities, or when they choose to play out a sinister role because of the illusion of power it gives them.

Knowledge, awareness, and control are the lessons real vampires must learn in order to harness their abilities. If

real vampires are not the immortals of fiction, they can at least be confident of one thing: for better or worse, they will keep the qualities they develop for many lives to come."

So much information this treacherous woman has implemented into my fucking head already. She then begins to feel on me...

"So, how much control do you have sir?" She touches my shoulder then works her way to my muscular chest, then to my firm abs and then grabs my cock, I snatched her hand firmly. Then said forcefully, "I have plenty of control." She smiled, "well, I see, so do you not find me attractive, Mr. Discipline?"

My big chocolate cock was rock hard, but I was not going to give in to her ways. I didn't want her having any type of control over me, not now, not ever. I pushed her hand.

"Do you not find me attractive, Mr. Discipline?" She repeated herself, waiting for my reply. Intrepidly I responded, "you are an attractive supernatural, however, I have different things in mind." She smiled at me once again. "You can focus on those later, I want you now."

She ripped my shirt off, I stopped her by placing my hand on her throat. My grip was stone, and I didn't let up, I squeezed her throat until she was begging for air.

"I said, I have other things in mind right now." This woman was horny as fuck, no stopping her from getting

exactly what she desired, which was me and my massive cock inside her. But at the moment, she was held at bay.

The night was old, and the sun was on the brink of rising. I attempted to fall asleep, and she came over to me, and she grabbed me in the most lustful way possible. I have never had a woman attempt to take me like this in my entire life. Her pussy was drenched, and my big dick was rock hard. She shoved my cock inside her drenched hole, through her drenched pussy lips. She moaned so loudly, and groaned so loudly, the woman looked possessed with so much rage.

The sex, I didn't want to give in, but 'sexual desires were enhanced,' and it took over intensely. I grasped her throat and flipped her the fuck over. I was on top of her, and I was thrusting into her yielding soft heaping wetness roughly. Pounding her into a dripping mess.

"Yes, yes, yes!" She screamed, "fuck me harder, fuck me harder. Yes, just like that!" I slapped her, and I covered her mouth with my massive hand. "Shut up," I growled at her, "one thing you must know, if we do this, I am in control. Don't tell me what to do. When it comes to this vampire shit, you may know more than me, but when it comes to sex, and handling a woman, leave that up to my mastery."

She nodded her head in agreement with me. I took her hands and clasped them together and placed them over her head, now pinning them on the mattress above her, and continued to keep stroking and thrusting harder and harder, while she was becoming weak, she was moaning, she was

groaning and humming through my hand. She moved her face to uncover her own mouth, "I'm going to cum, I'm going to cum.... ooohhhh, ughhhh, hmmm," she was cumming. She was drenched like Niagara Falls, soaking everywhere like a busted fire hydrant. I drained her of some energy.

I noticed something, this was when she was at her weakest point, when she was cumming. I then noticed, she let so many guards down here, hmmm, this could be something useful in the future to be aware of for sure. Perhaps she didn't realize how attentive I was as a human being, and now as a vampire those senses have heightened. I then followed her, I stopped enjoying it, so I forced myself to cum. "GRRRR," I growled into her ear cumming and busting inside her more powerful than a magnum .44 desert eagle pistol.

After we both came, we talked, I needed more insight on this shit, on her, on this life.

"You acted like you haven't had sex in a year, the men you kill, don't you seduce and fuck them prior to the feasting and killing?" She answered immediately, "not all of them, some, yes. But not all. Plus, I haven't had 'great sex' in years, get it right. And that was some amazingly great sex, mister Discipline."

I shrugged off her compliment, I paid no mind to it whatsoever, I wanted to know more. "So, what happened when you fed upon these men?" She began to tell me the entire thing, like she was spilling the beans and shit, "when I cum, I'm totally weak, so, I never cum, most of the men I kill, I take control of them, not like you just did with me now. And I kill them before I cum. Once I cum, I go through this crazy body experience and I do not think straight, see straight, hear right. All of my senses are fucked up. I'm like in a totally different world for like a good twenty seconds."

These are all vital information I will keep in mind. I exhausted her, and she went right to bed. I slept as well, however I could not keep asleep. I had to go out, and I snuck out of her lair and I ended up wandering the streets in human form. I went to the park that Precious and I would go to. The park her and I would spend some time together. The park where we were last together. I was thinking of her so hard and so intensely, I then heard, "hey Daddy," in a whisper, I looked but I could not see anything. I then tried to follow wherever the noise and whisper was coming from and all of a sudden, I see a form and shaped glow of a being. So shiny, it was blinding me.....

Chapter 5- Blood Never Tasted So Good

The form of the being was so shiny and blinding, I couldn't stare directly at it, then the glow was diminishing, and I could see who and what the being was, and it was Precious. Not just any precious or precious thing, it was my Precious. Her spirit came to me, she looked so beautiful, prettier than ever. I went to go touch her as I called out for her, but I could not touch her.

"Precious, my sweet and beautiful Precious..." I said softly. She smiled at me. "Daddy, just listen to me, I don't have much time, I can only appear to you twice, and this is the first, and I don't know when I will arrive or be able to arrive to you again, possibly I will not. So listen, the night in the park, as you know it was Alexandria, second, she finished me off. This woman or creature was the slave that I brought into our lives, I am so sorry Daddy. Anyways, I was taken to the hospital and I didn't make it, she made sure of that. Look, she wants you to be at the best of your abilities because she wants someone to do her dirty work, you are a hard worker and she wants to take advantage of that, she has no good intensions for you. You're already great Daddy, you just never reached your peak, and she just gave you more powers than you ever could dream up. Didn't she fuck up? You have to take her out, because eventually when whatever plan she has is finished and the goal is achieved, she will get rid of you, so it's either you or her at this point, Daddy... make the right choice, I know you will."

Her image was disintegrating. I was calling out for her, "Precious!!" She was in and out.

"I have to go, I don't know what is happening." She said sadly. All of a sudden, she was gone, her image vanished. Shortly after, Alexandria appeared to me.

"There you are, don't you know it's not polite to fuck a girl and then leave in the middle of the night without letting her know? You can turn a girl crazy like that, break her heart, and you know what they say, hell has no fury than a woman who is scorned..."

She went to attempt to grab me, but I was too fast for her, and I actually saw a cop who appeared and was coming out of a dunkin donut shop and I thought quickly, 'that's my way out.' I then jet over to him, and slap him on his face. Not enough to knock him unconscious, but enough to get his attention.

"What the fuck are you doing?" He asked me, and then I answered him, "what the fuck does it look like, dude?" And then I slapped him once again. He grabbed me and then turned me, so his chest was on my back, he reached for my hands, and pulled out his handcuffs. Of course I allowed him to manhandle me. He must have been salivating at the fact. To bring a black man, to the station. I was surprised I wasn't shot first by the police man. I smirked, I had a plan, and Alexandria saw me and made eye contact with me, as the police officer lowered my head to get into the back seat of his vehicle.

I arrived at the station and filed some paperwork, and I continued to create havoc, as I was placed in a cell. And for Alexandria to appear where I was, she would have to know or have an idea and then think of that place, in order for her to find me. But, I was blocking my thoughts, and that was making it very difficult for her to be able to locate me right away.

I've gained a little of her energy, she fucked up and she does not even realize it. She is going to grow weaker by the minute, and I will grow stronger and stronger until I am the best ever. Reaching my highest fucking level. Maximizing my abilities.

After being there for several hours, hunger began to take over, and I was in so much pain, I needed to feast, or I was going to die. I saw the officer whom was watching my cell, and I thought to myself, 'damn,' I needed to feed, fuck, my stomach had a mind of its own. I felt as if I was going through withdrawal. Like an addict, that needed their fix. I went into the officer's head.

"Hey, come open the cell." I controlled his movements, he got his fat ass up out the chair, and he was placing the key into the key hole of my cell, just as my mind was making him do. He opened the cell, and I feasted on his flesh, and then snapped his fucking neck. Damn, 'blood never tasted so damn good.' Now, suddenly, another officer came, he grabbed me, and he then hit me with a taser. Tasered my body. It felt like nothing I had ever felt before, and I was out like a light. The officer ripped up my paperwork, erased my name in the system, and took me with him. Took me in his car, I was out cold, I woke up sitting on a chair, hands tied behind my back. The officer then said to me, "you thought you could get away from me that easily? Well, you can think again." At that particular moment, I knew it was her, he then shape shifts into Alexandria. "Missed me? Haaaahhah," with her sadistic laugh. And then I answered her, "well, If I said, 'no,' would you believe me?"

She gave out a sarcastic gasp with her hand held on her chest as if she were shocked, and then said to me, "oh my god, you're so heartless, I taught you well, haha." I shook my head, "what the fuck do you really want from me, and why am I chained to this fucking chair? How did you find me? How did you know where I was?" I demanded my questions answered immediately. It must have been when I feasted, she could sense me.

"Well, first of all, I want you to not run from me, and second, you can't get out of these chains if that's what you were wondering. I teleported from the chair out of the chains, and appeared behind her, "you should've planned a little better, but I guess that's not your strong suit." I curled my fingers inward and created a fist. I then punched her, and she went flying into the wall, she touched her lip and she had a little blood there, yes, she was growing weaker, and she realized this. She got up and flew towards me and pushed me through the wall, and we transported back to her lair. All of a sudden, she gained this incredible amount of strength back. I get it, we were in her lair, there must be something there that charges her strength. We physically fought back and forth, and I then ripped her clothes off of her. I then began kissing her lips and biting the bottom of her lips aggressively. I pushed her on the bed.

"Yes, I see you love it rough, my kind of man." She said. I was not about talking, I was not even about the part of the seduction, but I knew this was my chance, I knew this was one mistake she made, this was one weakness she had, and that one weakness would be the death of her, and this big chocolate cock. I shoved my dick inside her so deep, she gasped and arches her back off the mattress as if her fucking soul was leaving her body, yup, now her soul is mine. She was moaning like her energy was weak and being takin by multiple lovers at the same time, yeah, I was taking that as well.

I thrusted harder and harder and my goal was to get her to cum for me. I felt her walls closing in, and her muscles contracting onto my thickness. "I'm cumin, yessss," that was my opening, her neck was exposed and I leaned in and took a bite out of crime. I couldn't finish but I got enough blood, just to get some of her powers and her energy. She pushed me off of her and I went flying into the wall. She elevated from the bed and remained in the air, her body didn't touch the ground, it was some fucking weird ass shit. I've never seen this before, fucking thunder and lightening, but there was no thunder and lightening. Her eyes were rolling in the back of her fucking head.

"Now I am angry," she said, yelling out ferociously. "Fuck attempting to make you a vampire King, I'm going to finish what I should have in the woods. I'm going to finish you just like I finished your sweet Precious." She had this ball of lightening in her hand and she pointed it at me, and I shut my fucking eyes. This woman was way too powerful, I couldn't stop her. I was gone for sure, as the lightening headed my way.

But all of a sudden, it stopped like ten inches before hitting my heart, and it just stayed there, it was radiant, but it didn't move any further towards me, it was like a forcefield stopping it from hitting me, even Alexandria was shocked.

"What's going on here?" She questioned, and all of a sudden, a shiny glow appeared. "I am what's going on here. Did you miss me, bitch?" It was Precious.

"What are you doing here? You're supposed to be dead!" Alexandria shouted. Precious now reached for Alexandria's heart and yelled out, "Daddy now!"

I swiftly ran over, I then bite Alexandria's neck and then I ripped her fucking head off of her shoulders with my bare hands, literally. Alexandria was finished, she was dead, she was fucking gone.

"Precious, I could not have ever done this without you, I was ten inches from toast. I would not be here as of right now, you saved my life." She said to me, "two things I always told you my King; one, I would never leave you, and two, I would only be able to come back to you one or two more times." I reached to touch her hand, but I could not grab her, she was just a spirit, floating backward and now fading into the smoke she created.

"Daddy, I must leave now, but you are what you have always known you were, you just needed a little help in bringing it out, I told you, that you and your soul would live forever. You will shine, you will obtain all that you desire, I believe this, now you must believe this, reach deep inside yourself and you will master everything in your path, and everyone…."

She then vanishes, and right before she went, I called out for her…Precious!!! Precious!!!! She was already gone……

Chapter 6- Resurrected

I was a brand fucking new man. I felt great, moving great, but only thing I was missing, was my Precious doll. She was never coming back, and I had to realize that. I died and was reborn a brand-new man, a King, a God. Fuck that, better than a God. Better than an Immortal. I was resurrected, rejuvenated. However, I felt a great amount of guilt with what happened to Precious. I feel like everything that happened was my fault. I then began to question myself, 'could I have done more? Was the timing off, should I have trusted my instincts that night? Should we have just stayed in that night, perhaps none of this would have happened? Should I have fought harder to get the female vampire off of her when I could? What if I had more time? What if I pulled back time? What if I could go back in time? Does time really exist? I would do so many things differently. Fuck, but what is done, is fucking done.'

I drowned in my sorrows. Drank my pain away. I went to the strip club. I was drinking like a sailor. Shots after shots. "Give me another!" I ordered to the bartender. All of a sudden, there were some women that approached me. Lustful and devilish flowers. One placed her hands on my shoulders. She asked me, "hey, baby, do you want a massage?"

I gazed at her with a menacing and dark stare. "First, don't ever call me baby, second, don't ever touch me without my fucking permission." She removed her hands from my shoulders immediately. The other one was smiling, "oh, he's feisty, he's aggressive, I like him." The one that had her hands upon my shoulders said dismissively, "well I don't, he's rude." The first one then hit her, and gave her a look, like 'calm down.' A look of, 'be nice. He could be reading big money all over him.'

She then said to me, "hey, we won't touch you without your permission. So, where are you from, hun?" I stopped her immediately, "don't call me 'hun,' either!" She looked at her friend, "so, what would you like us to call you then?" I stared at the both of them.

"Call me, sir, however, names are really irrelevant." The one who was the calm one, I guess she was the ring leader in this friendship, said… "You seem tense, let's give you a massage, would you like that, sir? We don't want your money, we want you comfortable."

Oh man the fucking lies, I could read their eyes, I could feel their vibrations, I could read their thirsty money hungry aura. She winked at the other girl. We went into the dark room, and she was feeling on me. Touching, and I was touching her back, shit, at the end of the day I was a man and I wasn't gay, but I was ahead of the games they were attempting to play. I then said, "let's get out of here." The other woman, who was not feeling me, because I would not allow her to touch my shoulders at first was like, "we can't just leave, we still have our shift."

I pulled out a gwap of cash and it lit both their eyes. I told the both of them, "don't worry, I'll pay for the rest of your night." And the one that said, she loved my aggressive behavior, that was the ring leader, the calmer one, the fucking hustler. She then said, "we are out this bitch, let's go girl." I assumed she was the fucking ring leader of her and her girl. We went to a hotel, all three of us, and we had a little fun. I wanted to tie the both of them up, and have my way with them. However, I was feeling so exhausted and I wanted to just pass out.

"We will have to resume this great fun, ladies, I'm not feeling it tonight." I then passed out. The women looked at me, with little remorse, and they then took my wallet. They were out of there, faster than a vehicle trying to run a yellow light before it turned red. There was no stopping them at all. I was knocked the fuck out.

When I woke up, I saw that no one was around me. I haven't got that drunk in years. I was looking for my keys and my wallet, and I couldn't find either one. I couldn't remember how I got there, but, I did remember the women I came here with. Where were they? One of them slipped up, and left her jewelry at the hotel. I grasped the jewelry in my massive hands and curled my fingers inward. Grasping the jewelry even tighter. I pulled my hand close to my nostrils, just to take a whiff of it. I smelled the jewelry with my eyes shut. I took a deep whiff of it, and that allowed me to know, where those two women were. I sniffed their scent that they left on me, and I sniffed the scent that was outside of the hotel. I could see their tracks, with my x ray vision. So, I began to follow those footsteps.

Suddenly, I just shape shifted, and I teleported out of there, I was so fucking angry. I then came to the place I teleported to. A home. I inhaled deep within the air, and I took a big whiff, and it was the same smell, these women left on me. Their natural womanly scent with their perfume. I found my car, and I knew if I could find my car, then I must be near where the women were.

Why? They must have been the ones that took my keys, and if they took my car, they took my wallet as well. I mean, I didn't need the car, I can transport and speed run wherever I wanted, and the money, I could make back more tomorrow or later that week. But, I wanted them back because they were mine. It was the fucking principal of the entire thing. Plus, no one was going to make a fool out of Discipline, and fucking get away with it. No fucking way, no fucking sir, and no fucking ma'am.

I then materialized within the home of one of the ladies, and they both happened to be there. "Well, hello ladies! I mean, were you both like not going to say 'goodbye,' prior to robbing my shit?"

They were in shock, and their eyes were wide open. One of the ladies then shouted out to me……

"How the fuck did you get in here?! And how do you know where I live?" The other one tried to run, and I was right in front of her instantly.

"How the fuck did you do that? You were just over there!" She pointed behind her. "Who are you, or what are you?!"

I grabbed her by her throat and lifted her up off the ground. The other one tried to run as well, so I threw the one in my hands across the room and ran after her. I grabbed her quickly and covered her mouth, so she wouldn't scream.

"Shhhh, silence, you pet." I said softly. She began to cry, tears were running down her cheeks. "Please, don't hurt me." She whimpered. I laughed. "So now you're begging? That's cute, I guess you were hot shit when you were taking my shit?"

She was gasping for air, "it was her, not my idea at all, I liked you, remember?" I really didn't see her stopping her friend, who the fuck is she trying to play now? I replied with a smirk, "throwing your friend under the bus, huh? Don't worry, I'm going to kill her, but as for you, I'll spare your life." She was panicking, "please, tell me what you need, and I will do it." Funny how people will do anything when their life is on the damn line. I gazed down at her and I was silent, and then I said...

"I just want my wallet you bitches stole from me." She was gasping for air, as she then began to grasp my wrist with both her hands, as she was lifted off the ground by me. Her feet dangled off the floor like five inches. "That's all?" She asked, as she struggled to breathe, trying to talk. "That's why you came all the way here? You could always get another one!" I shook my head in frustration. "Look, I'm finished playing games with you, and your friend, so here's how this will go…you will tell me where my wallet is in five seconds, or I will snap your pretty little fucking neck bitch!!!" I then started counting….

"One…. two…. three…" she looked around, and panicked some more, "uh uh it's…" she was stuttering and gasping for air…. I continued to count, "four…. five." She finally gave in.

"Okay, it's over there." She pointed to the direction of the kitchen counter. I looked up at her, I smiled, and then I said, 'thank you very much. Now, I will let you go, see, I am a man of my word. I will not snap your neck. But, I never said anything about me not sinking my teeth into it."

And then, my eyes turned gold, my fangs grew, and I grasped her throat with one hand, turned my head sideways, and sank my teeth into her neck, she collapsed in my arms and I let her body drop onto the ground. Then I slashed her face.

"Plus, you were too slow bitch, time is up. You really let me count all the way to five, before replying?" I stepped over her body and retrieved my wallet, yeah she was right, I could have gotten another wallet. But, that wallet had Precious' photo in there, the only thing I had left of her to glance at. Her friend was beginning to come back into consciousness. My head turned to watch her, but my body

didn't turn with my head. The only thing that moved was my head, and I turned it quickly, to the direction where her friend was, as she was coming back into consciousness.

I got my wallet, and I placed it in my pocket. And then I raced over to her, faster than a silver bullet. I didn't even allow her to say one word, I placed my massive hands over her mouth, and I sank my teeth into her neck. I buried my fangs deep into her. Right on the side of her neck. Sucking every ounce of blood and energy she had. Her eyes rolled in the back of her head after I dropped her on the floor. My eyes were red. Blood was on my hands, I then grabbed my wallet, just to insure everything was in there. Which was a good thing, these women just wanted money, they didn't care about my personal identification or anything like that.

I left the home, got into my car and was gone. I owned the night. I owned the streets, until I saw sirens from behind my rear-view mirror. Freedom is amazing, freedom is phenomenal, right until you see those red, white and blue sirens from the back of your car. As you stare into your rear-view mirror.

I pulled over, and there was a police car behind me. I checked and watched who came out of the patrol car, it was a female cop. I haven't seen a female cop in a long time.

"License and registration sir," she asked me, she then flashed her light into my car, and my wallet. "Is that blood on your wallet sir? Or is that something else on there?" I

stared at it, and then I stared at her, "what seems to be the issue officer? What seems to be the question you are asking me, ma'am?" I said, politely, and then she continued to say, "there's a series of activities that has been going on in the area, and you were speeding." I gazed into her eyes, "what type of activity miss officer? Is it some sexual activity? Did you observe, or hear a man handling a woman, ferociously? The point of devouring her deep, she becoming the object of his unbridled lust? His inner beast coming out. He is unleashing her beast. Taking her to a place of no return. Succulent lips and tracing every curve with his hands, before he devours her with his big cock….." I had her in a fucking trance, she was hypnotized by my words, and my power and more essentially, my fucking eyes. She couldn't move, she didn't speak, she didn't even blink, she was moving in closer, gasping for air. Yes, she was wet. With her eyes shut in pleasure, she moved her face and head closer to me. Then her lips were inches from touching mine, and I was two seconds from grasping her throat with my hands and sinking my teeth into her neck, and then all of a sudden, her walkie talkie went off.…

"We have a 21, 45, do you copy?" She snapped out of my trance, her heart lurched painfully at that alert that she received. And then said, "yes, I copy. Okay sir, you're good to go tonight, be careful, there's plenty of strange activity going on in this area. Its very dangerous, stay safe." She said to me. I smirked, "will do officer, you have a great night." I wanted to bite her, to see how she dies. Final screams, running scared, whispers, unspoken, kissed twice, before she was bit. Deep freeze, fatal burn, wicked lies, wicked ways, most likely to die. Without any mercy, hot blooded meets cold blooded. Shiver, absolute fear, malice, devious. Would her life flash before her eyes, would she think about the night before? The morning after, born to die anyways, afraid to die, ready to die, deserved to die? Unseen, blind spot, hush. Shhhhh, nowhere to run, nowhere to hide, nowhere fucking safe. Then I thought to myself….. 'oh, I hope I don't ever run into her again. Did I speak too soon? Should I have finished her off? Could it come back to, bite me, like karma? Nahh!!!'

Then I sped the fuck off into the night. The world, was in the palm of my hands at this point, and I could crush it whenever the fuck I wanted………

Chapter 7- Lust At First Sight

When that pineal gland is functioning properly, you now view the world at a God point of view. Your mind is completely free, and your senses are enhanced like they have never been enhanced before. I was still feeling grief from Precious' death. For the first time in a long time, I shed a tear. My tear ran down my cheek and onto the ground. That caused a big rain shower in the entire New York City. My emotions were extremely powerful. I had told myself that I needed to move on. I could not get sloppy like that ever again. Drunk? Shit, when was the last time I was that drunk?

So now, several years had passed, and I had several gyms I owned, and a couple of night clubs I had to run. I couldn't just be sloppy. I arrived at one of my night clubs, and it was a fucking banging and lit Saturday night. The night was lustfully delicious looking. And very promising for business. We were open like a few nights during the week, and we were on all weekend, from Friday through Sunday.

Saturday and Sunday were always our biggest nights. We could bank one hundred and fifty thousand a night, whether it was a Saturday or Sunday. Especially Sunday, weird too, you would think people are getting ready for the week, and would love to rest up on Sunday, but not out here, no way. They were party animals around here. Motherfuckers didn't sleep in New York fucking City. I know why Saturday was lit, I mean, most people out here worked a nine to five job, Monday through Friday, and they were off Saturday and Sunday. This was their time to unwind, this was a place for them to relax, have fun, escape.

I had that special aura or something, because for some reason women could not take their eyes off me tonight. It must be all these women I've been killing, they were sensing the other women's energies off of me. I mean, women were like wolves. Very intricate creatures, but they can sense things from a distance. But, that wasn't the vampire aura, that was just my natural Scorpio Dominant aura.

The bouncers greeted me, as I passed to the side of where the metal detectors were. "Hey sir, how is it tonight?" They asked me. I shook their hands, "well fellas, it's looking promising. Real promising tonight. Looks like some great business is going to be in the building here tonight. Big names!!"

I walked in, greeted the bottle women, and told them. "Sell those bottles ladies, whatever it takes, power of seduction, power of persuasion. Ladies, you've been doing this since you were born, you all know what to do, so do what you do best." And they all at once said, "yes boss!!" I went over to the bar, and I was looking around. I smiled to myself and my thoughts went wild, 'I fucking did it, I wish Precious could see me now, I fucking did it!'

A man then approached me, he was in a business suit, dark red blazer, and a matching red tie. His energy to me felt very strong, and he looked very prominent. He was dressed in a way that made him stand out completely. He then stuck out his hand, and asked me, "I guess you are the owner of this place, huh?" I looked at his hand, granted, I don't trust anyone, I don't just trust a person that smiles nonstop in my damn face.

I shook his hand, "who is asking?" I asked him right back, answering a question with a question. He then said, "I am Phil Scott." I looked at him squarely, "a man with two first names, huh? Phil Scott? Should I know you, well you approach me, like I should know you sir?" He then continued with me, "perhaps you should know me, perhaps you should not, but soon you will know me very well." I laughed, "haha, and why is that man with two first names? Why is that?"

He smiled back at me, "well, I am looking to buy this place, what is your price?" I shook my head at him and then rolled my eyes, "listen, it's not for sale, but I could possibly hire you as my general manger here, but I am the owner, and I will remain the owner."

He said, "we will see."

I wanted to know why this man with the two first names, matter of fact, who gives their child, two first names anyways? I wanted to know why this man was so confident in my club.

"Why are you so interested in my club? There are tons of clubs all over the world, and here in New York, why mine?" He then said to me, "your club is one of the hottest in New York City, that's why. I want to add it to my collection." I looked at him confused, "collection? What do you mean? You own a series of clubs? Look this location is prominent for me, I grew up in Brooklyn, New York. It's like my way of giving back to my community, and the fact that it is black owned, not many people would look at this place, and think it was black owned. I bet you didn't know this either."

He nodded his head, "yes, that is correct, and I want to take it off your hands." Damn, this man with the two first names was playing hard ball. He then said to me, "I want to add this club to my collection of clubs. I have one in Connecticut, one in Dallas, Texas, one in Atlanta, Georgia and I would own another in New York, which would be this one."

I laughed at him, "like I told you, its not for sale, but I would love to be partners with you on your clubs, and mine, I think we would have something pretty lucrative here for the both of us, don't you believe? With my fresh new innovative ideas, your savvy business style? What do you think?" He smiled at me and didn't say shit for like three seconds.

"Well no, it sounds tempting, but I like to work alone, no partners," Phil Scott replied. I wanted him to open his wallet, I needed to see his ID, I needed to know more of this man. He turned around, and gave his back to me, he was about to walk away from me when I grabbed him, I

placed my massive hand on his shoulder, "look, take my card," I suggested to him, "perhaps we change our minds, "I mean, if the dollar signs look promising, I might sell."

Now his eyes lit up, and he took my card. I mean, he would have never taken it, if I didn't lie. He then took my card and took out his wallet, and placed it in there, but before he could put his wallet back into his pocket, I told him....

"Hey, what are you drinking?" He said, "whiskey." I took him over to the bar, one hand was on his shoulder, as I was leading him to the bar. As he walked with me, and he was taking out his credit card to pay for a drink, I snatched his ID so fast he didn't notice. I scanned it with my eyes. Everything was moving in slow motion except me. The crowd, the DJ, the people on the dance floor, the bartenders, everyone. I had mental documentation of where this guy lived, how old he was, what his height was, etc.

"Hey, what are you doing here? Why don't you put that thing away, you are not going to pay here, its on the house, it's on me." I spoke to him casually. He smiled, then he said to me, "that is generous, sir." I shook his hand, and fake smiled with him then said, "hey, how would it look, for the potential owner of this place, paying for his own drinks?" He pointed with his index finger at me, with his mouth wide open, "uuuhh, yeah, my man!" I pointed back at him, "uuuuhh, listen, enjoy yourself." Then I walked away, and murmured to myself, "jackass."

I then walked over to the other bar. I walked over to it and I raised my hand, that's all I needed to do, and the bartender gave me a shot of Henny. I mean, she knew what I liked.

All of a sudden, there was a woman who approached me. "Hello there, how are you?" She asked me. I stared her up and down while I shook her hand. "Hello, how do you do, miss?" I replied, while I stared into her eyes, and quickly scanned her up and down, and her entire outfit with my gaze. "Enjoying yourself tonight?" I asked her. She nodded to me, "yes I am," then she asked me, "aren't you going to buy me a drink?" I laughed at her. "Why must I buy you a drink? Because I am a man, and you are the woman, and that's what the man is required to always do?"

She giggled, "uh, well yes." Then I continued to talk to her, "but, you women preach and beg for equal opportunity. Some of you behave like men, but today, it is the man's job to buy your drink? Correct miss?" Before she could answer I interjected, "I am about making the customer happy." I said to her. And she smiled, and so I was going to give her one drink on the house, just one. Who knew who this woman was. She could be someone very prominent. Then again, she could be someone whom is following up on me. Therefore, I should keep her where I could see her, at the bar, and keep her preoccupied. Because where there are drinks, there can be some preoccupied things. I raised my hand and told the bartender to come over to me. "Get this lovely lady a drink of her choice on the house," I ordered the bartender, "yes boss," she said to me. The bartender followed my instructions exactly. The woman then looked at me, but this time with much confusion in her gaze towards me. "Yes, boss?" She questioned me. I smirked, "yes, I run this lovely place you are in. I hope you enjoy yourself, have a good night miss." And then I walked away…her eyes then followed me in the direction I was headed. She asked the bartender, "is he really the owner of this club?" My bartender replied, "yes, of course, he was not lying to you when he stated that." She then said to the bartender, "most owners are in their little skybox or something, they are not hanging outside, never alone by the damn bar." The bartender shrugged her shoulders.

I went into a trap door, and it lead into my skybox. Now I can view everyone on the dance floor and bar. That woman at the bar that I granted a drink, was looking all over for me. I could tell, her eyes were wandering. She could not sit still, she could not sit down. She looked left, and then she looked right. I was gazing at her so firmly, my aura must have called her. The next thing I knew, she was staring at me dead in my eyes. My skybox was not see through, no one on the dance floor could see me, but I could see them. Therefore, I believed that to be so strange, who the fuck was this woman? Was she an immortal like myself? Did I know her? Did she know me? It's like I could hear her breathing, I could feel her heart racing, I could feel her energy in the skybox I was staring through. And it's like she could read my thoughts. Such a pretty face she had, a face that's probably gotten her out of speeding tickets, a body that has probably gotten her some free drinks, and words where she can get any man to get her and give her whatever she and her heart desired.

I headed back down to the dance floor, where I met up with her once again. "Hey, what's going on? You haven't moved from where we were last, what is it, the men here aren't grabbing your interest? They won't bite, you're young, go have fun, get your drink on and mingle. You have friends, bring them by."

She was completely out of sorts and she had no intensions on meeting or speaking with no other men but myself. "What were you doing up there so long, spying on me? How do you know I haven't moved from where I was? How do you know if I'm so young? You're assuming there, mister." She said smartly. I then replied to her, "how do you know I'm assuming? you play a good possum, I could be completely on point, but, you would not let me know I was right, would you?" She smiled, and I pressed the issue, "you could just be playing coy."

She smirked, "maybe, but even though, you know what they say about 'assume,' when you 'assume?' Huh? You make an ass out of you and…." Before she could finish, I interrupted her, "you know what I say with, 'assume?' the only time you may assume, is the damn position."

She smiled, "hmm, interesting, I like that saying better. And you still didn't answer my question. I asked you if you were spying on me??" I didn't answer her ridiculous question. I jumped around it, "actually, I own this club as you know, I watch everything and everyone." Hit her with a smart remark. Why would I tell her I was spying on her? I didn't care to flatter her. Men must be kissing this woman's ass all day long, kissing and sucking up to her all day long. Fuck that, not me. She must love when men

flatter her, well, I'm not every man, and I was not about to do that at all.

"So, what's up?" I asked her, "enjoy yourself, mingle." She answered me, immediately, "no, actually I want to only speak with you, I want to know more about you, and what other clubs you own." I smirked, "oh so that's it huh? You 'want' to know me? Or the other clubs I own?" I didn't wait for her to answer, I just continued on…

"Well, what you see is what you get miss. And I want to never have to work, live in a paradise island somewhere, and escape, but see, we all can't have what we want." She was persistent to know. "No, oh stop it, can you talk normal to me? Like a normal person. That's too plain, you have secrets, you're too mysterious." I laughed, nothing about me was normal, and then I said to her…

"The unknown will always intrigue the mind, don't you think? Plus, you're getting real personal with questions for someone that just met me. But did we just meet, or do I know you? Perhaps you know me already?" She just gazed into my eyes, but did not say a fucking word. This woman didn't want to get to know me, she wanted an opportunity, an escape, perhaps money, who gives a fuck what I did? Some assistance, perhaps? That is what gets her? Drives her. Turned her on? Looks like tonight I will have an easy dinner. And she would be served on my plate.

"Let's go somewhere a little quieter, shall we?" I insisted. She then began to nod her head in complete agreement with me. I brought her back to my secret hidden office. I turned towards her, while I poured her a glass of red wine that was on my table in the office, "what is your name?" I then asked her… and she answered, "my name is Cleopatra." I laughed, "are you fucking with me? that's not your birth name is it?" She nodded her head, and then she pulled out her driver's license, shit, this bitch was telling the truth, and I was shocked.

"Are you fucking kidding me? Cleopatra like the fucking ancient Egyptians? The Queen of Egypt at some point, that fucked with Julius Caesar and Marc Anthony?" She nodded, "that's right! You know your history very well there, mister."

I then continued, "Cleo was powerful, her beauty and her personality won her plenty of power. Is that just like you? And were or are you like that goddess? Are you someone powerful? I'm sure you are, right? I take you as someone whom gets what she wants constantly?" She placed her palms on her chest and gave out a sarcastic gasp, "who me?"

I smirked at her, I mean even though we were connecting, she was still a fucking problem, perhaps down the line. I had to get rid of her, she was asking too many questions.

"So, mister, what's your name?" She inquired. I answered sharply, "my name is Discipline." She began to laugh so loud, and then said, "now look who is playing games, come on that's not your real name, sir?" I then said to her, "why must that not be my name? That is what they call me. Therefore, it is my name."

This woman annoyed me, now it's time for dinner, her back was turned, and this was my opening, so close to sinking my teeth into her when suddenly she said...

"Ugh, I have work in the morning which is a drag, but I will be picking up my son later that afternoon, which is my joy." I stopped immediately, "son?" I asked her. She nodded, "yes, I have a son. This weekend it's his dad's turn, we share custody." I asked her, "how old is he?" She said, "he's only five and he's so intelligent."

Damn, this changes things. How could I kill her knowing damn well she has a child to get back to, a child that depends on her, but he does have the dad, but it's always best when you have two gender roles around you. Memories came back to me, what if Precious was alive, what would be different? And would it be different if we had our child, she was holding inside her at the time? Before she was murdered?...

I then blanked, I wasn't here, my mind was all over the place. "You can go." She looked confused, "excuse me?" I became furious, "did I fucking stutter? Get the fuck outta here!" I shouted. She stormed out frustrated, confused and frightened. She ran out of the club as well. I spared her life for her child, however if she ever stepped my way again and approached me sideways, I would be taking her out without a blink of a fucking eye.

As I was walking out of my office, I met up with Phil Scott, he was a little tipsy, I yelled as he ran into me, "hey the man with the two first names, how are you enjoying yourself, Phil?" He was super hyped, "this place is amazing, what was your name again?" I shook his hand, "just call me Discipline!" I retorted. He was heading out, "we will be in touch, Discipline!" He said enthusiastically. I smirked, "indeed, we will. Hey, I hope you have a designated driver there, sir?" I asked him. Then he pointed to two gorgeous women, and I looked over with him at them, and they were waving to us, and both Phil and I waved back.

"You animal, two? Don't kill 'em Phil, take it easy big dog!" I said to him. He then laughed, "we will be in touch." I nodded my head at him and watched him walk out with the two women. He was in the middle, with his arm around both of them, each woman on his sides, they all walked out together. Shit, Mr. two first names, Phil Scott, was not lying, my club was banging, I perhaps had one of the hottest clubs in the city. But to me, I believed I had the hottest club in the city, but that's just how I thought, what I believed, but I never cared to enjoy myself in my own establishment. I am always focused on the business aspect of everything, I can't be slippin,' that's like me getting high on my own supply and that is something you just can't do.

It was the following day, and I had Phil's address from his ID that I scanned with my eyes and kept in my mind. I arrived at his home. Snuck in there when he was not there, swept the rooms for information. And I went there again when his family members were home. His children and his wife. So a couple of days go by. He gives me a call at the club. Because, I gave him the club information. But my

cell and the club's phone number is on there, the business card. He asked for us both to meet. I tell him to come to the club. We were closed, it was a Monday afternoon. We sat at the bar, then I invite him to my office. He says he wants to buy the place for sure, and he wants me to have no part of it.

"Listen, Discipline, I made up my mind, so what is your price?" He would pay me handsomely for the clubs, but I would have no hands in it. That was his deal.

I said, "no price, no deal." Then he said, "this will happen regardless if you are in compliant to it or not." I said, why don't we just team up like I was saying the other day? I believe we both can turn this business venture into something lucrative for the both of us." He then said, "no offense Discipline, you look like a stand up man, a man of his word, and a man about his business. However, I don't do business with your kind, like I said prior, no offense." I then asked him, "what do you mean, 'my kind,' you don't do business with?" he then elaborated, "I just mean, I don't do business with negroes, that is all. It's just me. I don't have any middle men, I work alone, no partners, and especially no negro partners."

I then said, "I urge you to reconsider, because if you go into the ring with me on this, you will lose. We go from me being potential alley, to now fierce competitor." The man with two first names, Phil Scott, laughed, " ha-ha, you will not even be a competitor Discipline, because I'm buying you out. I'm buying out the competition, therefore, there will be no competition." I shook my head, then I said, "okay, you were warned, so listen, I want the hottest club you own, and I want it signed over to me. I don't care what state it is in." I then started up talking again, right when he was going to talk, and said, "as a matter of fact, I want you to sign over your clubs for Texas, Atlanta and Connecticut to me, now."

He laughed, "hahaha, you must be sipping on the Kool-Aid." He said sarcastically. I then said to him, "why does everyone use that reference, is that an ethnic joke? Is that a racist or stereotype of a joke?" He then looked at me more seriously, "I will never do that." He said to me. Then I replied back, "well, I was hoping you were going to say that," and then I took out three photos. One of his wife, one of his daughter and son, I then asked him, "should I fuck your pretty wife? Or should I visit your son the football player, and daughter the ballerina? I mean, my niece knows who your son and daughter are. Come on, you want to make this difficult? You want to do this the hard way, or the easy way?"

I really didn't give him an option. He immediately called his lawyers to draw up a contract. I had him sign over all the clubs he owned to me.

"Fuck, Discipline you are a savage, yet an astute business man, do you have a heart?" Phil Scott asked me. I pointed to my left pectoral on my chest, and said back to him in reply, "It's cold, if it's even in there." I then continued to tell him how things were going to go...

"Now, there will be no middle men, especially a man with two first names, I think your parents are strange for that one, anyways, there will be no middle men, understood?" He nodded his head to me, and then assured me, "you'll pay for this," he threatened. "No, I won't, but you'll pay me, thank you." I said to him. After he signed everything over, I asked him to be sure, "everything is signed?" He then told me, "yes, everything is signed over to you." I smirked, "perfect, now, man with the two first names, Phil Scott, I hope you do not take this shit personal? It's just business!"

My eyes turned gold, my fangs grew, his eyes got wide staring at me, and he shouted out in panic, "what the fuck are you?!!" Then I said, briefly, "im the man, that just made you sign your life away."

And then I bit him. Sinking my teeth so deep into his neck. I could not watch over my shoulder or wait for the pay back. This man lost a lot, who knows what he would do. As far as his children, I had no plans to hurt them. Perhaps, I would have fucked his wife, and had him watch just to hurt him, if he still wasn't going to deal. But, all that talk about him not doing business with my kind, and the pay back talk he was spitting out, I could not risk it. I took all I needed from him, ID, finger prints, cell phone, I saw he was receiving texts, 'meet us at this warehouse? We have some shipment issues.' The text read this. Therefore, I called the number, and pretended to sound like him, the guy on the other line said...

"Hello, look, come later on tonight, I will text you the info, don't be late. We will all be there tonight." I then said, "no problem," pretending to be this guy Phil. I read this thread of conversions, what was this man into? Looks like, there was more to this guy with the two first names than he lead on. So, I needed an advance on some cash, and perhaps this would be it. I wanted to open another fitness club, so I went to go visit some mobsters later that night that Phil apparently was a part of. They were having a meeting in a deserted warehouse and it was all five of them. Each one, ran a borough in New York, as there were five boroughs in New York.

"What's going on fellas?" I asked that just to begin conversation, but I really didn't give a fuck how they were doing. So, one gentlemen said, "do we know you?" I smirked, 'no, but I know all of you, and I'll do the talking here." These men looked at each other like, 'who the fuck does this guy think he is? Or does he know to whom he is speaking to?' I gave them instructions.

"Listen, I want and need an advance from each one of you. Cash, check, whatever is clever!" They all laughed, I was angry. "Uh, that's not funny, I'm actually very serious. I want cash from each one of you now, like right now! And I'll help triple all of your businesses and territories."

They all took out their pistols. I then said to the gentlemen, "fuck, I thought this was going to be easy. Wishful thinking, I guess. "Fellas, I promise all of you, for your safety, this is not a problem that you want. I'll pay you all back in interest. Trust me, this can all be lucrative for all of us. What do y'all say?" They didn't speak, they just allowed their index fingers to talk, as those index fingers ran the chamber and those bullets came out the barrel and all flew at me all very quickly. Those bullets all came at me at once. My body dropped to the ground. They went back to their business. In about 5 seconds, I rose up back on my feet.

"Ugh," I grasp my stomach, my chest, my legs, but the wounds closed up as I had rapid healing and the bullets reversed from out of me and the bullets dropped onto the floor, and then I asked the fellas...

"So, I guess you all have trust issues? I was going to give y'all interest, now I am just going to take all y'all shit, and fuck y'all up."

These grown men were yelling, and shouting, "what the fuck!!!" I swiftly struck all of them at the same time. With lightning speed, hitting each and every one of them. And the last one I ripped his heart out.

"Those shots weren't too bad, very nice aim, I'm impressed. But next time, 'put some fucking heart into it,' motherfucker." I ripped his heart out and I had that shit in the palm of my hand. And then I sucked the blood from it. I took all the wallets out of their pockets, their cell phones and got all other information I needed. Credit cards, ID's just in case I needed finger prints in money vaults, and bank accounts. Cell phones, and their finger prints from that as well, in case I needed passwords, to unlock everything. I got the money, shit, I should open a club in each of the boroughs, just so I can say, 'I damn near fucking run New York.'

I took all their ID's so if I needed, I could shape shift into each one of them with no issues to obtain whatever I wanted to obtain. Nothing and nobody would stand in my fucking way, of what I wanted. I see it, and I want it. If I wanted it, it was already mine………

Chapter 8- Love Bites

I didn't head home right away. I arrived at this local bar, heading home was the last thing on my mind. With this new life, home never felt like home anymore. I sat at the bar, and this lovely lady sat down right next to me. She was ordering 'sex on the beach.' I snickered to myself, and she looked over.

"I'm sorry," I apologized to her, "that choice of drink always gives me a laugh." I said. She smiled and asked me, "hello, what's your name?" I replied, "it's Discipline." She stares at me with a flat stare, her gaze stared me up and down, as if she was measuring me up. Wondering why I would have a name as such. She then asked me...

"Really? Like really? I'm fucking tired of you men and your lies" I smirk, then I told her, "Discipline is what they call me, what I prefer people to address me as. However, I do go by another name, my real name. My government name, and if you care to know that, then you will earn it. And as far as your statement for, 'all men,' no one told you to deal with all men."

She was astonished with a facial expression like, 'how dare you!' With her mouth opened wide. I guess she never had a man speak to her the way I just did. "I'm not like that at all, it's a figure of speech." That's what she said to me, defending her statement. I then laughed and then said to her, "bad figure of speech. Look, if you want to deal with all men, that is your problem. It's a free country here

in America." She let out a deep breath of frustration, "I told you, I am not like that, I am not dealing, nor have I dealt with all men." I got her again, "okay, so, your statement means what? If you systematically, and consciously place all men in a certain category, that's what you will always obtain and attract. However, not all men are how you perceive them. A woman that says, 'all men are the same,' clearly has never met a Dominant man. She clearly has never met Discipline."

She raised an eyebrow in a sense of curiosity. We then began to talk a little bit more. I asked her, "what if there were no systems? What if there were no machines? I mean, no real machine can amplify, real power. What if there were no guns? Only powers? Superpowers?" she raised an eyebrow again to me. And I continued, "they put all their faith into machines, they can target and aim at whomever they choose, but they can never touch God. Does God give life? Does he take life? If he does both, what does that make him?"

She had no answer for me, she exclaimed softly, "my goodness, that's deep." Then she asked me, "what powers would you love to have?" I then gazed into her eyes firmly, "what powers would I love to have, that I do not have already?" She laughed at me, "ha-ha, I'm serious, what powers would you love to have?" I told her, "I'm serious as well, but if I were to have a power that I do not have?" I paused and thought about it, then I answered her, "it would be to bring back a life that was taken." If I had powers, it would be to bring Precious back, but, that shit is not happening, she is gone forever, and there is

nothing I could really do with that. Nothing to do but to accept what is. She was a little calmer towards me after that talk, and there was a power I wanted, and I didn't tell her about, and that was to be everywhere. To have the ability to entice every damn mind in the entire world.

Talking to me, it was like she grew comfortable around me, I told her, "don't be so quick to judge a book by its cover, you could learn something from a man. Not all of them are placed in the same category as you would believe. Know this, a woman will never love a man truly whom she cannot learn from." And then she said...

"I mean, you're right, you do have a point, it's just that 'Love Bites.' It really does. It sucks. Her choice of words were just the worst for a time like this, when hunger is kicking into my system. I stared into her eyes, and I said, "come to me." I had her in a trance. Blowing magic into her ear...

"Come to me, then cum for me. Let's get out of here." She gazed into my eyes and she didn't look away, nor did she blink... "yes let's go, please." She said to me in agreement. I paid the tab, and we left.

I ripped off her clothes as soon as we got to the room. I took off my tie, and I bound her wrists together and I tied the lead end to a piece on top of the bed. I took off her sheer cut lace nylon panties, I licked her body from head to toe. To the point of where I reached her pussy. I sucked and tug on her clit. Love bites I left on her inside thigh. Love Bites I left on her legs. I ate that pussy like it was my last meal. I traced the number 8, on her clit. Flicking my tongue now, back and forth. Side to side. I spread her pussy lips wide apart. I played with her pearl. Explored her. Teased her. Controlled her in so many ways. Dominated her entire existence. Manhandled her. Pinning her legs back towards her ears. She can complain about her legs later. But when the endorphins kick in, and the oxytocin and dopamine are released from her pituitary gland, not only does she forget where she is. She forgets feeling the pain. Mostly because she is not thinking of the pain.

Heels in the air. Slithering my hand towards her throat. Tight grip. Squeezing the flesh around it with my strong muscular fingers. Feeling the blood rushing throughout her body, turned me on even more. Pinning her wrists to the bed with my big hand. Curling my fingers inward into her scalp. Grasping a fist full of her hair. Tugging, just to anchor her head towards me. I see what I want. I take what I want. No question marks. She's already invited me in. Now I take her like she's never been taken before.

I shoved my thick, long, chocolate cock inside her drenched pussy hole. Stroking through and between her drenched, begging pussy lips. That pussy hole was so tight, it squeezed my cock like a vice grip. Walls closing in, my thrusting was spreading her walls wide open.

"Cream on my cock, cream on my cock." I demanded. She did just that, and then once I came with her, my fangs extended, and I sank them deep into her neck. Drinking her entire blood. Love does bite, and it can drain you out of your life. I growled at the moon. She was dead.

I got dressed, and I was out of that hotel faster than a man running home because dinner was ready, and he'd been starving all fucking day. I got out of there, faster than a bank job. I fucking owned the fucking night. I then met another young lady, and I was going on a rampage. Murdering all the pussy I could get and feasting on their flesh.

I could love a woman from the bottom of my heart. With every fucking cell in my being, and still hurt her. Still punish her and hold her accountable for her actions. Why? Three things; one, I never forget who the fuck I am. Two, no one controls Discipline, but Discipline. Three, I didn't get to where I was today by following, I fucking lead. I'm a difficult man to love, and to get along with, I know that. Does love bite? Perhaps. But, it also bites and sucks. Whether it's people in my life, the things I engage in, or pain alone, my assertive character is different from the norm. However, if a woman was able to love me properly. Accepting me for what I am. Who I was, as I her, she could get things beyond her wildest dreams. If a woman could love this lunatic, tattooed, chocolate maniac, savage monster, I would never let her go.

Unless it was a hard limit of hers that we agreed upon and discussed prior to this relationship, she is to do what I demand at all times. How I want it, when and where I want it. No exceptions.. When it came to other men…when it came to immortals even, they may be good, I just have way more to offer. I met this dominatrix of a woman, yet she was a masochist woman at the same time. I said, to her...

"This gives me power over you. Now, I will not use that power over you, however, if I have to in order to control you, I will. I will withhold this big, good chocolate dick from you to control you, until you learn and understand what this life of mine entails. If I must hold pain from you because that's what you crave? I will. You will know where you belong, who the fuck I am, what you are to me, and what this pleasurable, peaceful and serene, dynamic entails. You will understand the magnitude to this lifestyle. Tranquility, which is only to be interrupted by misbehavior, or when we fuck or play. We can play games together, but, you are never to play games with me. Because, I said so. Also, because you will find yourself playing checkers, with a man playing chess.

Nowadays, it's difficult to find a person to connect with you emotionally or mentally. Difficult to find men, who aren't so quickly trying to get in your pants. Behaving like they never had women in their lives before, or never seen pussy before. They say, they love pussy, but they never devour that shit. They mention they want you, but they never take that shit. They're soft, unassertive and passive. When it pertains to me, I will imprint my King essence in your soul, that anyone that tries to entertain you outside of me, will need to know me well in order to understand you. I am that, irreplaceable. So, it's a lose lose situation or a win. The choice is yours.

When I take, I take completely. I am always in control, no exceptions. You need to show me more gratitude. It's not something I should say, it's something you need to wise up about. Because, what's taken for granted, will eventually be taken away."

I then asked her, "do you take your looks for granted? Do you take your gorgeous body for granted? Do you take your life for granted?"

She gazed at me confused but didn't know what questions to answer first. I then continued...

"You're not here for play, unless I fucking say so. You are not here to be pleasured. You are here to please. To please a King, among men. Only complete obedience will be rewarded, and if you cannot provide this, I will gladly give you nothing. Lose yourself in my insanity, as you question your own sanity for the love of these moments. The irony is, you find peace in my chaos. The tighter my grip around your throat, the more you let go. The tighter the restraints, the more secure, and the more you feel at home. You've waited a while to feel this. Dreamt about this perhaps. Thought about this. Fucked yourself to the idea of this. Now, here we are.....show me how much you need me. Show me how ready you are to receive your destroyer, and your creator. Show me how ready you are for my big dick to organize your organs.

The time for fear has eradicated in a cloud of lust, desire, and wetness. You know you never adored the superheroes in the movies. You were rooting for the bad boys. The villains. These are who you idolized. So tonight, show me who you fucking idolize now! I will bury myself so deep inside you, that you will feel hollow when I'm not around. MINE. You know where the fuck you belong, and I don't need to remind you now."

Even if I could only have her for one night, I would show her the most ferocious love, and I would make her mine. She would feel it as well. She would know where she belonged. But, if she need reminding, I will reassure her with the bruises she would witness on her flesh. The soreness she would feel the following day. How drenched she would become, when she would sit at work thinking about me, and the moments we've shared. When she is destroyed by the extent of my sadism. Becoming appreciative of my Dominance. I now commanded her….

"Now on your knees, stare up at me with those pretty fucking eyes and say, 'can you fuck my face Master?' Then say, pretty please?"

She did as I commanded, but she wasn't about this life. She didn't love me. She loved the idea of me. Therefore, I could not let her live. I took her innocence, not that she was really that much innocent, and then I took her life. I was the beast of the night. There are things that need to be said, perhaps they're cruel, they're harsh. Callous. However, it's needed.

"You need to feel it. You need to hear it. You will always be humble. And if you do not come humble, you will be humbled." This is something I reiterated.

These women needed to know this. "It's one thing, to enjoy the act. It's another to want to please. The need to taste me courses through your veins like an addict going without their fix. It's that moment when I know they are in the mindset, where I need them to be before I shove my big chocolate beast in their mouth. Where I make this particular woman's mouth, not a tool for sex, but a fucking experience in itself. As for now, I make her wait. Then I make her wait some more."

I told her to keep her hands on the wall. She was not to remove them until I get back. She couldn't remove them until I say so. She said she was loyal, she said she would do what I wanted. The strength of this woman, but she was submissive to an immortal like me. And I didn't use hypnotism or any threats. She wanted to serve me, so she claimed. I put that to the test. I said to her...

"I'll be back." but I didn't mention when. I was out for quite some bit, peaking into the window from a distance. I never came back right away. Several hours went by, and then I showed up. She was still there, but she had moved from where I told her to stay. Her hands moved from the wall as well. We made passionate love, then I fed on her flesh.

Another that was not enough. She wasn't loyal like she said she was. Couldn't take it. Another one I felt just not ready for me. Another one bit the damn dust. A woman can talk all the shit she wants. Things you can't do, things she wants you to prove so she can utilize as reverse psychology. But when she's face down, ass up, or on her knees. Only things she's going to be saying is, "please? Can I?" And, "thank you." And if she's really disrespectful, she won't get any of this good pleasure, but a vicious spanking, a kneeling in the corner, a time out or hog tied.

A woman can say she's this, she's that, but her actions speak louder than how her gums flap. Yes, I get it, a lot of men say plenty, and deliver none. That makes women change, or behave a certain type of way. You see, women need to be wanted. It's a cry for attention. Whether it's a slap, a spank, choking, a kiss, an argument. They love that they can get under your skin. They love to feel needed by you. They love to be used, or be of use. Don't listen to them when they say they don't. Whether you're using them for pleasure or non-pleasure. They love it. It's a stroke to their ego. To be that one. Even to be the one, that you use for, that you don't use another for.

No matter if there are others, if she is a first of something, or the only place, thought, city, action, behavior for you, that pleases her. It makes her feel special. Women know exactly what it takes, exactly what to say, to push a man's button. The more she knows you. Your personality. Your mannerisms, the more power she has to utilize to push your buttons. This is why sometimes they throw temper tantrums and act stupid because they want attention. It's a cry for attention when they are misbehaving. And it works in their favor every damn time to a weak emotional man.

Myself, I was never born regular. I read between the lines. I'm always a step ahead, and when you think you're playing a game, you'll find yourself playing checkers with a King playing chess. I am in control at all times, even when you think I am not. DOMINANT, in every sense of the fucking word. Men are many things, but Masters of nothing. Pain must always come prior to the love. I will provide pain before pleasure, and she would then learn to appreciate both. If the pain is too much to bare, they are not ready for what I would be willing to provide. These women in this generation are nothing of what I've seen in the earlier eras. Times have changed. They behave manly. They are aggressive. They are slutty. They wear less and talk plenty. They have fake personalities, live fake lives and they crave real men? These women in this new generation are very confused.

Mere mortals. Mere human beings do not know how to love properly. They think love is crazy, and making love is crazier. They are cursed by their own limitations. I believe they are inadequate when it comes to such things. Providing insufficient satisfaction, whether that be emotional, mental, or physical. But a God. A Master. The greatness, not the best, but the greatest. Not only is remembered forever, but their powers are limitless. An immortal. Taking her imaginations beyond your physical limitations.

Lay back, take notes, and I'll show you how a real Beast, a real Sadist, a real King, a real Man, a true Scorpio, a true Dominant loves a woman. Some people don't have it in them to hurt another person. Whether it's with the truth emotionally, or marks on their body physically. Hurt them good, or hurt them bad for their own good. That's fine, but this lifestyle is not made for the weak. And that pertains to both parties. Physically, mentally, and emotionally. If you're thinking about it. Asking if she's okay, you're not built for this. That's why you discuss hard and soft limits ahead of time. That's why you grant her a safe word. I don't even allow a woman to scream, beg or tell me what to do in bed like, "harder, harder, spank me, pull my hair." I'll slap her in the back of her head...

"Shut up, let me do my thing, bitch. I know what I'm doing. I'm the Master of this, shut up and let me teach you. Don't tell me what to do, or I'll pause, or I'll pull out right when you are on the brink of climax, or I'll do the opposite of what you're ordering me to do to you. I don't take demands lightly, shut the fuck up, and take all of me, or nothing at all."

Anyway, if I hurt her, it is for her own good. She deserves it. She's earned it. If I mark her, I mark her as mine. She should be so lucky. I claim my territory in the most potent way possible. The most potent way I know how. She is mine to use. Mine to abuse. Mine to cherish and love. Mine to take whenever the fuck I want. However the fuck I want. Wherever the fuck I want. Discipline therapy. I am her escape. I am her stress reliever.

I always say, hair pulling is essential. Especially if you're already giving her that pain from the back. Fat, long chocolate dick slamming into her. Between her begging lips. Dominating her drenched, submissive hole. My control is her release. I literally feel when I pull her hair, them walls open and embrace me more.

You should learn how to pleasure a woman by how wet she becomes. How her moans and breathing change. The look in her eyes, as she falls in deeper love than ever before because of the release of dopamine, and oxytocin dripping from her brain. The endorphins kick in, there's no longer pain, but wetness. She forgets where she is. Forgets her name, but screams yours. Soaking, and those lips begging for more. A gangsta and a gentleman. Hold the fucking door open for her, and slap her ass as she's in front of you walking through it. I will hurt her. Especially if she begs nicely for it. Only the ones who hurt you, are the ones whom can heal you. No woman has truly loved a man, she has never hurt, or shed tears for. My love doesn't exist without pain as I've stated before. There will be pain involved, she will not escape that. I will test completely. Her mind, her soul. Especially her body. How much can she take for me? How much is she willing to withstand? I will slap her pretty little face. I will grasp her little fragile throat. Squeezing the flesh around it. The blood suppressed from her brain, down to her pussy, the endorphins will then kick it. Dopamine and serotonin engaged.

When I speak to her, while I'm inside her. The pain will become her pleasure. The pleasure will be the pain. The pain will change her. It will make her love. It will touch her heart. It will ignite all her senses. It will empower her. It will make her appreciate pleasure. Therefore, I say...

"Suffer my Queen. Suffer my slave. Suffer for me my slut. Give me every once of your pain. Give me what belongs to me. Pushing through your pain threshold, you grant me the key to your heart."

I then met another woman, oh she was Russian, with an accent. A lot of discreet behaviors and manners. Dressed properly and spoke well, perhaps I won't feast, I then thought to myself. We went back to my place, maybe I could just enjoy her time. If we fucked then we fucked, if not, I didn't mind. I spoke firmly....

"Adhere to my demands, and I'll show you how conducive this is to what you truly desire, baby girl." I called her. Granting her a nickname of my choosing.

"Let your imagination take you beyond your physical limits. Let my hands, my tongue, my lips, my thick, chocolate, muscular long dick know how to pleasure you, because they know your body..."

Body language is a major component of human interaction. We communicate more of our conscious thoughts and intentions with words but, when it comes to feelings and desires, a lot of what we are saying is conveyed on a subtler level. Submerged below the level of conscious control and coming out in how we position ourselves, what we do with our eyes and hands, how close we come to another person and many other cues.

I think about sixty percent of human communication is nonverbal. That's fucking more than half. A woman communicates her romantic and sexual interest in a man (or in another woman) in mostly nonverbal ways. Her eyes, her hands, how she positions her body. Just to name a few. Words enter the picture too, particularly if she is bold, and always in the end stages. But mostly they confirm what the body has already said and verify that the conscious mind and will are in agreement with the blood and the vitals. If you are reading her correctly, what she says when it comes down to, "Here's my phone number" or, "I'm free this Saturday" or even, "Your place or mine?" will come as no surprise.

She doesn't care to use her safe word with me. She yearns to give her pain to me. She aches to hurt for me. I have her whipped, and I don't mean with my big chocolate dick, a strip of leather or length of cord fastened to a handle.

She loves me, and I love her like poetry. Like art. Like music. Like control. She was like heaven and I put her through hell. Her body was like paradise and I put it through misery. I love seeing her pain when I stare into her eyes. Love and Lust. Pain and Pleasure. The glow on her face. The brightness of her smile. The look in her eyes. The bruises on her flesh from my impactful, yet delicious slaps on her plump ass cheeks. Big hand print. Big, strong, powerful hands. Reminders. Reassurance. That is me. Because of me. For me.

Eclectic messages from my brain, soaking into her female estrogen. Now she's wet between her legs from this thug seduction. Discipline passion. Discipline intensity. Discipline therapy. Only given by me. I could bend her over. She'll be whispering how much she's in love with my intelligence, Dominance and my gangsta. The anticipation driving her insane. Awaiting my next command.

"Don't move a muscle, turn around, don't turn around. Spread those legs for Discipline. Don't make a sound. Nor even a moan for me. Shut the fuck up. Give it to me. On your knees. Now crawl to me. You've come here to be taken. Destroyed. Overwhelmed. Dominated. Then loved and protected afterwards. By me. By a powerful man. By this chocolate King. You do not want mediocrity. Therefore, you wait patiently."

Now as I place my finger between her begging lips. Into her tight, drenched, torrid walls. Finger stroking so slowly. Medium speed. Quickly. Now slowly once again, like I was down shifting and working the clutch of her vehicle. Her eyes shut, she's moaning so ever softly, she is humming her moans. She remembers the rules. But later I'm going to have her moaning forcefully, when I give her permission to moan that is.

My big hands reach over to her head. Stroking her hair, curling my strong, big muscular fingers inward into it. Grasping a first full of her luxurious hair. I then took my finger out of her drenched walls and placed it in her mouth. Her eyes were shut. Savoring the taste. I literally have her wrapped around my finger. Like a snowflake, one little touch from my hand, and she melts. She was hot faster than the sun beaming on a barren land. Heat instantly around my presence. Her heart beat races. I could feel the pulse on her neck. She was like a piano. As I was touching the right keys, it was like music to my fucking ears.

I came from behind her, I spread both her ass cheeks apart. With all ten strong fingers of mine. Utilizing my big tongue to bless her. Before I utilize my big dick as a weapon to destroy her. Put her in such a euphoric state, she forgets where she is. Tongue in her asshole, tongue in her pussy hole. Tongue on her clit, I don't fucking play when I'm in that bitch. I want her to bust more powerful than a .50 desert AE desert eagle.

"I want those juices," I commanded. "Yes Daddy," she replies. Gushing like a busted fire hydrant. Juices streaming down her thighs. Tongue climbing on her walls like Spider-Man. She's drenched like Niagara Falls. Her feverish moist flower adores me. She's ready for her big chocolate treat. I spoke softly but forceful....

"You're going to have way more orgasms than that until your body is weak, and you can't go anymore. Let's see what your body is made of for me."

We then got it on. After the great sex, I could not even conduct an efficient conversation with this woman, we just didn't have that connection. I was bored, looks like she's not, nor will she be one of them.

"Say goodnight." I said to her. She looked at me and smiled, "uh, what?" My eyes turned gold color and I then bite her on her neck. And that was that for that woman. Blood was on the side of my mouth and my eyes were dark red.

I've walked away from some good pussy in my life. I've rejected many beautiful women in my life. Things that vanilla (average, ordinary) men wouldn't have the strength to do. One thing I'll tell you about a Scorpio, even though there are different levels of the Scorpio, and even though we are the most sexual and powerful sign. One thing I will say about us is, we don't just fuck with anyone. We require some type of connection as we are the most intense sign of the zodiac. For me, what makes me the best at pleasuring my partner is how well I know her, and how well we connect. Intellectual conversation releasing dopamine and serotonin from our brains. We are engaging in intellectual intercourse. If you are on this level.....When you involve yourself with an individual with no vocabulary, you dumb yourself down to their level. This is what happens when you witness the sapiosexuals with the non-sapiosexuals (that's the only way I'm going to refer to them as. I don't want to get extremely derogatory, but you all get the type of men or women I'm talking about). It becomes more difficult as we get older to sustain efficient conversation. Its like, people don't even read anymore as well. And because of this, you have awkward interactions.

As a hardcore sapiosexual woman, it is extremely difficult for her to find men that measure up to her degree. I mean women are already emotional to begin with, now you add a sapiosexual to her resume, good luck trying to pursue her. When it comes to words women love two things; music and books. Some of these women, they're in these mundane, mediocre relationships, because they have needs as well, or they remain single.

There's plenty of idiotic and stupid people in this world. Don't underestimate stupid people in large groups as well. You're never going to meet someone on your level. This is what makes us all individuals. As a sapiosexual man, you must have a woman that stimulates your intellect as well as your loins. It gets boring if not. However, if you elevate each other, or if you elevate the other one to your level, that's a different story.

I am a different type of Dominant. Yes, I am gangsta, and aggressive, passionate and intense, but highly intelligent as well. Scorpio, wise beyond my years. And now that I am at the point of greatness, possessing these immortal powers, I am on a level, that's un-fuckable. Untouchable. One of the things that separates me from other Dominants, is I have this innate understanding of the human's heart and possess the ability to delve in the human mind. Within these vampire powers I've been granted, has made me unstoppable now. I am not smart, I am intelligent, that's a major difference.

Two things that bless you; giving, and your genuineness. Authenticity, not counterfeit. Since women are the most emotional creatures on earth, this makes most of them very sensitive. You may say the wrong thing, and get them started. Started how? Ball out crying, very defensive or fuel and ignite a large fire. When a woman or man can open up their heart, many good things will come into it. You ever see those women with terrible attitudes? Short tempers? Negative souls? Where does that come from? How do they get them? Past relationships? That negative and bad energy is still in them? Can be many different things.

You are the universe. Every cell in your entire being is eavesdropping on all your thoughts. "Where have you been all my life?" She could asked me, I would have said, "you weren't ready for me yet." I don't believe in accidents. I don't believe in a coincidence. You create your own destiny. Your own luck. Why is it that the shy girl found that confident Alpha Male? She set that in motion. She knows she craves more courage. Who can help her with that? She knows she yearns for more confidence, who can help her with that? She sent vibes to the universe and his soul dragged his body to her. Or she was seeking, and she found him visually. "Dope souls need Dope souls." Until a woman, or a man finds themselves, they will ruin everyone they encounter. Or they will just not be ready. Doesn't it feel amazing to be touched by a person who fully understands your mind? A person who acknowledges your flaws, and loves your soul anyways?

When there is a deep and genuine connection, you will witness her doing things for you, she will not for another man. This generation is sex crazy, and think making love is crazy. He or she is drawn to you in a way that opens his or her heart in absolute vulnerability. Commingled with you in heart, body, spirit. They realize they have nothing to fear. Their flaws, insecurities and secrets are safe with you. They let down their guards. Let down their effort. Surrender in love with you for real without restrictions. It's like when you kiss....

Kissing and sexual energy are linked. Erotic kissing involves the lips and tongue. That is part of love play. When couples kiss with their tongues, also known as French kissing or soul kissing, the tongue reflects and connects their hearts. While their lips give and receive affection between each other. I appreciate sexy lips. Kissing deeply is an exchange of energy. It is emotional. Sexual chemistry is powerful. Sometimes when you are angry with your partner, you may have rough sex to ease the frustration, and once you release y'all think y'all make up. But, I bet you're not kissing, and even if you are it's not sensual. You aren't connecting. It's just all the anger has gotten you riled up, and your disposing that off. That tension. It's not like you're making up, because I promise it will be a reoccurrence of the same shit you were arguing about. It's like a pattern. Patterns turn into habits. Now these habits turn into behaviors.

Kissing her while you're inside her is a different level of intimacy. She is more than the pleasure. It is a ritual, where you exchange energy, emotions, thoughts, consciousness. That's why when you see girls speaking or behaving a certain way, you can tell who she fucks with, or has fucked with. When you're both engaged in sex, you are one. It's important that your vibes resonate. Each pump and thrust is an affirmation. When a man enters your pussy, what type of vibe and energy is he giving? Is he happy or bitter? Is he a positive thinker? Does he love himself or love you? When a woman makes love to you, is she happy? Is she positive? Does she love herself, and you? She has trust issues? Is she blessing you? Is he cursing you? Is your partner refueling, healing and recharging your soul, or draining the life out of you? Are they dragging you down to low frequency energy, negativity, un-fulfillment, depression? Or are they elevating you? Empowering you? Into the high frequency of love, life and happiness, King, Queen, God, Goddess, immortality?

I say sex is powerful all the time. You need to be mindful. Master how your energy is exchanged, received and returned back to you. Temporary forevers. Pleasures are temporary. But the side effects can last forever. Sex is a therapeutic medicine when done right. When two musical instruments do not resonate to each other's beat, the music is awful, really awful. And so is the sex. Engage in more cuddling. Love. Talking and conversing with one another before, during and after sex. Hugging. Holding hands. These things help with each other being able to orgasm. And when you orgasm, the body and mind start the emotional well being. It's imperative to maintain a healthy well being for emotional strength in today's stressed and negative world. By you choosing who you have sex with, you're building a bond to what is conducive to you, and what you desire. That bond becomes stronger through a creation of respect and love. That opens doors to intimacy, trust and loyalty.

Respect and loyalty are not upgrades in relationships. They are requirements. So, do I just fuck anyone? No, not only is my sex amazing, but I know what energy you're bringing into my life, and what I'm bringing into yours. It's imperative I know you, that's the only way I'll know how to work you. Physically, emotionally and psychologically.

I always speak of the power exchange relationship, with Dom/sub, and a woman is the most powerful creature on this earth. Dominance is the most prestigious thing on this earth. Similar souls attract, inevitably. All these thoughts, but I'm not destined to find true love anymore, look at me. I am an animal. I am a monster; a regular woman could never accept me. We would never work, even if we tried. I am her killer, I feed on her type of people. I'm cursed for eternity.

Another woman came along, petite, cute, she was a fiery one. We went to a hotel, I brought out my hand cuffs. I am a competitor in practically everything I'm engaged in. Everyone wants to be a beast, until it's time to do what real beasts do.

"So, you want to ride, baby girl? Then ride." I said to her. She can't do it efficiently. She can't do it with no hands. It's a little difficult with her hands isolated. My strong, muscular big chocolate man hands grasp her ankles, just to hold her in place.

Now she feels my strong and big hands tighten around her fragile neck. As she continues to go up and down like an elevator on this strong, big muscular chocolate. Moans get louder, eyes roll back, and breathing begins to change. Slapping of flesh sounds as though it's like back ground music, as her moans over power. I further open her flower. She feels her muscles contracting on this big beast. Her thighs getting tired.

"Keep squatting on this animal, I didn't say stop. I don't care if it hurts. I'm not trying to hear that. This is what you wanted? This is what you asked for? Then fucking work, slut!"

I fuel her voracious appetite. "If you pause one more time without my permission, I will reach for my thick wooden paddle, and that's going to keep you locked in. So, giddy up, now let's see what your body is made of."

I loved her energy, but I had to eat, and after I made her cum, she was weak, so I went in and bit her, killing her as well. I didn't stop until her eyes rolled in the back of her head, and I took her energy and blood, and ended her.

It was now morning, and as you know I was a day walker as well. I then met this woman as I was jogging outside by the park. We sat down for a little bit. We engaged in conversation…

"I'm curious about you. You seem so innocent. Let's go somewhere." She stared at me confused, and replied, "what type of girl do you take me for? Boy, I'm tired of running, let's talk for a minute." "Don't call me boy," I said to her. She then giggles, "okay, then what are you? A girl?" I then said to her….

"You can call me great." She then laughs. "Why are you great?" She asked me… I remained quiet. "So you're not going to reply? She asked once again and then she said….. "I'm going to have to find out or something? You're not great."

Here's the reverse psychology in play, but I didn't fall for it. I still wasn't going to tell her, or prove to her to give her peace of mind. Therefore, she can say to herself that she knows me well? She then continued....

"Especially if you don't know how to speak to me." In my mind I was thinking, (bitch, I could fuck you up, entirely). She has no idea what or who she is dealing with. But I see what she's doing. But I maintained my composure. "So, teach me how to speak to you. I'm willing to learn." I said to her… So I approach her like this, just to see where her mind was at. Just to listen to and observe what she would say.

She laughed, "first of all, learn how to ask me." She paused. "And say, please." Now I busted out laughing, "ask you for what?" I chuckled, and she answered me…

"To take me places, my number, etc." I then said to her, in reply to that....

"That's not going to happen." I said this softly but forceful. She then asked me, "why is that?" I moved closer to her face. Gave her one of my stern looks, just so she would realize how serious I was. "I won't chase you, I'm not into those games. However, I'll work to gain you, there's a huge difference." She stared at me squarely, "why is that, sir?" She asked. I then educated her....

"Because, I don't mind a little hard work. But as little as I will work for you, I promise you will work three times as hard for me." She pulls back with a smile, "oooh, I love your confidence sir, and a man of integrity is rare. I respect that. But just because I respect that, doesn't mean I'm going to let you hit it." I smirk, and then asked her, "who said anything about sex? I see one of us has sex on their mind. If we engage in anything, if we become anything. My goal. My job will be to make sure you feel safe. Not comfortable. Comfortable is when you forget who you are, and what this is. I plan to always overwhelm you. Keep you on your toes as if you were wearing stilettos. Surprise you. Leave you helpless. We would go dancing, and we can do that all night. My choice. You just get ready when I say, wear what I want, and be ready to engage at my time. Share these special moments. Then again, you probably don't have rhythm," I said to her, and then she was offended....

"Hey!" She exclaimed, while she gave me a flirtatious love tap on my shoulder. "You know what's sexy?" I asked her. She stared flatly, and then she asked me back, waiting for my reply. "What's that?" Then I said, "an intellectual conversation." She didn't believe me, she didn't believe this encounter…

"You're too good to be true, who are you? Stop playing games." She pressed the question. I smirk, "perhaps you say this because of what you're used to. What you're used to seeing, and what you're used to hearing."

She was craving intellectual stimulation. She throbbed at my every word. My mind. Insatiable.

"I speak to you like no one before me, so your mind, body and soul has no choice but to listen. I snatch your soul, without the hint of sex involved. Every cell in your being reacts to my energy. But the whole time I'm speaking, you're probably imaging how big my dick is."

She giggled then placed her head down, "no I was not." She's lying, I then started gaining this new power I had, but never really used to it's full potential, which was telepathy. I was able to read her mind very well, accurate and adequately…. I then continued moving closer to her earlobe, just so no one could hear me but her. Whispering softly in her ear...

"Concentration on the feel of me slamming into you. The perpetual friction against your clit, and how I could possibly do anything to you right now. But would remain devoted to your pleasure. Your muscles contracting against my thick long chocolate dick........but we won't get into that."

She sighed. "Sir, you are fresh." With a smile on her face. She didn't deny it. I could see the images she created of me in her head taking her. She thought I was fresh, but she loved it, I could read her body language. I continued.

"I'll have you discussing me in front of your lady friends. And when I'm finished marking your mind, you will beg me to mark your body." She then asked me.... "oh, you're so sure about this huh? Get out of here. However, you do have a way with words, but it's not like you're blowing my mind or anything. But I'll see it when I believe it." I then said to her, to counter what she was saying....

"No that's not a challenge. I don't have to prove anything to you. You will earn everything. And you know it's true, that's why when I speak to you, you stare into my eyes, like you're hypnotized. More than 90 percent of the communication we put out there is non-verbal. Why are you so not trusting? Guarded? I know why. I see pain in your eyes. I see, many have spoken and never delivered. I see past disappointments. I see, many have never fully measured up. The way you sit, the way you tilt your head back. How you twirl your hair when I speak to you. How your foot taps repeatedly because you're nervous. But how can you be blamed, it's my incredible Scorpio sexual energy that you feel throughout your body. How you bite that bottom lip of yours, every single time my voice raises."

She shook her head at me, "what are you like reading my mind or something?" I smirked, "well, yes I am actually." She laughed, she wont believe me, to her I am an ordinary man, because she has no idea whom or what I am. She stuck out her middle finger to me, as a sign of, 'you're lying,' type of shit. I then told her, "the middle finger is the most sensual one, and the ring finger comes in a close second. I witnessed a few times as you play with your pearls between your middle finger and your ring finger, alternately wrapping them around each. Your brain is going into overdrive right now."

She pulls her hair aside to bare her neck, an instinctive, 'I submit' signal. Come on, I'm figuring her out, she's fucking OVERWHELMED. Each movement she did had an irrefutable meaning by itself. A woman's words can lie, but never her body or soul. Always listen and pay attention to those. Listen to her soul and read her body.

She let out a little giggle, "that was impressive sir." I then said to her, "oh how I will bite that bottom lip." She demanded I tell her more,"oh yeah, tell me more." I now had control, and then I said to her, "you didn't even say, please?" Yeah, I flipped it back on her. Now she puckers up her eyes. Turned her head sideways and says, "please?" I shut her down, "no, too late." I replied sardonically. I gave her a little, and I now allow her to fiend for more.

"Plus, what makes you entitled to my greatness anyways?" I smirk, "and anyways, you're probably terrible in bed." Her face fell in astonishment. "Oh no you did not just say that! You damn asshole!" She sputtered. I then smirked. "You won't even know until you try me." She said. Now look at her, now practically going to and willing to give me her panties, to prove a fucking point. She then said, to boost her ego up herself. To intrigue me, to make herself seem desirable. "I could be the best you ever had."

Now, I put her on the damn spot, "so now you're inviting, huh? I thought sex wasn't on your mind?" She tried to flip it on me....

"Well, you're the one speaking of this!" She accused me. I told her..."So, who cares if im speaking of it, I never said sex wasn't on my mind. The question wasn't directed towards me." And in my mind, I'm thinking (and no you won't be the best I've ever had. You've never had real sex, until you've dealt with this true Scorpio King). But I'll allow her to think that. She has no idea. But maybe one day she'll find out, lets see how things go. Let's see how persistent she is. Let's see how good she becomes. Let's see how obedient she is when she's hungry. She was good, but I was better.

We connected so greatly, but, I found out from her, she was engaged to be married, I fucked her. But I didn't kill her. I should have killed her right then and there for not telling me upfront. But, I allowed her to live. At least I knew that she was going to get married, that I wouldn't see her again. She was probably just trying to enjoy her final time out as a free woman. Maybe she just wanted some chocolate she always fiend for but could never have, who knows, who cares.

I met another woman; this woman was a lioness. But a lioness who thrives on Discipline. I told her the rules right from jump so she could understand where this was going to go. I got her to the room, and now here we go....

"You need to understand, you are my submissive. Not my girlfriend. I am your Dominant, not your boyfriend. I am your Daddy. Your Master. Your King. Your fucking Sadist. When you are given the right, these are the only ways you address me as well. For these names are powerful. Strength, and have different and such significant meanings. Since you forgot, I have to remind you. You will be reassured by the bruises you witness on your flesh. You will be held accountable for your misbehavior. Your little disobediences. You're not the average woman. Your life consists of; rules, Discipline, guidance, and when you get out of line, I will not hesitate to put you back in your place.

You will know your role, or I will teach you. You will love being good for me, as I prefer you to be. You will hate being bad and disappointing me. As you will receive nothing for your misbehavior. Punishment is the last resort. I never want to punish you. But if I have to, trust me, I will not hesitate to. Don't unleash my savage, he isn't pretty. You will take me to a dark place I keep hidden away. A place where I hear voices in my head. I do a great job in controlling him. But he's ruthless and has no compassion. He won't listen to your cries. Your tears. Your apologetic mess. He thrives on your pain. He's set on destruction. You give him ammunition. Ready to teach you a lesson. Brutality is his home. The bitch in you, fuels the asshole in him.

You have all the power in receiving what you need, because I will never give you what you want. Be conscious, I am the Master of this. I have a memory like an elephant, conscious of your likes and dislikes. I will use those to keep you in line. You misbehave for a spanking, because that's what you like, I'll make you kneel for an hour in rice. Overstep, you will get my thickest belt never seen. Fuming? Nothing cold water can't take care of. Talk too much, you get my spider gag, or ball gag, and now you shut.....the.....fuck.....up. You will never want to argue face to face, or go back and forth with me, baby girl. You will always be in one or two positions; on your knees, and I could make you wait an hour before I touch you, or face down and ass up. That's the reality.

You love to display masochistic behavior, be ready for the dark. Be ready to look at true evil in the eyes. Be more afraid of the monsters you run from, and less of the ones you run to. 'Discipline' is the most prestigious. Most conjuring. The worst of them all. The catalyst to change. Experiencing it, you will never be the same, nor view normal the same again. Your mental muscle memory. Your body's muscle memory, your soul's muscle memory. Repetitions, you will thrive. Watch how you evolve.. A hungry submissive is always an obedient submissive. You will receive nothing from me, but the things you earn. You will work for everything you get, and you will learn to appreciate whatever I give. Then and only then you will receive this prestigious gift of mine. Me. My Dominance. My mind. My power. I will give you pain before pleasure, and you will learn to appreciate both. Come humble, or be humbled. Why? Because I don't crave it. Why? Because I don't ask for it. Why? Because I don't wish for it. Why? Because I don't compromise myself for it. Why? Because I fucking demand it!"

She won't beg? She's too stubborn. She's too much of an alpha woman? A boss? Independent? She will learn alpha. She will learn boss. She will learn how a Queen has no shame in bowing to a King. She won't kneel? She won't worship? Why? Because she's never had to chase a man before? Why? Because social media, or friends have brainwashed her? Because she thinks she is the highest or highest ranked of women? Because perhaps she's accomplished so many things? Whatever she's accomplished is irrelevant when she's face down, ass up getting pounded. So why isn't she going to kneel again? Because she never had to beg a man before? Because begging is beneath her? Now I put begging above her.

"Hello, I am Mr. Begging now. You kneel, and you glance up at me with your hopeful eyes, and you start begging. You want to be a Queen? You are a whore first. A woman that can crawl has potential to fly. You want to be elevated? I can make you function at your most optimal level. Show me how powerful you are. Crawl. Then fucking Beg."

Because I am not a man to her. I am not a boy to her. I am not ordinary to her. I am a King to her. I am a Daddy to her. I am a Master to her. I am the phenomenal one to her. The all powerful to her. I am her great creator, and I am her all mighty destroyer. She won't beg? I bet she will beg for this hand. I bet she will crawl for this thick, long chocolate to be sliding in and out, between her begging lips. She won't beg? I bet she beg for this monster to touch her cervix. She won't beg? I bet she beg to squirt all on it. When I say. When I want. No? But what if I pull out? I take away her pleasure. I bet she begs then. She won't beg? I bet she begs to touch herself. She won't beg? I bet she begs for the most prestigious aspect in life. She won't beg? I bet she eventually begs for this pain. This callousness.

This pleasure. This aggression. I bet she begs for, 'harder.' She won't beg? I bet she begs for chocolate. She won't beg? But her fucking body betrays her. Her eyes beg. Her lips beg. Her throat begs. Her hair begs. Her body language begs. Her soul begs. Her mind begs. But I want to hear it from her mouth. Why should she beg? Because she will earn it. Why should she beg? Just off the mere fact that I fucking said so, that's why.

"So, beg my slut. Beg, and then beg some more. You promise to be mine at all times, I promise to destroy you and heal you every time." She was out of sorts. Out of body experience, but she understood what I said, well she heard it. She was not too fond of that idea, so I had to get rid of her. I gave her too much of me, I told her too much. She was either in or out, but I could not just let her walk, therefore, you don't want to be in this life, I take you off this earth. And by getting rid of her, I fed once again. All women I believe were born to be submissive. That is why they are healers. That is why they are mothers. That is why they are nurturers.

Women will say many things, but we all know before any type of physical interactions, displaying resistance is irrelevant. Physical, that's easy. You will receive the best you never had. But to focus on your mental. Your soul. That's power. That's control. That's work. See, power doesn't require a total transformation in your character or any physical improvement. Power, and seduction is a thing of psychology. You'll do this, you won't do that, you'll try that, you won't try that. Bullshit. See, a hungry submissive is an obedient submissive. When you know the reward at hand. You will do anything to please your Dominant.

Granted you have hard or soft limits, however, when hunger takes over. When need overpowers want. When you relinquish complete control. That's when true pleasure begins. You will crawl, you will beg, hurt, cry. Why? Because I say. It will occur because you care to please me. Why do you please me? Simple, because pleasing me, will please you. You want it, earn it. Earn your pain. Earn your pleasure. Earn your reward. The chase is on......

Chapter 9- Silver Moon, Drenched Night

Everyone wants to be a Dominant, until you have to tie a few knots, or work a little hard. Women are like vehicles. There's different makes, models, body types, some are fully loaded. Some are not. Most men want them fully loaded, but don't want to pay that price. It doesn't impress me to hear a woman say how great she is in bed, her skills, etc. all of those things are irrelevant to me. You're dealing with an immortal man. You're not going to do to me what you think every man likes, or your last liked. You will please me how I like. So, your skills on your résumé, I'm deleting all of them. I met a new woman......

"Your training begins baby girl. Let's train your ass. Like literally. Trained to please me. Trained to take whatever I wish to give." I said to her matter of factly.

A lifestyle of this magnitude. A man of my character. I can turn the coldest woman, warm. Alpha woman into a little. A savage hearted, soft. A spoiled brat, a loving and giving submissive. It doesn't matter how long it takes. What methods and techniques that are implemented. It's the results that matter in the end. Algolagnia, when you are going through the motions. The endorphins, and oxytocin released from your brain, throughout your blood streams because of this intense activity. You will not even feel it as pain, it will now become your pleasure. Testosterone is at an all-time high. Your libido is raging. Adrenaline is rushing. This euphoric, intense, exhilarating experience. Lose yourself in my savage. In my insanity. In my brutality. In my sadism. This energy is potent as if it were a drug, and even if you fought it, the urge would keep coming back. Lose yourself in my sin. Beast mode doesn't end in the gym. When all the good shit hurts at first. When 'forever' takes work. Call me insane, as you question your own sanity for the love of these moments. So today baby, we train you. Train you to please me. Whenever, however, wherever, for whatever. To excite you intellectually. Cover you spiritually. Stimulate you mentally, and after the apodyopsis, undressing you with my eyes, satisfy you physically. You will have the best sex of me and with me, in your dreams, in your mind, way before I can even lay a hand on you.

This new woman, I told her to call me, 'Alpha.' I didn't give her my name.

"So, my pet, when you're going through the motions, don't cry out for God, not only is he busy, but he won't save you. Call for Alpha. Beg for pain. Hurt for the Sadist. Moan for the King. Ask for me to go too far. Scream for 'harder', tear for your Master. Release your sweet juices for your Dominant. Surrender what you are, for what you can become. Surrender your mind, body and soul to my control."

The night was wet, and young. I look at the lion in the fucking jungle for example. It is the prominent King of the jungle. Even the elephant knows he is the King of the jungle. The lion has the formidable personality of a King. Just look at him. Well you can't see it in any pictures of a lion, but the highly distinctive mane he has. It resembles a natural crown providing an excellent intimidation display! The more casual and laid back 'I don't give a fuck' attitude! I can't think of any other animal to take the coveted King's role. I cannot think of any other carnivorous feline. Even the heavy plant eating mammal the elephant, is aware the lion is the King of the jungle, like I said. King of beasts, apex predator. Royalty. Naturally Dominant. Stare into his eyes and you will witness strength, resiliency, pride, honor, power, courage. Designed for combat. Built for war. Brutality is home.

The lion has amazing fighting technique. He's calculating, strategic, and methodical. He will assess his prey before he attacks. Hunger is the prime incentive. 'Dominate' is his primal instinct. However, there's perks to being King. The lioness does most of the hunting (they are quicker in speed, they weigh less, and they do not have mane, which helps significantly. Allowing them to disguise themselves from prey), lions sit back and wait for the meal, wait to eat first. For there are perks in being the Alpha, the King, the Dominant Lion. It's not that they're lazy, it's just lions are stronger. It's their Dominant role to protect the pride from intruders, etc. Most lioness desire to be around him, and most lions desire to follow or be like him.

Usually the most Dominant alpha female lion, will mate with the most Dominant alpha male, because she desires a strong cub. A strong cub to eventually take over a pride one day, and have a better chance of survival. One of the male's jobs are to, establish and maintain Dominance. Lioness provides. Lion instinct.

Myself, I associate my energy and behavior like a lion. I can turn it on and off whenever I please. During the day.

The poise, calculating, strategic and methodical business man. Night, the sadist. The savage. The Dominant. The beast incarnate. The fucking vampire King. Control and pressure is where I excel. Physicality is where I thrive. Power is the norm, Dominance is a way of life.

The moon was full, and it fueled my hunger, and my strength. There was something in the fucking air. Women are coming to me. Attracted to me like I was the shit, and they were flies. Like moth to the flame. Women are like wolves. They can see, smell, hear and feel power and Dominance from afar. I mean, honestly, show me a woman who never craved to be Dominated, show me a woman who never craved to be taken and pursued, and I'll show you a damn liar. It doesn't matter if she was twenty-five, thirty-five or forty. My power will inspire her to feel like a young child once again. I will treat her; however, she's behaving.

Women are perhaps the most potent and emotional creatures on this planet. Because women are so beautiful, intelligent and powerful it's so easy for them to Dominate weak men without a lift of a finger. Women Dominate men in different forms; whether it be with their looks, their bodies, their idiosyncrasies, their minds. You may think you're in control, meanwhile they are one step ahead of you. I'll use the analogy of the game of chess. The Queen is the most powerful piece on the board, however, the King is the most prominent, and that must always be understood. Because if the King is captured easy, or in a sense of losing control, the game is pretty much over. In order for you to be able to Dominate your opponent, or in the game of chess, one must understand their opponent thoroughly, or the game that's being played. It's like you know their next move before they make it. If I can't beat her in an intellectual argument or conversation, I will with my physical Dominance and strength. And if I can't physically, I will emotionally. And I will display how I play and know the game is played much better. Speaking of better, let's make her better. While I was speaking to the woman I was Dominating….

"Slick mouth, I'll take care of that for you. No, it won't be a spanking, that's what you love, want and expect. Plus, that's too basic. That's not even punishment or Discipline. How would you learn from that? You wouldn't, you would just repeat the same patterns and behaviors, so you can get the same results. Repeated patterns, turn into habits, and those habits form behaviors. Leading to you being in complete control psychologically of me. But, you're going to learn quickly, so your first lesson begins today."

I had this one woman, she never experienced something so primitively strong. She's never been challenged, but the look in my eyes invaded her every thought. Every Moment. And her fears. Doubts. Insecurities eradicated. My gaze made her legs weak. Gave her goosebumps. Watered her pussy. Leaving a feverish dampness that was uncontrollable to her. The steady cadence of my voice, left her in a hypnotic state. Magnetic. She gave herself to me over the depths of my words. The sounds of my voice soothed her. It smoothed the rough edges of her stressed consciousness. Sometimes she needs a hard, slow, wet mental pounding of hard and big dick. Not frantic pumps, just attempting to get off. Or get yours. I'm talking; slow, hard, deep, long, strong, methodical, passionate, intense, jarring, stiff.... brilliance stroking her pituitary gland, that takes her ideas, dreams and her thoughts to a whole other world. Her thoughts squirting everywhere. I spoke softly to her, but forceful…

"Have you ever had a connection so deep, feelings, goosebumps, butterflies occur within you? Great sex is not achieved through multiple positions and deep penetration. Some may possess a lot, but unsure how to actually utilize what they have. The best sex happens with deep heart connection. Knowing how to breathe, speak and relax in moments of ecstasy is orgasmic. Afraid to love, and trust is what fully keeps a person from experiencing life, magic and true pleasure. When your heart is desired, it's because selflessness breeds love. If your mind is desired, it's because conversation breeds connection. If your soul is desired, it's because energy breeds an intangible bond. If you're wanted, it's because nothing can replace the impact of your presence.

Do we take our senses for granted? Your physical appearance will never compensate for what your mind lacks. And that's substances. What if the entire world was blind? Who would you impress? Imagine what we would be capable of as a society, if there was a magazine on the top shelf. Or a pageant for beautiful minds that were as popular as miss universe?"

Whether a man is a bad guy, a bad boy, if he treats her well, you think she cares? Fucks her immaculate, you think she cares? Let's flip it, let's take a nice guy who treats her like gold, but can't fuck her properly, is he still treating her like gold? You think she cares? Now, for that little thing in their life he lacks? Does she just shrug it off? Of course she does. Women love bad boys, women love danger, even if it screams 'death.' However, you know what makes a bad boy even more irresistible? A bad boy who has his shit together. A bad boy who is a good man. I mean, if she's pleasuring herself when she has a man to do that, isn't that embarrassing? Does she now have uncertainty within herself? Does she now believe maybe it's her? Does she feel undesired? But, wait a minute, how is he not satisfying her if he knows her? So, he doesn't know her? Because, if they connect on a deep level, and they know each other, aren't they going to know and learn how to satisfy each other? All these questions here are rhetorical. You see, I am not a savage monster. I am just ahead of the damn curve. I said to the woman, as humbly as I could say it...

"Do you know how fortunate you are? Be thankful, be humble, be appreciative and be grateful. Do you know how many women are deprived of pleasures in this world constantly? Embrace your desires, your fantasies and urges that constantly come back. Women do not experience some of these pleasures, and they have men. Men whom are inadequate of providing such things, therefore leading them to be single, pleasuring themselves. Mentally, emotionally and physically." She had nothing to say. I was inspiring a desire for her to get on her fucking knees. Waiting on all fours, for my next command.

"Crawl to me..." I spoke softly, but forceful. As I stared down at her, and she met me at my feet. Gazing into her begging, her 'fuck me' eyes. Watching her submit. Surrender, waiting for me to give her what she needs. What she's earned. What she deserves. That first whip of my big chocolate man hand, on her soft round ass. The impact my hand creates as it kisses her flesh. A loud gasp and relief escapes her soul. Her journey begins now. An undeniable wish for my big, strong, chocolate man hand to grasp her throat and command my darkest desires for her to fulfill.

These things that I would do to her, these things that I would provide to her, become the only things that feed her cravings. Constant wetness between her legs became worst, with my growls in her ear. Begging to fucking cum for me. She constantly begs. Now she knows what it's like to be taken. Controlled. To be a real woman. To be owned. To be mine for the moment. Mine for the night. I'm official, I'm not a referee but I definitely made her pussy whistle. The best sex is usually with the ones you shouldn't be having sex with. Love. Sex. Rope. Duct tape. Handcuffs. Restraints. Slaps. Marks. Bites. Bruises. The one who gets her pussy the wettest, is most likely the least good for her.

"I'll take what I want from you. Don't act as if you don't like it," I growled at her. "Now, when I'm grasping your hair, spanking your ass. Thug style, hand around your throat, while I'm fucking you all wild. Altering your moods and behaviors. You're a good girl, but different woman around me. I see that. A brand-new woman. Lose yourself in my madness. You need that. As I push, pull, grasp, hold, and take you down. It will feel as if you're being taken and fucked by so many different lovers. The Beast. The Dominant. The Sadist. The King. The Alpha. The Master. The Monster."

All these masculinities in me, inspire the femininity in her. I make her feel like a real woman when I tell her what to do. I make her feel like a real woman when I touch her. I make her feel like a real woman when she wants to dress up for me. Dolled up, just so I can rip that fucking dress, fuck up her makeup and mess up her luxurious hair. Thick, long, Dominant chocolate dick, driving into her submissive, drenched hole. Hugging my girth snug, with those begging pussy lips. I shouted at her...

"Yeah, just like that! You love being my bitch, my whore. My good girl, my naughty and nasty pain slut, my prize."

She loves to moan and roll her eyes in the back of her head when my thick, hard long chocolate dick is slamming into her round ass. She is knowing damn well I won't take no for an answer when it comes to that pussy. And I don't give a fuck if I only had her for one night. I would love her so intensely, I would make her mine entirely. She doesn't struggle, because she knows it's mine. I destroy her body, and my big chocolate beast massages her insides. Body begging. Pussy vibrating. Clit throbbing. When I've stroked her soul to absolutely no return. When she feels nothing of her former self. When animal instincts become stronger. When it's too much. When she's ready to let it all go. Through the clasped hands. Through all the restraints. Through the sweet, rough kisses of darkness. Through the perfect blend of helplessness. Breathlessness. Torture. Vulnerability. Through everything she has given me. From the last bit to share. Through the last gasp of air. She begs to cum…

"Please, can I cum? I'm cuming." I made her come faster than 911 in white neighborhoods. And I made her scream like she's never screamed before. Oh I know she has never screamed like this prior. Why? She has never fucked with an animal like me before. The regular men in her past were practice, and this was the fucking test. This was the big game. My cock penetrated her so rough, a little blood came out, right onto my cock. She looks at it, and says in surprise, "I'm bleeding? But it feels so good. Well, I'm not on my period. You are an animal Mr. Discipline, yes!! But a little blood never hurt nobody."

She stepped into the bathroom to go clean herself up. She came back into bed, "you were like a desperate, howling demon." that is what she said to me. I gazed at her, and then she asks me....

"Please do it again? And rougher." She begged. I looked at her, and my eyes turned a gold color, they were bright, and my fangs came out. "Don't worry," I said to her. "See, my sex is so good, it's to fucking die for." Hissing at her ferociously. Now, she screamed, and before she could run away I grabbed her, and I sank my teeth and feasted upon her. My fangs dug deep into her neck, and then on her chest. First, I murdered the pussy, then I take her out. If it's one thing a vampire has, it's patience, but sometimes even that runs out. Vampires have a high sex drive, and even we won't jump ahead, until we are invited in.

Humans fear what they don't understand, and they hate what they fear. Clearly, I showed her a demon, a potent demon she was asking and begging for. But, when I gave it to her in the flesh, so she could see it for herself, the demon made her scream. She screamed out of fear, fear for her life. She deserved to die.

The following day arrived, and I was a special breed of a vampire. I was what you would call a 'day walker.' Its like after I killed and fed on Alexandria's (the one who turned me into this immortal in the first fucking place) blood, I gained most of her energy and her powers.

I went into one of my fitness clubs that I owned, and I was just exercising and getting my blood pumping in my human form. I broke a sweat or two, and I was ready to go. I left my club, showered and started my day. The night arrived, and it was beautiful. Full moon, and drenched atmosphere. In the night I was the strongest. I felt the most alive. I ran into someone that night, she was strolling in the park, no one else was around. I ran up to her, and asked...

"What is a lovely lady like yourself doing out so late?" She gasped for air, "listen, I have pepper spray, okay!" I was in my human form, I mean, damn lady, I didn't even display to you my eyes or fangs yet. She then said to me, "I mean, I love the negro people, but…." I interjected then, cutting her off, "no, you actually don't, if you must mention that, you definitely don't. Perhaps you are unaware, perhaps you are aware. But, let me explain something to you, I know you just want to seem like you do, you actually have a problem with as you say, 'the negro people', don't you?"

I already knew this bitch had to die, just off the fact of that remark. She frantically answered me, "no, that's not true, I….I..." I cut her off again, "well, you are lying." She shook her head, no. I nodded my head, "yes. I mean, I can read your mind miss. And that's all you're thinking about. Yes, you do have pepper spray in your bag, oh and you have a knife in there as well."

Her mouth opened wide as she was shocked that I guessed right. But, I had x-ray vision and I could see what was inside her purse and knew better than her what was in there. So many buried things in her purse, she probably forgot was in there. She then asked me, "oh my god, how did you know I…?" I continued to cut her off, "shhhh, just listen, this will be quick. And you are probably wondering when it will happen, right? Will you get a chance to run? Yes, I notice your eyes moving left and right, are you looking for something to strike with? You think, how far will you get? Will I chase you? Will it be painful? And I could answer all this for you. See, you will not get far, you will not find something to strike, it will happen very soon, and it will be quick. Will I chase you? No, because, well you will not get a chance to run. Will it be painful? Just a little bit."

I didn't waste any more time with her, "and don't worry about loving or not loving the negro people anymore," my eyes turned gold and my gold fangs grew. And before she could scream, my claws came out and I slashed her neck, I aimed for the jugular. I aimed for that vein, and when I did that, blood gushed out, and I drank the blood that speared out of her neck. Blood never tasted so damn good. But it felt good killing her, just because. Yum. That night, I went on a killing spree, taking everyone I wanted, and getting rid of their bodies in the process. But, there were some bodies I left behind. I knew something would eventually catch up to me. But, for some reason I did not give a fuck. I was a day walker and a night walker. I had businesses that I owned that operated during the day, and some at night strictly that were my cover. But, shit will always catch up to you, and it may not be now, it may not be when you expect, but it does. And I was right...

Suddenly, I came across that woman that was at the club, Cleopatra. How did this woman find me? "What the fuck are you doing here?" I then questioned her. She found me at the park. It was weird, normally I am able to sense a presence and I could not feel hers.

"Is that a way you greet a woman, or any person? She asked me, and I just gazed at her. "My goodness, so rude!" She said to me. I was not entertained, nor was I pleased. "Who are you? Why are you here? I know you're someone that knows me, this shit is not a coincidence."

I was asking a series of questions and I wanted her to answer them. She knew I was on the money, she then said to me, "you're right, your energy is picked up by me, and I feel you. It is so potent. I know you're someone powerful, a warlock, a vampire or a God? I can sense your energy. It is so powerful, no way a mortal possesses this type of energy that you possess."

I gazed at her up and down. "I am all three of the things that you have assumed me to be." I stated. In this moment I knew, and I believed she was something great. I knew she was someone great. I knew she was someone of extreme power. I could feel her energy as well. And I felt she could hide some of her energy as well from me. And that shit was amazing, scary but so amazing. I then asked her, "you're a witch, aren't you? You've known who I was from the beginning, you just needed clarification. The clarification brought you here. It brought you to me. No need to hide, no need to lie. Let's put everything out in the open, I know some women and men how they feel about the truth. I know how such human beings behave and interact, and how the truth affects them. Right now, it's a moment of truth, and you cannot escape it. What the fuck are you? Who the fuck are you?"

She stood there frantic. She didn't know what to do, I thought her number one impulse was to destroy me. She started moving her hands around and speaking in tongues, reciting this ritual. She was a witch; a witch is what she told me.

"You're right, Mr. Discipline, I am a witch. Not any ordinary witch, but a powerful one. Perhaps the last of my kind." She moved her hands around and all of a sudden, the atmosphere changed. The clouds in the sky were rupturing. She was creating a storm and it all balled up into her hands. She had a ball of thunder in her hands and she was going to strike me with lightning. She moved her hands quickly, like a dismissive wave and the lightning was headed my way. And I had to stop it and I did exactly that. It stopped in its tracks. It's like I almost stopped time. I was even impressed with myself. I've never done that before, just by merely putting out my hands, and my palm facing her, I controlled the lightening coming my way.

Alexandria had been right, she told me, I had plenty of powers, and I would discover them when I was in some time of need for them. I pushed the lightning back towards Cleopatra. She got blown away by her own storm, her own creation, but she did not die. Because, she knew when to move quickly, right out of the way. I shook my head, and thought to myself, 'what the fuck do I need to do?' Damn this bitch just won't die, she was definitely some type of mystical creature. Someone, all powerfully great, and I was going to get to the bottom of it.

"What the fuck do you want from me?" I yelled, as I questioned her. She shrugged herself off and came back up onto her feet. She was so powerful and resilient, persistent and resourceful. Maybe I need someone like her on my side. I need to know her power, I need to know what the fuck she possessed. I needed to know what the fuck I was dealing with. Perhaps she could be more useful alive than dead?

Darkness was settling in. A thick fog, smelling of brine was creeping through the crooked and pockmarked streets. I then began speaking to the moon, 'you set the night sky ablaze. So far away, yet your persona is large enough to hypnotize millions from just a sheer glance. There has to be a reason this woman is in my life, she is annoying, but there has to be a reason."

Cleopatra looked up at the moon, and then asked me, "are you talking to yourself? What are you looking at?" I didn't answer her, I just continued talking to the moon, with my head up, eyes gazing at the sky...

"Our relationship extends across vast galaxies as we share this moment in time." I then started speaking to her…..."Your haunting calmness mingles with my spirit and intertwines with my thoughts. This is a lovely moment we share, a connection more precious than earthly gem, and as I watch you slowly fade as the time passes, I have solace in knowing that we will soon be reunited again to bid a farewell to the waning day together." Then I growled with my head up, looking at the sky. Silver moon, drenched night…..

Chapter 10- Come To The Dark Side

I put my head down, and it was now facing her. We were both face to face, eye to eye. I spoke sharply, "come to the dark side." She had nothing to say to me, but one thing, "oh, so are you talking to me now? I'm confused, you had your head up and gazing into the sky, talking some nonsense. Now, you are addressing me?" I then continued to attempt to get her onto my team…

"You won't beat me physically, I doubt you will outsmart me psychologically. You might as well join me, bitch!" She then said to me, "who are you calling a bitch? I am no one's bitch. You asshole."

She was persistent, and she came at me with full force. Full force, and she did not stop. And I disappeared. My flesh vanished. My image was invisible, but my laugh was sadistic, as that was the only thing she heard, as I was laughing non-stop, and left her clueless. She was looking all over the place for me. Just looking up and down, left and right for me. She would attempt to follow my laugh, perhaps thinking that would lead her to me. And then I reappeared, and I grabbed her, and teleported us both out of there, and into my world. My dark lair.

I tied her up. I tied her up with my eyes. Utilizing telekinesis. Controlling objects with my mental. With my emotions. With my energy. I placed her body in a chair and tied her up. I wanted answers. I wasn't making no other moves until I fucking knew who and what I was fucking dealing with.

"Now, you're going to answer all of my fucking questions, I asked you when we were over in the park. One fucking question at a time, one way or another." I demanded. "Now, we are somewhere else, a totally different atmosphere, perhaps now you can focus on me, and not what you're attempting to do to me."

I noticed, that she had power with the atmosphere around her, so let's take her out of her element, and see how she performs. She tried to struggle out of the rope I had her in. "Don't struggle," I said to her, "you'll only make it worse for yourself."

I gave her some advice. I gave her a chance to explain herself. I asked her, "what the fuck are you, and I would like to know that now!" I demanded once again. She then said, she is a mystical witch, she told me that she had been tailing me ever since the club, and that she has also been intrigued by me. She knew I was something great, and she wanted to find out more. She wanted to find out why? She is a witch with magical powers, but she feels my powers, she feels my energy and she knows that I am a greater power. I needed to know what the fuck a witch possesses. And what the fuck are they entitled to do? And what are they not entitled to do? I then asked her...

"So I know that once we are in here, you are powerless, but outside you have such a great power, and why is that?" She then said to me, "that's because, I utilize the atmosphere to my advantage."

See, I figured that was the case with her. I placed my thumb and index finger to my jaw, cupping my chin, and now stroking my goatee. And then I began to think. I paused for a couple seconds and did not say a word.

"OK, so that storm shit, that huge disaster that you created, you get all of your power from the universe? Like, is it that you can just create hurricanes, and tornados with emotions? You get all your power from the earth and nature?" I asked her. She answered. "Yes, I do." She began to open up to me a lot more. She was thinking to herself...

'Was my life pleasant before I met him? Was I content? What's missing now? I'm pretty sure I've never truly been happy. I've always struggled to find where I belong, but how can I belong somewhere when I don't fit anywhere? Sometimes I find myself picking a fight with him just so he will talk to me. All I want is a little attention from him. Good or bad. It's sick. I know. But living in the land of indifference has changed me. I reside here day and night until the moment I snap from this indifference. Then I lash out, rebel against what has become this norm. Although it's not right, the reprieve from the emptiness when we argue is welcome. If I left, would he follow me? Would he fight? Would he even notice? Why is he asking all these questions? Does he want to get to know me? Does he want to know what I am, perhaps? He can protect himself. Why does he want to know?'

I then answered the questions in her head, "I'll tell you, It's all the above. Everything you just thought of!" She looked at me confused, "were you just reading my mind just now?" She asked me. "Yes, I have telekinesis abilities, and telepathy. The ability to move objects and control objects with my mind. And the ability to communicate with my mind, and read mind and souls. Reach beneath the surface and communicate soul to soul. I have this innate understand of the human heart and mind. You could have all these powers and they are impressive, but you are still a mortal. Myself, I am not a mortal. You are in the presence of the 'Immortality of Discipline,' the most powerful entity you will ever encounter in your entire life."

She then asked, "how do you do that?" I did not answer her. "You were telling me more about your kind, and your powers. Continue," I demanded from her. She said, "You ever feel a part of you is slowly dying? Your heart is empty? The weight of the world perpetually sits on your narrow shoulders? Something is missing from your life?"

She was a witch, in my control for the time being, but she was dangerous. I can sense it. She was pretty, and I could see that was one of her powers as well. SHE WAS A VISION in green with a long tight dress. Her hair was long, straight, and dark. Her big brown eyes were simply dazzling. She had a doll-like face with red plump lips, and she moved with the grace and prowess of a feline. Shit, I'll tell you right now, I hate cats. Unpredictable, leave you out to dry, can't trust them. And she was just like a cat. Slick, clever, and perhaps she would always land on her feet.

The night in the club, I could see her soul. Broken. Hurt. Black. I could feel her energy, and when she walked, all the men stopped in their tracks. When she gently brushed her hair away from her face and her skin gave off a gentle glow, looking softer than silk. I couldn't help but feel drawn to her like a June bug to a porch light. And I began to realize that shit. Never in that time she had ever wanted

137

to meet a man as I, as badly as she wanted to meet me. It was as if I had a magnetic pull and the ability to make her forget about everything around her. All but me turned into a blur as her senses focused on my presence. The pull she felt served as a reason to approach me, so she walked to the counter, with no control over her body, sat next to me, and flashed her sexiest smile.

I'll never forget that night, her scene was like addicting. Completely intoxicating. She smelled like a bouquet of roses, orchids, poppies, heaven, strawberries, hell, danger and candy. What a feast for my senses! She was the personification of lust, temptation, and dreams come true. She was like sex incarnate. My eyes wandered down her figure, intrigued by her choice of clothes. She then continued to educate me…

"In days of old, witches were blamed for anything that went wrong. Cow died, crops failed, someone got sick, all blamed on witches. 'Real' witches are nothing like they are portrayed on TV or in Movies. There is nothing supernatural about it. Witches get their 'power' from nature, from the earth itself. Some, including myself, will tell you that spells are not much more than glorified prayer. We don't ask a higher power to do something for us. We ask for help in making things happen, then we do a bit of work to make it so. Simple example. Pray to God for your garden to grow. A witch will ask a Goddess to assist, then the witch will sow the seeds, thin the young plants, weed, fertilize and prune as needed. I know this is not a real word, but I call what we do Inter-natural. With nature. On the other hand, I do have some abilities that most do not. I am an empath, I feel other people's emotions, and I hate it. I can see spirits, when they want me to. I communicate with animals. Again, when they want to. But I would have these abilities whether I was a witch or not, so witchcraft has nothing to do with them."

This is crazy, my goodness, I should have fucking killed this bitch when I had the chance. Now look at the trouble I have put myself in. I asked so sharply, "so what the fuck were you planning on doing with me? Did you think you can just come here and kill me or something? Did you think you were dealing with a mortal?"

I walked up close to her, so she could feel how powerful, how serious, how dangerous of a force in myself she was dealing with. "Even if you did kill me, I swear, I would have taken a piece of you with me, believe that bitch!! Were you planning to do something reckless? What are your intentions? You came to my club, you tracked me down, you were trying to kill me in the woods? I don't know what I'm going to do with you, yet. Be careful what you ask for, be more careful what you come looking for. Sometimes you want the bull, and sometimes you end up getting the fucking horns. Who are you fucking working for, witch?"

She shook her head. She didn't answer that question. "I told you, your energy draws you to me." She responded emphatically. Humans were inclined to get themselves in danger. They were drawn to evil creatures like moths to flames! Witches and vampires were danger. And when it comes to danger.... humans naturally assume they were hallucinating and try to forget all things supernatural, as they are impossible to be true. At least in their eyes and their minds they believed this. Plenty of thoughts running through my head, then another thought of what to do popped into my head. I was thinking, 'shit, maybe I could keep her captive. Second, she could be lying to me, maybe I can torture her and make her tell me the truth. Maybe I will torture her for just fucking fun?' I then asked her...

"Why are you a single mother?" Something completely off the subject. "Why are you not married, with a man? You and your baby father cannot work things out?" She shook her head, no. "Ever since my kid's father, I haven't found a decent man. We are not together, because, we have differences. He's just not on the same page as I."

I gazed into her eyes, "you ever looked in the mirror, and thought to yourself, perhaps it's not men, or him. You may have a lot of issues with yourself you haven't come to agreement with. You're pretty fucked up. Mentally, emotionally, and perhaps physically." She shook her head, then said, "what are you, a vampire and a psychologist? Is this our little therapy session now?" I then continued, ignoring her question; but then it could be the men...

"A man will constantly feel insecure with himself when it pertains to his woman, because, he knows he does not deserve her." I said to her. Then I continued to educate her more... "Two rules as a man; step up or step aside. If you know you cannot fuck, appreciate and love a Queen or Goddess properly, allow a man who is adequate and self-sufficient enough to. Only a King can appreciate a Queen. If you get lucky enough to be with a Goddess, and you do not level up to her status, when she encounters Kings, it will be a struggle for her, as you place her in a tight position. She will never look at you the same again. There are individuals on this earth, whom are ahead of the curve. By, 'curve' I'm referring to the average. These individuals originate from far distant stars, solar systems, planets, and galaxies. These highly evolved individuals carry a plethora of wisdom and special abilities that hibernate deep within the core of their being. There are stars that are encoded with activation encryptions that will unlock their knowledge and talents at a pre-determined or spontaneous time on earth. When you vibrate at a high frequency, watch how many toxic people fall back from your life, because, they just don't know how to approach you. Or you will see, how you eradicate your existence from their life all on your own. Pull out your notebook, Discipline is about to educate once again....

Women never appreciate what they can obtain so quickly. Women never want what they can obtain so easily. Women actually want, what they can't have. They want what they say they don't want. Then they don't want what they really want. They are the most inconsistent, indecisive, emotional creatures on earth. That is why a decisive man that is comfortable in being assertive, bring healing to their mind and soul. Conscious and spiritual men and women, will always attract people that need healing. Even if they don't, they see you. And your energy makes them behave accordingly. Your energy introduces you prior to your speech. Yes, I acknowledge your body and your face, however, I'm looking at your soul."

I don't age, however, for mortals, it seems as if the older they get, the more difficult it becomes when attempting to obtain a sufficient conversation. Is it because, no one has time? Wait, I got it, no one cares to put in time. No, wait, perhaps that's not it. Perhaps it's, no one knows how to converse? Are they spoiled? Yes, and they take it all for granted? Yes. There's so many other ways to communicate efficiently now, without physical interaction and all nonverbal. Yes. Telekinesis and telepathy.

"I am real, and I have true powers." I said to her. "Everyone is naturally telepathic. They just don't know of their power, or haven't mastered it yet. The communication of mind to mind. Soul to soul, is unparalleled to anything you can ever have, pertaining to a relationship. It is powerful."

She wore a smile, like a loaded pistol. Her body was precious flames. Her soul was deeper than the ocean most men would drown in. Her mind was intricately aesthetic. One touch from me, and she will feel electric. Eclectic messages from my brain seeping into her female estrogen. Wet between her legs from my Discipline Thug Seduction. I could heat her up faster than a sun beaming on a barren land. With a gaze, with a word, with a touch. Understanding, I will know how to open and touch each of the centers of spiritual power in her entire body. Her root chakra, her basic trust. Her sacral chakra, her sexuality and creativity. Her solar plexus chakra, her power and wisdom. Her heart chakra, her love healing. Her throat chakra, her communication. Her third eye chakra, her awareness. Her crown chakra, her spirituality.

Certain foods enhance chakras as well, she will not admit it, but I am her food for thought. I am her soul food. She asked me, "do you care to live the rest of your eternal life like this? People fearing you? You don't want to be loved? You don't want love?"

I thought about it, and then I answered her, "when there is a hint of fear and desire, that is when true pleasure begins. Would I rather be feared or loved? I wish I can have both, but if I had to choose, I'd choose fear. Why? Fear lasts longer than love and respect. Pay attention, for example a man can attempt this..... begin to get his woman angry to her core. As angry as you can get her. Be the man that is the blame for it. Make sure she knows you are the blame for her temper. Pay attention to how she behaves. To your face. Behind your back. To her family. To her friends. The things she won't keep her mouth shut about when it pertains to you.

You'll see fear, when your friends stay close to you, because of the power you have over other people. Therefore, they feel empowered as well. Whether it's women, money, the way other people bow down to you, physically and emotionally. When you snap a corny joke. You're not funny. But, people laugh. When someone speaks behind your back, but to your face they shake your hand, or remain quiet like a cricket when you walk pass. This is all associated with fear. Love is so fucking great, I swear this to you. But fear, lasts longer. Fear keeps someone in line. That fear is there to let them know, they can't get away with shit. You may have a boss, and even though you're super cool with each other, there's still a level of fear. That fear, keeps you in check. Not to take advantage of, or etc. Even if things are bliss, it's that fear in the back of your head, that doesn't allow you to lose control, because you're aware of the ramifications. Be less afraid of the monsters you run away from, and more of the ones you run to. Discipline, is the worst kind of monster. I mean myself, not just the act, the practice, or tool you implement to obtain better behavior. For a woman, she will always fear me, because she would respect the way I Dominate. The way I handle her. But you will respect my character. My principals. Even though fear is more prominent, respect correlates with fear."

She had nothing to say, so I pressed her, "nothing to say, huh? You weren't this speechless since I first met you at my club and told you I ran the place."

She let out a sarcastic laugh, "ha-ha, perhaps I am just impressed." I stared at her, "perhaps? Or you are?" She didn't reply. My eyes followed her every fucking move. It was as if she were an exotic animal of some sort, and I was studying her. She thought to herself...

'Maybe I was overreacting, and he was acting normal, but it seemed as if he looked at me in a peculiar way—not bad, but a way that made me feel analyzed. Normally, I'm not affected by having men's eyes on me. I was sure of myself and knew I was pretty. I knew I could steal the attention of a room simply by walking in, dressed to impress, and ready to seduce my prey. But my undeniable attraction to Discipline is making me shy and totally breathless. I'm coming down with a case of utter attraction to him. I'm normally good at ignoring men and never really give a damn about their looks or sexual interest in me. So why in the hell am I so fascinated by him?'

I then told her, "you keep doing that, and I think now you know I can read you, you're thinking harder." She gasped, "oh shit, I forgot." I shook my head at her, "anyways, I'll answer your question. Women do not respect, or trust men they can manipulate. But, they go crazy for a man that can manhandle them. As a man, if you can't control your woman, you are the woman. You cannot control me, or manipulate me, therefore bringing you closer to me. It's a natural reaction. Men don't speak to you the way I speak to you, because I don't give a fuck who you are and what you've accomplished. You're still a mortal, just like everyone else." She raised an eyebrow. I then continued…

"Women are not built to control men. It's not in their DNA. There is a strange feeling of vulnerability. A strange feeling of helplessness, restriction, overpowered, mentally, physically, or emotionally that turns women on."

But meanwhile, I can't fucking read her mind anymore. Perhaps she was closing her thoughts? Fuck, she's now become the only woman I cannot read her mind. How did she do that? She is blocking her thoughts on purpose? But how? She has great powers, I must find out more, she's holding something back. It's almost like I can't get in. I must let her go, like a dog and cat game, like a cat and mouse game. I'll give her a head-start to run. I spoke softly but forcefully...

"I'm going to let you go, but, the next time we meet, it will be an unpleasant meeting." I forced on the rope with just my eyes, I then released her, and she got up from the chair. She thanked me, and then she created this tornado.

She kept spinning and spinning and spinning, until she vanished from my presence. The sun was about to approach, it was bedtime. And I haven't slept in twenty four hours. Plus, I had a potential investor. I had an appointment with an important investor, Miss Susan Wilts in the later evening.

Waking up, I sighed deeply, inhaling the freshness and warmth of the cozy place where I lay. The memories of the previous night were still fresh on my mind. I got up, showered, put on lotion that had some coconut oil in it, then I put on some cologne. I then went to my big closet, deciding what color suit blazer to wear. Went to my motorized tie holder, pressing the back, then forward button, searching for a nice tie to match. I had a tie in almost every color. Normally, I was always ready, if I knew I had something big planned that day, or later that night, I already knew what I was going to wear in my head, before I laid out those clothes.

But last night, I was thrown off balance, I felt. Anyways, I was off to this meeting with Susan. Sleeping was weird. I hardly did that. Ever since the attack, that turned me into the savage monster I was today, I had never felt safe since then. All I had was nightmares. It had been some long years of running, chasing, and hiding. Sleeping the whole night without waking up covered in sweat with a racing heart, was also something new.

The meeting had commenced. After the encounter with Cleopatra, I met with a potential woman business partner, because I wanted someone to be able to run the clubs in Connecticut. Atlanta, Georgia. Dallas, Texas. Quite frankly, I love working with women. Why? One, they are more compliant, and submissive. They get the job done better and faster than any man, and there's no competition with them. Alpha males always want to be the top dog, most people hate male management. In a group of plenty of Alpha Males, there's a few looking to get to the top, and they don't care to step on each other's toes to get it.

I mean think about it, you could have a long-time boy, I bet your girl would ride harder for you than him. Women are just built like that. And they loved to listen to Discipline.

"Hello there, mister Discipline," she said. "Look, I'm sorry, but I'm still laughing about that name! People need to know who you really are, people need to know your real name as well. You see, that is what makes people want to keep coming back. It makes you pop out more, free bottle service is not enough anymore between VIPs. Customers like to feel special, they like to feel like celebrities. If you're closer with customers, taking pictures, it makes them feel that special as they're celebrities themselves. It's like a sense of power."

I then said to Susan, "listen, the unknown and the mysterious will always intrigue the mind. Don't you think so?" She said, "it's not enough, you need to be around more. People will be more intrigued when they know, who you are. Giving them a little access, then taking it away, will keep them coming back. Like an exciting movie or book, and all of a sudden, you get to the juicy part, and then, well, bam!! To be continued! Seeing your social media, pictures, perhaps videos, these things would all help out. Trust me." She was good, she was intelligent. She was business savvy. I wasn't hard headed, I was always open to new ideas and discussion, as long as I felt they would be conducive to what I wanted to build. But, I believed, the cliché saying, 'if it ain't broke, why fix it?' Yes, I believed that as well. I said...

"Look that's great to know. However, do you know who the damn CEO that is associated with McDonald's is? Do you know who the CEO that is associated with Dunkin' Donuts' is?" She shook her head, no. I then sat there with a smirk, "exactly. There's a CEO for these major, prominent companies, but do you know who they are? No! Corporations in these companies still run, why? Three things about business; advertising, people, and placement. You have the right team running it to please you, the right promotion and marketing team, and location, location and location is key, and you don't need to be seen!"

She was in complete agreement with me as she nodded her head, 'yes.' I then said to her, "it's all about that Demand and Supply." She gave me a confused look; "don't you mean Supply and Demand?" I laughed, "no, see they've been teaching it in schools and in life all wrong. And they've been teaching it everywhere else all along, all wrong. It's Demand and Supply. You see, the Demand comes first, then whoever is supplying, profits." She said, "interesting, I never looked at it that way. Regardless of all that, people need to know who you are, they need to see you. I mean, you're a person to only come out in the dark, you are barely around in the light, what are you, a damn vampire?" She then began to laugh, and my laugh followed her laugh.

"Okay, okay, I'll get on social media, I'll take a few more pictures. Let's do business!" I said. She then smiled and shook my hand and gave me a kiss on the cheek, "happy to do business with you, sir."

I might as well join with this woman and sign the contracts, when I get to more clubs there will be more money and that's always the better. She could run them, I can be a silent partner. And I can get her to run the other clubs as well. Money never scared me. Show me the dollar signs, I'll ask you, 'where do I sign?' Show me the dollar signs, and I'll give you 200 percent of my dedication and hard work. I said to her...

"Well, we're all about the nightlife, welcome to the dark-side. She smiled, and then before she left the club, she said to me....

"You are about to be more successful and lucky than you already are, Mr. Discipline." I replied with, "come on now, where I come from, you make your own luck and success. It's just a matter of opportunity. Opportunities are out there every day, its about grabbing it, success is a choice, but it begins with opportunity......"

Chapter 11- Psychological Bondage

Susan left my office. And then she walked out of the club. It was time to feast, I was getting hungry. Walking in the ally, I saw a lovely victim.

"Hello there, miss, what are you doing here? It's late and it's dark! Really, what is a lovely lady like yourself doing here, by herself?"

She stared at me, and my eyes were bright gold, and she then began to run. "Shit, am I that ugly? I asked myself. Shit, am I that intimidating? Maybe I should have smiled? Damn, I didn't even get a chance to show her my gold fangs."

I chased after her, but I didn't run like she did. Actually, I walked, and she wasn't getting too far. She ran into the woods, so scared, so naive. And she lost her way home, she was so frightened, she forgot where she was running to. I then attacked her, I tackled her down and then I swooped in there and claimed her. I growled in on her. I feasted upon her fucking flesh, and then I left her body there for the vultures to have that shit.

The afternoon arrived, I went to go check on my fitness clubs, as they were doing very well. I saw a female cop in there now, and in there she spotted me right away. She kept eyeing me the entire time, and every time I looked over her way, she would look away. I thought to myself, 'has she seen me somewhere? Or was she just attracted to me? But, a woman would not constantly be staring at someone, nonstop. It did not make sense.'

I then walked up to her, because obviously she was showing interest with her body language, but most women will never approach you, and say hello. They will for sure throw hints, but they will never approach. Therefore, I approached her....

"How are you ma'am?" I said politely. "Hello there, sir. You're all over, huh?" She said right back. She knew who I was, I knew it. But, where did I know or see her from? I gazed into her eyes, and I could tell that the intensity of my gaze made her stomach feel like it was filled with crazy butterflies, as her body reacted with tingling sensations on her neck and palms. Every time I looked at her face, and she looked at mine, I bet she felt the undeniable allure. I said to her...

"How do you like the facility? And where do I know you from?" Completely changing the subject, and avoiding the question. She looked around here. "It's a great facility," she said. "I have a facility in my headquarters! But I also love coming here as well, you have amenities here, my facility in the department doesn't have." I laughed, "but you know what your facility in your department there does not have, miss?" She asked me, "what is that?" I smirked, "well, it doesn't have me."

She looked me up and down and started laughing. She was blushing and I asked her, "headquarters, huh? What do you do for a living?" She said, "I'm a police officer." Come to think of it, this woman did look familiar now.

Very familiar, wait a minute, it was actually the female officer that pulled me over. I wondered if she remembers me? She had to, she didn't answer my question when she asked me, that I was everywhere. That alerted me, on the fact that she knew who I was, or she has seen me somewhere. I took mental documentation of that, just because I did not revisit the question, doesn't mean shit went unnoticed.

Who the fuck she think she's tryna play? I will make myself more discreet quick, scarcer and vanish, rid her of my presence immediately before she does recognize me, if she didn't already. I mean I had her in the palm of my hand that night, she was ready to do everything and anything, bending to my will. She could've followed me any-fucking-where. Her energy, could have brought her to my energy, just now or vice versa. The thing about seduction is, it has all to do with power. It's all psychological, take everything she has, then give her everything she fucking needs. So, I excused myself quickly...

"Well, you have yourself a great workout." I let her know chit chat was over, I entertained her a little, but I'm always about business. No matter the woman, no matter her relationship status, they crave attention. If you give them a little bit, then take it away, they look for you. They crave you, they chase you, as if you were cheese, and they were rats. To them, it's like now you become the provider. No matter what it is, and in this particular sense, it is attention. The chase is on. As if you were really a cat, and the woman was the dog. As if you were bread, and they were birds. As if you were zebra and they were lioness.

The night was young, my night club was packed. Saturday nights, were usually like that, but, the new year was approaching. The month of December was very promising. People want an escape, they want a release. All that Christmas shopping for friends, family, cousins you only see once a year, secret Santa's you have at work, for your boss or coworkers that you secretly hate. Families you only really see once or twice a year.

The club was like an escape for many different people. A place where they could release. Be someone different for just a night or two. The environment changed people, and yes, so did the music and the alcohol. I mean, when people hear music, serotonin dripping from their brain, it can cause so many emotions.

The same female cop that pulled me over, the same female cop that was at the gym, is the same female cop that's now at my fucking club? Out of all the clubs, in the city, and the other ones I own, she is at the one I am at? This fucking moment? Something is fucking up, right now. I smell something fishy! This is a coincidence three times? No way. I don't believe that this is a fucking coincidence. She is here for something. And I am not going to wait for her to approach me, or look around snooping to ask me any questions. I walked right up to her and asked her...

"What are you doing here?" I questioned her. Then I approached it differently, just so she wasn't aware that I was aware. "Looks like we meet again." I said to her. She then said, "well, well, well, looks like we do meet again. You are everywhere, huh?" This is exactly what she said to me at the gym. This woman is onto me, but she is not

153

about to make a scene in a public place. "Busy man!" She said to me, shouting out, because the music was so loud. "I feel like this is a big world, but at the same time, small world. Big city but look how we keep running into each other." I smirked, but it was a fake business-like smirk. "Yes, indeed, and out of all the night clubs, you are here." She then answered, "yeah, I live in the area," she said. "I'm looking for some nice spots for me and my friends to come and party, release, or perhaps escape."

You fucking liar, she was good. First pulls me over, clearly you remember who I am. Then my fitness club, now in my night club. Bitch is tailing me. I need to check if she put a tracking bug on my attires, my car, my places, I don't know. She said this to me, while she gazed firmly into my eyes. Then I insisted……

"Well, this is a nice place, one of the best clubs in the city. And I own it." She was intrigued. "Oh well, your club is very nice, just like the fitness club. You own that as well, am I right?" I interrupted her. "You are right." I said.

Man, she knew I owned that, she was playing dumb. We had a long ass conversation in my fitness club. You want to play games bitch? I'll show you how I play it so much better. She then asked, "let me talk to you for a second?" She pulled me over to the side...

"There has been a lot of activity going on around the club, around the gym, do you know of anything like that?" I try to play stupid to see if I can cover my case, get more answers out of her as well, "what type of activity or activities are you talking about now?" She just gazed into my eyes, did not answer right away. She waited for like five seconds to respond, and then she answered me….

"There's been a series of killings, but not just any regular murders. These victims have been murdered by bites. Bites on the neck, weird. No knives, no guns, it's something that I haven't seen before. I mean you read books and watch movies pertaining to monsters, beasts, vampires, witches, etc. However, you never see it for real, I'm not saying this is what that is, we are still investigating. It's just, these types of murders seem fiction. Just like what you read in books or see in movies. You know, things that are strange, strange things that have been going on around here?" She said. I kept playing stupid.

"Do you care to elaborate on that? I mean, people die or get killed every day, and then babies are born every day. The world is overly populated as it is. That is the circle of life, eh? It's just so weird what's going on around here, isn't it?" I said coyly. She then went more into depth...

"The killings are happening late at night, as well. They are hardly going on in the day time!" I then stated, "well, freaks come out at night? We have all heard that saying. I mean, one of my establishments are a night club. Different type of people come in here all the time." She agreed with me, "yes, that's why here is a good place to ask."

Who the fuck was she fooling, not me. Bitch, sit the fuck down, we both know you are stalking me. Because, you think I know or I am responsible for all these activities going on. "I don't know what else to tell you, officer, like I said, people die every day." She gazed at me squarely in my eyes. "You have a smart remark, or a joke for everything?" She asked. I didn't answer, in fact, I just changed the damn stupid pointless subject. She wasn't going to get answers out of me, what was she doing here? Both her and I knew, but if you want to play dumb, I can play dumber. I know what she was doing here, but I'm throwing her a curve ball, and she can't hit the target. Let me change the fucking subject now.

"But are you here to have fun or are you here on official police business, I mean I'm looking at that dress, and you don't look like you're here on police business?" She then smiled at me. "Where are you and your friends?" I asked her. So, then she pointed over there to my right...

"Ok good, I will send you guys and ladies a couple bottles of our finest champagne on the house." I smiled. "That's so nice of you, thank you," she said to me. Appreciative of my fine gesture. I then indicated, "well, you know, I like to try to take care of the ones that fight crime and keep us all safe. So, in reality it is I that must be thanking you. Therefore, thank you." I said with a smile on my face, then I walked away quickly and went to my skybox.

The night was coming to an end, and I remained in my skybox just to observe what was going on for the night. I loved the box, people didn't really pay attention to it, but I could see everything from here, every corner, every spot in the entire club. I loved how I had the stripper poles and cages built in. It brought a smile to my face, I thought once again to myself, look at all the shit I created myself, with just a few dreams, no resources yet, just imaginations, and

I then fucking turned that shit to a reality. The club was getting ready to close, it was like five in the morning, and I don't normally stay till the end, but I wanted to remain there. I was sometimes there as the first to come in, and the last one to leave the building, sometimes the first inside of it. People were walking out, and I left the general managers there to take care of the closing of the facility.

I then started walking to my vehicle, I could sense a big presence. A presence that was perhaps watching me all night. As I was walking to my car, I spoke in front of me, "is there a reason why you've been following me?" I stated that and asked the question to a woman whom was behind me, and she stopped in her damn tracks.

"How did you know that I was?" she asked me. "In fact, here is a better question for you. How did you know a person was following you at all?"

It was the female police officer, who was at the fitness club, who was at the night club tonight, who had pulled me over, the night I savagely and brutally killed those strippers that took my wallet and tried to hustle me.

"You know, I always thought there was something weird about you?" She said to me. I laughed, and then I asked her, "why would you think that, officer?" She was not shy to voice her thoughts about me either, "well, the night I pulled you over, you had blood on your wallet a little bit." Now, the truth is coming out. My instincts did not fail me. "Then I saw you at the fitness club and the night club earlier tonight. I asked you about activity going on, and you didn't even look shocked. Either you are a calm man at all times, or you just didn't care. But if you're a successful business man, that would indicate you always know your surroundings. Competition lurking, how much income is in the area. How does your demographics appear?"

I nodded my head, "that's impressive officer, and you are right about that." She then said, "so, why would you act oblivious to what is going on in your area? Because, I can tell by the way I spoke to you the last few times, I can tell you keep up to date on everything. Why would a man not want, nor care to know that there has been suspicious activity close by his clubs? That can hurt business. And why would you want to hurt business?"

Damn, she was fucking good, but I don't hear her accusing me of shit yet. I don't hear the handcuffs coming out of her back or front pocket, unclicking to be placed on my wrists. Nor do I hear a, 'you're under arrest.' I then asked her bluntly...

"So, what the fuck are you implying, miss? Because, if you're not arresting me for anything, or accusing me of anything, I would love to leave. It's late, well, its early, I would love to get some rest. Or perhaps you have been tailing me this entire time, because perhaps, you want me to fuck you?" She laughed, "oh please, you are full of yourself, ever since I met you." I smirked, "oh yeah, have I been? And then why the harassment? You're in denial, the accusations are a cop out, you cop. That's your excuse to get close to me." She was furious, "don't flip this on me. I want you to come in for some questioning. She then pulled out her handcuffs.

First, she pulls me over on a DWB (driving while black), now she wants to bring me in on some suspicions of her own, where is the evidence? Even though she is right on the money. Shit, can't a black man get a little peace? Shit, I guess I must create my own peace.

"Just come with me to the station for some questions, if you're clean, you can walk free." She assured me of this. I then stated, "what's your probable cause? Take me in for what? Are you bored? You need someone to arrest so it looks like you're doing your job? Are you even out on the streets watching and making sure things are being upheld to the law? Are you even on the streets fighting crime, or you are in the office all day pushing paperwork? I mean, you brought out the handcuffs? Look, I don't know what type of kinky sex you're into, but I like to do the tying up, I like it rough, but if we must, I am always on top. Shall we discuss hard limits and soft when it pertains to the bedroom? Okay, well, I'm not submissive, I'm more Dominant. And no woman will ever handcuff me."

She got even more furious, "this is not a joke, sir, you are coming with me." I shook my head at her, and said, "I'm not going anywhere with you." She took out her gun, and I said to her, "well, damn, I wonder if I were a white man, would you pull out a gun on me as well? I want you to understand something, look miss officer, I promise you, this is not a problem that you want nor need. Just turn around, be a good little girl, and head home before this gets real ugly."

She released the safety, and her index finger was on the trigger, I thought to myself, 'shit, this is about to be ugly.'

My claws and fangs grew, and my eyes turned gold, now I was angry. I growled loudly, she was frightened, I slowly walked towards her and she shot me like five times and my body dropped. She then gasped for air, she was relieved that she killed me, well at least she thought she did. She turned around and reached for her walkie talkie.

"We have a gun wound, suspect shot by myself in self-defense." This bitch was lying, how was it self-defense? I did not pull out a pistol, a knife or any weapons on her. And meanwhile as she is talking, I rise back up onto my feet reverse way of how I fell backwards, like it was a rewind of a video or movie. Her back was turned, and I quickly walk up from behind her, grab the walkie talkie and smash it with my one hand into pieces. Then I said to her...

"It's funny, I've been stabbed, I've been strangled by people, and I've been shot by some mobsters, but I never get used to the shootings, they still itch a little bit. And by the way, I told you I like it rough, do you?"

She screamed, and began to run away from me, damn she was fast, but I loved to watch her run. I'm not used to women running from me. Yes, run little bunny rabbit, the wolf will be there shortly. The wolf will be there shortly to hunt, to feast. She would find her way to me soon. Or vice versa.

She jumped into her vehicle, and I was already laid down in the back seat. My goodness, this woman is making it way too easy for me. Such an easy kill now, and now no one would be the wiser. She started the car, and then began to drive off, honestly, I didn't even care to feast upon her, I was not hungry, I just wanted to kill her so bad. I couldn't allow her to walk away from this, she was way too annoying, and she knew way too much. I then sat up from the back seat...

"We just keep meeting and bumping into each other, it must be fate, so did you really think you could get away from me that easily, miss officer? Did you miss me?"

She screamed, and I grabbed her by the throat from behind, "you're screaming, but tonight you haven't answered any of my fucking questions. Shit, all I wanted was answers, this might hurt a little bit, actually I'm lying, it's going to hurt a lot, but you might enjoy it."

I thought to bite her, then I thought, I would make it look like an accident, I slit her throat with my sharp claws, "have a safe trip officer."

She drove into the street rail, and the car did cartwheels down the hill. I jumped out of the vehicle. I was floating in the air. I remained suspended, and I didn't drop to the ground. The vehicle stopped upside down, and I focused hard and my eyes were menacing, and from out of them came red lasers, and I lit her car on fire. I flew away, I didn't walk away, I didn't want to leave any footprints, I was that paranoid, or maybe two steps ahead of everyone. I had to kill her, but make sure she was burned, because, my finger prints were on her neck and throat. If forensic would look into that, they could get me as a match, but aint no one going to check for a burnt corpse now.

I wished her a good night, "have a good night, you annoying bitch!" I just could not allow her to live, like I said, aside from all the other shit, the main thing was my DNA that was all over her.

I got home, I showered and rinsed myself off like three times, I shampooed my hair like three times, I took a toothbrush and scrubbed underneath my finger nails with hydrogen peroxide. And then I burned the clothes I had that night, shit, her DNA was all over me, and I have businesses to check up on, I can't afford to be locked up, even though they would not be able to keep me in my fucking cell, nor any damn cell. I don't need shit on record, or in files. I don't want people knowing who I was, or anything like that. I wanted to remain as low key as possible. I owned this fucking town, but they didn't know it yet. But the damn publicity, the papers, the bad image for the club. I have a lot to lose, but not really a lot to lose.

I went back to the club area, and I got into my car, and I drove it home. I didn't sleep, it was still dark outside, but it was morning time. I had to clear my head, therefore I went for a stroll. I passed by a group of men, they were on the corner shooting dice. They looked at me, and I looked at them, and I gave them a head nod, and they reciprocated. I passed the men, but there was this fine ass lady that walked by, and even though I was far away, I heard one of the men say to the lady, "hey, yo ma! Why don't you come over here and blow on these dice and give me some luck! Make me some money, come on, don't act like you've never done it before!"

She said to the man that asked her this, "leave me alone, asshole!" He then got aggressive, and began walking towards her, I swiftly flew in front of the man and said to him, "chill, the lady said, leave her alone. No harm, no foul, you could go back to what you're doing."

He stared me up and down, then he took his hand, placed it on the end of his fitted cap, and he turned his hat backwards. "How did you get here so fast? I thought you left? Anyways, don't get involved homeboy, this ain't about you. This between me, and this bitch right here."

I then said to him, "well, now I'm in your face, therefore, it is no longer between you and the lady." He then said to me, "my nigga, if you don't get out of my face in two seconds…" then I cut him off, "what? I mean, if you're going to do something, just do it, don't talk about it." I saw he had a knife in his back pocket, and I could feel he was going for it. I hurt his pride, he's completely embarrassed in front of his boys, and this woman he was trying to pursue or whatever. The only way he felt he could redeem himself is by reacting, physically. Verbally he was no match for me, nor psychologically, and he was going to find out he was not physically either. Yes, I was reading his mind. Before he could pull it out I said to him,

"look, I urge you to reconsider what you are about to do. You're misguided, I get that, and you are a brother, just like me. I really don't want to have to do this to you."

Therefore, I exposed myself to him, so it would frighten him enough to make him back off, or better yet, run away. My eyes turned gold, and then my fangs grew, he said to me, "damn, nigga, what the fuck are you?" His boys got him, to come to defend his honor, I started shaking my head, and one of them pulled out a pistol, I swarmed over to him quickly, and grabbed the pistol out of his hand, and crushed it in the palm of my fist. There were four of them total, and I made waste of them quickly. Man, I hated black on black crime, but I could not allow them to escape, didn't trust they would keep quiet about the animal in me they saw. They could tell one person, and that one person tells another, next thing you know, the police finds out somehow. Now all the heat is on, and I was so close to closing that deal with the Susan lady.

After I feasted on their flesh, the woman was still there, shit, I thought she would have left as soon as this fight between myself and the four guys broke out. No, she was still there. Typical woman, where there was danger, it drew her close.

I walked up to her, my eyes were red from feasting, I had a little blood on the side of my mouth, I gazed into her eyes, and I said forcefully, "run!" And she screamed loud as she ran. I let her go, I spared her life. I thought about it, she would forget all that transpired here. She was so embarrassed, so frightened, she wouldn't have the strength to explain what happened tonight with anyone. How would she explain it? "Oh, I was walking, saw some guys shooting dice in the corner. One of them tried to holla at me, and then a monster, or man came to defend my honor, but wait, he wasn't defending my honor. Then he beat up the four guys, and he killed them, he had red eyes and fangs."

See, her story would not make sense. How can one man fend off four guys by himself? A monster? They would tell her, she watches too much movies, better yet, she was delusional.

I then headed home to get some rest. The following day, I got a call from Susan. The deal with Susan Wilts went through, and I was going from a couple of clubs, to now having a club in all of the five boroughs, because I fucking ran New York. Now I go from myself, to now having a co partnership in two more clubs. One in Los Angeles and the other one in Miami. This is great. All about fucking expansion.

The police officer's car was discovered, that following day as well, and the identity came back as the officer woman. They said her name was Jane. They reported it as an accident, there were witnesses that saw her drinking a lot. She was speeding, they assumed, and the car ran off the road, breaking the rail, and tipping over several times, and then the car was lit on fire. There were no signs of malice, no footprints indicating of there being another person. And she ended up driving alone that night. This is what the autopsy, the officers, homicide and other detectives said in the police reports.

There was some heat at my night club, as the police were questioning everyone there, because as far as anyone knew, it was the last place she was before she perished. The officers then approached me, and I greeted them, and took them to my office. I answered the chief of police and all the other detectives the best way I could, I made them feel stupid. One thing I should've done was destroy the surveillance video of the club that night, I fucking forgot, but I thought again and said to myself, 'it was good that I didn't, because if I did, it would definitely be something to have on me.'

These were all the things that were running through my head. Like, 'why would the cameras not function on that night alone, but they did the day prior and prior to that as well?' That is exactly what they would have asked me. They viewed the video, and it displayed her and I talking majority of the night.

"Officer Jane spent a great deal of the night speaking with you sir. What did you both speak of?" I was beginning to get frustrated, but I did not let it show, I kept my damn cool and answered the police officers accordingly. "We talked about plenty of things; one was fitness, I don't know if you gentlemen know, but I have a few fitness clubs out here as well. And if you gentlemen want to swing by, a complimentary workout is on me." I pulled out my card for the both of them. "So, officer Jane and I were speaking of fitness, she is a member at my club, and if you need evidence just check our records of names and phone numbers that have checked in from the last couple of days." The officers looked at each other, "yes, we will need those records," I put out my index finger to them indicating for them to give me a second, "hold on one second, I will make a phone call and have those records sent to me." I made the call, and within minutes, the check-in list of members were sent to me, and I displayed them from my phone, and I had the secretary fax it to me as well. I gave them the list of names that were on there. And her name, the officer was clear as day there.

Jane Fisher. They both looked at each other like, 'shit, we don't really have shit on this place, nor this guy, let's leave. He's too good, he's too smart. Before his educated black ass sues us for some dumb shit and wins.' I could read their minds, communicating to one another without word or anything verbal being exchanged. Just their body language, just their eyes. I then said to the two officers...

"So, did you both get your answers, did I help you both out?" They glanced at each other once again, and then the first one said, "okay, no further questions for you sir, just don't leave town, just in case something else comes up, we may have further questions."

I shook both their hands and smiled, and said, "good day officers. By the way, let me ask you both something, why would I leave town? I have clubs to check up on here."

They looked at each other, why did they keep doing that? It's like one was looking at the other for help? Who was the alpha out of the both of them? Did one wipe the other's ass for him as well? I mean, shit! They had no response for me. Dumbasses. Then as they shut the fucking door, my mean, dark mug appeared. Susan Wilts showed up right after them………….

Chapter 12- Look Me In My Eyes

Susan walked in right after them, she gasped in fear, then let out a deep breath prior to her actually walking in, "may I come in?" She asked my permission. "Come on in Susan." I then told her. "Hello Discipline, lovely day huh?" she said sarcastically, with a gasp of air coming out of her mouth. I could sense a wave of fear enveloped her. She was scared, she was worried, I could see it in her eyes. I could read her body language. I could feel her energy.

"Look, it will all be over soon, an officer passed, they must do everything in their power to investigate, even though they don't investigate like this for every other individual but, when it's one of their own, forget about it." I assured her. She was nervous, and it showed, she then began to have second thoughts...

"Look Discipline, this is why I came here, I came to tell you that I don't think we can do business, this is crazy, and I don't want to deal with these scandals and drama, it's not good for business. Maybe we can do business, but let's just exclude business in New York."

Susan was not from New York, so this was definitely something new, and it made her a bit apprehensive. I mean, she didn't have a reasonable excuse to back out of this agreement, the plans, and businesses we were going to establish. We were going to have this partnership one way or another. She was going to play ball, I would make her. I gazed into her eyes, and placed my massive hands in her hair as my muscular fingers stroked it...

"Look me in my eyes," I said softly, but forceful. "This is what you want to do, you want to have an establishment here in New York. You want to eventually expand international. Canada, London, perhaps the Caribbean like Dominican Republic. Puerto Rico. Jamaica. Bahamas. Not just state to state. And we will make this a lucrative journey for the both of us, and you want this," she repeated after me, "I want this..."

She was compliant to my telepathy, I worked way too hard for this to be taken away from me by uncertainty and scared money.

"This is what you want to do, we will expand, and we will resume business as usual." She said softly to me, "yes, Discipline, yes. This is what I want, yes." And then she started to walk towards the door, but before she could walk out of my office, I said to her, "go home, you didn't even come here today to speak about this. You came here to ask how I was with all this drama, and you look forward to resuming business and to expand this brand of ours and get into a major lucrative journey for the two of us."

I seeped these messages aloud into her mind, while I was hypnotizing her with my eyes the entire time. She did not blink, and neither did I. I then snapped my fingers. My middle and my thumbs touched, and she snapped out of my hypnotic powerful words. She then blinked twice, and she shook her head. Then she smiled, as she started to touch my broad shoulders.

"Discipline, I hope you are okay, with everything that has been going on, I support you one hundred percent, and

I want you to know that I am here for you one hundred percent and will love to continue our business ventures. I was thinking about further expansion."

I looked up at her, "really? I am listening, what did you have in mind, Susan?" I asked her. She then continued, "well, I was thinking perhaps internationally, Canada, London. And even the Caribbean, like Puerto Rico, Dominican Republic, Jamaica, Bahamas?"

I cupped my chin, and started stroking my goatee, "wow, interesting. This is new Susan, when did you come up with this stuff?" She shrugged her shoulders, I have no idea, just now I guess, I know we never talked about this, but it just came to me, like the idea was slapping me in my head. She smiled, and I smiled right after her. "This is going to be a lucrative journey for the both of us," she said to me. "And do not worry, it will be great no matter what is going on, it will blow over, keep your head up."

Acting as if she was reassuring me, bitch, I made you say all this shit, don't get gassed, don't get hyped. And I played the game well. I gave her a worried look, as if I were worried about everything that was going on. She smiled, and my smile followed hers once again, we then hugged and then I said, letting out a gasp of relief, "thank you for your support, I hope you are right, and this will be a good journey for the both of us. I said, "let's make a toast." I took two glasses, and I poured into the glasses some wine, I then held up my glass, and she raised her glass to match the length I had it raised, I then said, "to new partnership, and to a lucrative journey!" She nodded her head, then I said, "salud!" And she repeated after me, "salud!" After the glass of wine, she then walked out of my office, all smiles. I smiled back at her, and when she shut my office door, my smile disappeared. I then got serious. I took care of some paper work before I headed out. Checked inventory, revenue, guests, etc. I thought to myself, 'man, I need to hire more general managers, and one assistant, so I don't need to be here as much.' But, I kind of liked it, I mean, I'd rather bury myself into work than go home. Home never felt like home anymore.

I then began to head out, and all of a sudden hunger kicked in once again, I fucking hated when hunger kicked in, because it meant, I needed to feast upon some fucking living beings. It was either feast or die. And I was loving life way too much right now, then to just vanish from this planet. Therefore, that meant, the fucking hunt was on. So, it was time to feed. The moon was full and that is when I was at my strongest ever. I saw a prime fruit lurking in the park, and I was so hungry, I was ready to pounce like a fucking lion pouncing on fucking zebra. Talking about hunger, it was like a two for one deal. A buy one get one free. A male and a woman, a couple? I took the man out with the quickness. Talk about an eat and run, an eat on the go. A fast meal, and who said, there's no such thing as a free meal?

The woman noticed her companion was nowhere to be found. She looked left then right, and even called out for him, "Jim, honey, where did you go? Honey, where are you?" As I was on the verge of hunting upon this delicious looking feast, and tackle her down, I was going to take a bite out of crime, suddenly, a woman comes out of nowhere, and just kicks me and I go flying. I haven't met a woman with such strength since Alexandria, the female vampire that turned me so many years ago. And I fucking ripped her head off and killed her. Therefore, it could not have been her. Whom or what was this? I picked up myself off the ground and the victim ran away yelling and screaming for her life.

"Now my meal is gone, I guess you will be her replacement!" I said to the woman that kicked me. The woman said to me, "well, that's what you get for playing with your food, didn't your mother ever teach you this when you were younger?" She told me this, and I grew furious…

I teleported to the woman that kicked the shit out of me, that sent me flying, and I returned the favor as I balled up my fist and let it kiss her in her pretty little face. Then I sent her into a tree, but she lifted herself up. Who or what was this woman, this was not a supernatural, because I would be able to feel how strong her presence was. But, she was not a mortal either. I could smell her blood from here, and it was too strong. I thought, 'hmm, perhaps she has some prominent blood?' I then asked her to know more…

"Who are you? What are you? And where the fuck did you come from, with that powerful kick you have?" She brushed herself off and stood up and spoke to me, "I'm Julie, I am the chosen one!" I laughed, "the chosen one? The only thing you are now is a nuisance to me." She then continued to enlighten me, "I know what you are, you vampire, I am your destroyer. I am a vampire slayer, and I kill your kind for a living, yes, I have a little strength that is supernatural, I was given this by the Gods to take your kind out. You did me a favor when you killed Alexandria years ago. She was the last of the best, the last of her kind, and I know she turned you."

How does this woman or creature know so much about me? What the fuck is a vampire slayer? Those kinds of things or people really exist?

"Listen bitch, woman, creature, or thing, I don't know how you know me, or what you think you know, but you're not fucking with me, or are even on my level." Then she laughed, "you did me a favor killing your maker, she was difficult to keep up with and find, and after you killed her, I've been keeping tabs on you. But, you too are a difficult man to keep up with. You do not stay at one place too long. You are constantly moving. But I finally got you right where I want you. Ironically, we all came out of a woman. You came from a woman, placed on this earth, and now a woman takes you off of this earth, permanently."

I laughed, "you don't know shit about me, shut the fuck up, you sound like a damn robot. Look robot bitch, this is not a fairy tale, and there is no damn happy ending for you. This time the bad guys win." She said, "oh I don't know shit about you? I know you killed, officer Jane. You ran her off the road, you burned the car."

How did she know this? Anyways, I would then play it off, to fool her as if I was oblivious to the fact. "That's a crazy imagination robot bitch, too bad no one would believe you. You're a robot remember? Following some

173

boring, stupid script. And you don't make much sense."
She pulled up a video from her phone, and showed it to
me, clearly you see my face and officer jane's. The
confrontation, and the car, and all I've done. She then said
to me, "how do you think the car was found? I called it in.
But, I never exposed you, I'd rather bring you into justice.
I want the pleasure of taking you out."

I smirked at her, "you should have turned me in, not
only are you a robot bitch, who clearly can't follow a
boring script whoever you are working for gave you. You
are a stupid, robot bitch, and now I end this shit..."

I ran into her and pushed her on the tree again, her back
was against the tree, and I put my hand around her throat. I
then lifted her off the ground, but she kneed me in my
balls, and she had this garlic spray that she sprayed into
my eyes, I felt blind, I growled, and hissed. I felt nothing
like it, and I was not prepared for this. I could not see, and
that gave her a huge advantage over me. Then she was
hitting me left and right and I had nothing to counter her
with, but slightly guessing where she would be. She had
these special gadgets like rope, nets, etc. I could not get
out of, and a net she launched at me, I was hanging from
the ground, she was joyful in glory. I demanded her...

"Fucking put me down now!" What type of net was this,
I could not get out of it. She had me in check, she
definitely did her homework on what could get me rattled.
What could tame me. She then said, "I'm actually going to
destroy you, the world will be a better place without you in
it."

Suddenly, as she was going to get rid of my existence from this entire earth, and I had my eyes shut like, 'this is it, this was fun while it lasted, Precious, Daddy is coming. We will meet soon.' And as soon as I thought I was going to die, I heard thunder and she was hit with lightening.

Cleopatra appeared. She swung at her and knocked her out, then she cut me loose, and Cleo looked at me, and said, "go ahead, finish her." I lifted her up and I bit her on her neck. Why? I could have snapped her damn neck. Ripped her damn heart out. No, I wanted her blood. From the moment I met her, her blood felt so powerful to me, and I wanted it. I drank her blood and absorbed her energy, now I had the blood of a vampire slayer coursing through my fucking veins. I then howled at the moon, I felt so fucking lifted. So strong, it was a different type of energy.

Cleo looked at me, "why do you always howl at the fucking moon Discipline? That shit is just weird. And then you were speaking to it the other night? You two want to be alone or something? Get a room and shit?" My eyes were bright red gazing at her, and I hissed, then I said, "shut up, and help me get rid of her."

Then Cleo and I got rid of the vampire slayer, Julie's body. And we did it together. I took the vampire slayer, Julie's phone, and erased the files she had and then I smashed the phone into pieces, and burned it with my eyes, just to be safe. Cleo stared at me, "I think you have a temper issue. Perhaps you need anger management?" I just stared at her firmly, but I did not say a word. She then asked me, "why do you care to smash that woman's phone? she is gone. Who cares about her damn phone or what is in it?" I stared back at her, "I care. "Why the fuck are you here?" I asked. She then asked me, "that's how you say, you're grateful to a person who just saved your life?" I shook my head, "I didn't need your fucking help, I had her right where I wanted her, I was playing possum," she laughed, "oh yeah. You were hanging from the ground, oh yeah, you had her alright." I hissed at her, "well, thank you, but I didn't need your help, plus how did you know where to find me, and where I was? Plus, this doesn't negate the fact that one of these days, I will kill you. You're not getting a pass for this!"

She laughed, "aww, damn, I don't get a pass? Oh shucks, darn it!" With her sarcastic remarks. She laughed, then quickly became serious, "look one day, I will kill you, before you kill me. And I am always keeping tabs on you, Discipline." I shook my head, "my goodness, all you women!! Can you all just stop stalking me?" I questioned her. She laughed, "you're a high commodity Discipline, we are all some crazy bitches for you, I guess. No but seriously, you and I had a common enemy. That slayer is not just a slayer of vampires, she casts out witches for some reason as well. So, I didn't just do you a favor, I did it for myself as well. Plus, I wasn't about to let someone kill you before I did. I will be the first to kill you and go down in history for putting you out of your misery."

I laughed out of sarcasm and then said, "listen, you will not get that pleasure, because I will be taking you out prior to you ever getting a chance to get to me. Look, thanks, but no thanks, and stay out of my fucking way next time! I told you the next time we meet, I would be at the cross roads with you, and there will not be peace, it will be war, it will be havoc, and it will be the end of an era." She scuffed at me, "whatever you say, and we will see when I see you, and you're welcome, asshole! You're never nice to me, asshole."

I flew up into the tree and flew away. It frustrated me, the fact that I could not get in her mind, nor affect her in anyway emotional, like I do the other women. The constant challenge, wait a minute. I got it! Moon dance. On a full moon, I'll take her to dance, one dance, and that is all I need. One dance and she will be mine. She will put her guard down and then I will get her. Once I get her, I'm going to kill her....

One look into my hypnotic eyes for a good amount of time, she will be putty in my fucking hands, and that is for certain. Allow her to bask in my fucking presence, and feel my powerful energy. She will not be able to resist me, then I will have her under my spell. Then I will have more opportunities to take her, all of her. And have my way, and then I will take her out, and rid this world of her existence.

Chapter 13- Take And Devour Her Innocence

I was in heavy thought of Cleopatra, I focused on her greatly. She felt my energy, 'Cleopatra, come to me." I called out to her in my deep thoughts. "Come to me. Come to me. Now!' She then came to me, she appeared in my presence instantly.

"I felt your presence, and you called for me? I guess you're ready to apologize and say thank you for saving your life, the other night as well, correct?" She asked me and she was waiting for an immediate reply. I then answered her, "well, no, I'm not apologizing, but I do want to thank you for the other night. I would love to make it up, allow me to take you out, dancing perhaps?"

The chess game then began… I looked into her eyes, and she gazed back into mine, she was skeptical, but she accepted my offer, "yes, that sounds promising." Then she snapped out of my trance, and then she asked me, "wait, don't you hate me? Aren't you still planning to kill me?" I laughed, "hate is so dramatic, I dislike you. I don't know you enough to hate you. Allow me to know you more, than I can hate you." She started laughing, "well damn, aren't you the charmer," she said sarcastically. I then continued to assure her….

"And as for killing, well, if I wanted to kill you, you would already be dead. You are here right now, because you know you want to be, if not, you would not have come when I called. Like I said, if I wanted you dead, you would already be dead." She may have been a witch, but she could not have picked up on all of my powers. I shape shifted into a Lion, and I frightened her, "or I could have been sneaking into your place, where you lay..."

I then turned into a fly, then an eagle. "You see, I could have destroyed you plenty of times, but, you entertain me. Plus, let's face it, you won't kill me, as much as I won't kill you. You are like the good superhero and I am the villain. It's like we need each other. You complete me. What would superheroes do without bad guys? What would villains do without superheroes? It would just be plain boring." She smiled at me. Then I continued....

"Therefore, shall we dance?" She nodded her head, "you have a point there, yes we shall." I was pleased, then she paused and asked me, "but wait, how are you certain you know I won't kill you? And if you are, how are you so certain?" She turned all the lights out. The street lights, and made it completely dark, and she became invisible. I laughed, "oh, you think darkness is your ally, see I was born to be into the darkness. It became the only thing that made sense to me. I fell in love with sin before love. I fell in love with the dark before the light."

I was talking and looking left and right and moving around. Meanwhile, I could feel her presence near. It was getting stronger in certain directions I was moving, and it become weaker in other directions. Therefore, I went to the direction where I felt her presence the strongest.

"Light is boring, and it can be blinding to someone that was already molded in the dark for so long. I am the King of Darkness and you know why these shadows will always betray you?" I then grabbed an invisible image to my left, behind me by the throat, and she appeared visible in my massive muscular hands, gasping for air...

"That is because, these fucking shadows belong to its master, and that is me!" But, I then released my grip from her throat, she grasped her neck. "Impressive, very impressive," she said, as she gasped for air. I said to her, "you won't kill me because deep down, you need me, and I won't kill you, because deep down, you entertain me. So, the reality is, this is all about you. This fucking problem we have here."

I said this to her, with a smirk on my face. I noticed something with this woman, she does not fear death, she welcomes it. Interesting, if I were to punish her, her punishment would be more severe. There's much pain and suffering this woman has endured, I can feel it. From her past, coming to her future. What doesn't kill you, makes you stronger. What doesn't destroy you, makes you stronger. I told her...

"Tomorrow, we dance, tomorrow we dine, tomorrow is a clash of immortality. As immortality comes in all different forms." She stared at me then said, "you and your riddles, why can't you speak like a normal person. Why can't you do what an ordinary man does?" She asked. I answered her, "ordinary? But, what is ordinary? I mean what is normal to a lion, is chaos to a warthog."

The following day came, and then the night arrived so quickly, and we met, oh she was so lovely. She was dressed in black and red. "My two favorite colors, throw in some blue in there, we would have a triple threat." I said to her and she smiled at me. And I continued, "darkness and blood."

She then stopped smiling, as she said to me, "you sure know how to make a woman feel good, huh? Warm and tingly inside, huh?" She said sarcastically. I smiled as I answered her question, "I do my best." Sarcasm right back to her with that one. "Your ass actually looks real juicy and plump in that dress, shit, my goodness!" She shook her head at me, with a flat stare, "are you going to be an asshole all night? Or are we going to dine and dance already?" I smirked, "well, do I need to choose?" She answered, "hahaha, you asshole! You're trouble there, mister."

It's funny, when a woman tells you that, you are trouble, or you're so bad, normally she is already visualizing having sex with you. We then dined, and we wined, and we then began to dance, I pulled out my hand, and asked, "shall we?" She didn't answer, she just placed her hand in mine.

Normally, I like to just tell a woman what she's going to give me, where we are going to go, and when I am to be invited, but as a vampire, it's a lot different with this lifestyle. I could never sink my teeth into her until I was invited. I gain her trust, her vulnerability. I would take everything she has, and I would give her everything she needs. FREEDOM. Therefore, constant consensualness was required. Constant assurance was require. We danced calm, we danced slow, we danced sexual, we danced romantically. We danced hard, we danced passionately, we danced until we controlled the entire floor. Until we controlled the entire room. I stared into her eyes, and I captured her attention. She didn't look away at all, I spoke into her face...

"It's interesting, isn't it?" I said to her. Then she asked me a question pertaining to my question, "what you mean?" I gazed into her eyes, and then continued...

"This moment of two beings, who once loathed each other," she cut me off, "no I still loathe you. Get it correct!" I smirk and continued, "don't cut me off, you know I can feel you, it's beautiful, you know? Like hypnosis? Physical hypnosis, like your body relaxes....your eyes drop a little bit. You fall into glances when they become stares. Don't fucking look away!"

I cupped her face in my massive hands, brought her back to my eyesight. "Fall!! Fall!!!" Her eyelids dropped, and I saw it all over her. "Look me in my eyes, yes, look!" Her eyes opened wide back onto my eyes, "let everything fall away," I kept talking to her. Smooth, softly, not forceful. "The moment, the past, things outside of this, duties, jobs, responsibilities, situations, the actions, let it all disappear, fall! Life is for living, life is for exploring, for the moments that matter enough to remember. This is ours. Fall, and I can see it, you are putting all that weight down, all those guards down."

Out of all the women that I slayed, even though she is a witch, why is she so different? I cannot figure it out, why can I not bite her right away and be done with her already?

Then I fucking figured it out. Trust! She lacks it, trust, she can't provide it. Trust, she fears it. She is constantly in control, and she has never been able to let go. But in this moment, there had been a shift of power. There has been a shift of terror. There has been a shift of magic. In this moment she stopped resisting, because she didn't want anything to get in the way of what I can do to her, not even her. She herself does not want to get in the way of what is next to come for her. She falls for me; her apprehensions melted away. Her insecurities quieted down, her busy thoughts are calm, her past is forgotten, that smile of hers lets me know, she is completely here. However, she is gone as well, ready to float above earth, high as a fucking kite, stone cold sober. All of this while staring into my beautiful hypnotizing eyes.

She's ready, willing and able to be everything I need in that moment, she is mine, she FALLS! My control becomes her release. Her neck was exposed, my eyes turned gold, and my fangs came out. They grew slightly, she was ready to die, willing and able under my damn spell. I'm going to bite her, as hard as I can. Tattoo her my teeth marks, as my jaw will clench. The pain will be intense, her pussy will be drenched, she will squeal, she will scream, she will attempt to fight. Maybe she will? Maybe she will not? Then she will go weak, she will go numb, her body no longer her own, her blood no longer her own. More pressure, higher pitch, I will unintentionally growl, the vampire King will take over, crushing her prefect skin, warped. Gone and rid her existence of this earth, finally...

I just couldn't do it, I stopped myself, but it was more than that, it was more than the damn feast. Damn I hated her, but not really, I wanted more. Of her. Of us. I wanted to know, the 'why', the 'if' the 'when.' I needed to know why she was so closed off, of her past. I wanted to know if she had goals. What did she believe was in the future cards for herself? What has brought her up to this point in her life? What has made her choose the life and path she so religiously leads now? I needed to know the, what if things could have been different for her? Why they are different for her? I needed to know, when this all came about? Therefore, I pulled back, she blinked in confusion and stared up at me, and she snapped out of my hypnotism.

"What just happened? I felt like I was in a dream." She directed her attention to my fangs that I had put away. My eyes turned its natural beautiful brown color.

"Listen, I must leave, have a good night." I said to her, as I was attempting to rush out of there. I did not know what was happening to me. Was she becoming my weakness? No, not me, I was Discipline, I was harder than the concrete. I was fucking tougher than Nigerian hair. I did not know what it was, however, I had to get the fuck out of there…

She then yelled out for me, "Discipline, why are you leaving? This dinner and dance thing was your fucking idea!" she then whispered to herself, "fucking asshole."

I needed time to think, how long I've been so used to being a vampire, that I was never able to feel like this before, not for a long time, hesitant to feast, to feed especially upon a woman. I never had a problem in that area at all. And I just couldn't do it. Was it the fact that she helped save my life? Did I feel like I owed her? Like some type of loyalty to her? I don't know if it's a subconscious feeling of, I owe her. I never intend to feel like this for a human, a mere mortal, oh hell no. Was it the fact that I liked that witch bitch a little bit? Perhaps it was a little bit of everything? I had no explanation for this, this was bugging me the fuck out, shit!

Prior to dinner, Cleopatra and I exchanged numbers, I wanted better access to her therefore, I demanded it. And she was blowing up my phone, and then texting me, 'hey, asshole, where did you run off to? You didn't even feel like yourself. What was it? Stomach bloating? Was it cramps? Did you need to take a number two? Do vampires even shit? No, wait ya'll drink blood, so do you piss out blood? Oh, I get it, you must have had your period, so you ran off on me?'

She was right, I was not myself, but she was still making stupid jokes, therefore I avoided her phone calls and ignored her texts. Man, one thing a woman can't stand is when you show them a little attention, then take it away, they hate being ignored. Especially, women whom are so used to getting so much attention. One thing about seduction is, taking everything, I mean everything. That includes what she wants and has, then giving her everything she needs.

I had to go to the night clubs and the fitness clubs, those were my businesses. I figured, I was not going to kill Cleopatra, but I was not going near her either, it was best I stay away from that witch. I avoided going to the club every night. I made sure things ran smoothly enough where I didn't need to show up there constantly. But I would stay late at times, randomly. I was supervising my night club, meeting with Susan Wilts, my prime investor of the clubs, and business partner and all of a sudden, Cleopatra comes over...

"Listen, we need to talk." She was very demanding. I turned over to Susan and shrugged her off, and I said, "not now." She grabs me, and says, "yes, now is the best time." I turn to Susan, and apologized, and said, "this will take just a minute, I'll be right back."

We went heading towards my office, and when Susan looked away, I grab Cleopatra by the arm, and we got to my office, "what the fuck are you doing in my place of business? I worked hard for that deal with Susan, for months and you could fuck it up in like a minute, with your messy shit. And then I would really fucking kill you."

She raised an eyebrow, "then do it, yeah, kill me." I shook my head, just leave, it's better if we do not ever cross paths ever again, okay?" She was a stubborn creature, "no, I'm not leaving, I need answers, you left and didn't mention a word. You get me to the point of trusting you, get me to the point of putting down my guards, then you fucking leave, you asshole. You typical male, and you're not even like a human being, you're a...well....you're a.... I don't even know what the fuck to call you."

I was furious, then I said to her, "asshole, that seems to be the common word you love using for me lately." She then answered me, "I said all that and all you heard was, "asshole? Men! They hear what they want to hear, but they never hear us women. I'm not asking you to listen to me, I'm not trying to be domineering or demanding, I'm just asking you to fucking hear me."

I was looking away from her, as I had a lot on my mind, then I stared at her and asked, "what? Excuse me, what were you saying again?" Frustration built, as she let out a deep breath, then a grunt, "ugh, this is what I was talking about, you damn men!" I then said, to her, "the problem is not men, it is you. Once you begin to place all men in the same category, that is what you will encounter. I heard everything you said, I can manage different sets of tasks efficiently. I was just asking, because I knew it would piss you off, and I wanted you to feel how I feel right now, I was trying to close another deal with the Susan woman, and you are now here."

I was already furious from the interruption of the meeting I was engaged in with Susan, I grabbed her by the throat, "I can end you right here, right now," she head butted me. I mean, what woman does that? She then clinched her fingers, and balled up her fist and her fist kissed my jaw, but it did nothing, and then she kicked me, I fell to the ground. I lifted up into the air quickly, my eyes were thunderous, and my fangs then came out. I grabbed her, I didn't even touch her, I just lifted my hands, and I elevated her off the ground, and I used the 'come here' gesture with my fingers and she floated over to me. I balled up my hand into a fist, and that created an invisible chain around her body, therefore she could not move, and she just floated to me...

"You have no idea how powerful I am, you idiot, you're fucking with the wrong man, bitch." I threw her heavily into the wall. She waved her hand as she got right back up and she attempted to hit me, with a bolt of thunder, I blocked it. And I took the thunder and lightning and made it disintegrate. I said to her...

"Guns, knives, weapons, systems, magic, you mortals put so much faith in. You could aim, whatever you want to aim as you please. However, you will never be able to strike, or reach a God!"

Both of us were furious, and we ran towards each other and we collided. It was like a clash of two titans. She hit me, and I hit her back, I grabbed her throat and she was gasping for air, and I leaned in and kissed her luscious lips, and I bit the bottom part of her lower lip, and she then kissed me back. I ripped her clothes off, and I pushed her up against the wall, I grasped her hair and kissed her lips again, this time rougher. I took her panties off, ripping them in two and I shoved my erect big chocolate dick into her wet begging pussy hole. I thrusted into her pussy like there was no next week, like there was no tomorrow, like there was no time to waste. I utilized my dick as a weapon to destroy her with. Tame her anger and soothe her craziness.

She moaned so loud, and I covered her mouth, and I continued to fuck the hell out of her. She was like an animal in a cage, waiting to be released. She cried out, her voice so high with the fright that it surprised her, like she was starving. Starving for this, starving for me, starving from her own desires. She sucked the air that was ever so faintly scented. She felt my strong desires in her cervix, this congealing fire in her breasts. And this passionate strength of big dick that was inside her, it swept along her legs and up her spine, radiating out from her belly.

The hunger was dangerous. The hunger came upon me by inches, then it made her explode unexpectedly. Her eyes shriveling until they rattled in their sockets like stones in the pocket of a child. Her heart beat become noticeable to me, I could hear, see, and feel it more intensely. I was in so deep, and I could see it in her eyes, in the way her breathing changed. I clasped her hands together and I took them with one of my massive hand, and I pinned her hands above her head. I had her vulnerable, she was exposed, she was helpless, ready for me to take all of her at any given time. I thrusted roughly, she was clutching onto my broad shoulders. I stared dead into her eyes and witnessed her eyes wide and frozen. Her curled lashes wet from the overwhelming fuck I just gave her, from sweat, from tears, from excitement, from desire. I pulled my big cock out of her...

"On your knees," I commanded her. I placed my hand on the top of her head, and held her head in place. I came intensely, into her mouth, making sure she swallowed every drop.

"Swallow all of it, don't miss one drop." I demanded. I growled following that. A pretty bitch down on her knees with a pair of soft, full lips wrapped around the big head of my big dick. A hot, wet tongue twirling all over it, then gliding up and down my shaft, wetting it up real slippery-like, then slapping at my big chocolate balls. She was using her tongue in places that will get me dizzy, urging me to give her my hot, creamy powerful nut, once again. She wanted more.

"Mmmmm, what… you think you're ready? If so, sit back, ass cheeks should be on your heels. Then relax and let me see you try to deep throat this big cock. That will make your eyes water more and cough as your throat throbs. Fucking rock my cock, gargle my balls, and suck me from hell straight to heaven bitch."

As she then attempted this, and I wanted to feed her voracious appetite, I paused it. "Wait, I still have shit to discuss with Susan, no, we can't."

Cleopatra was upset, "are you fucking shitting me? Go on and tease me why don't you, huh? Get me dripping wet more. My pussy in need of you. My mouth begging for your big juicy and meaty cock, and you have to go?" I replied, "yes."

I had a dick and tongue game that could make any woman forget her name. An intellect, that could enhance any woman's soul. I put my pants back on, and she had no clothes to put on herself, I transported us out of there using my telepathic and telekinesis abilities and took us to my place, "see yourself out, after you take this," I gave her one of my dress shirts, and a boxers to wear, "this will get you into public without having to walk out naked, bring my shirt back, get the fuck home immediately and change into your regular clothes."

She then said to me, "you know, you could have just teleported us back to my place, where I would change into my clothes. But I guess, you didn't care to make it easy for me, huh?" I gazed at her firmly, then I said to her, "just fucking do what the fuck I am telling you, I don't need to hear no lip." I said in a forceful tone.

She was in complete agreement with me, "understood!" I then left, I needed to get back to the meeting I had with Susan, so I freshened up and didn't change my clothes, that would have been the first fucking thing she would notice. You're reading this, probably saying to yourself, 'oh, she would not have noticed.' Trust me, women notice, everything.

I left Cleo hot and bothered, literally. Her body, missed me immensely. And she needed me already so badly. Her pussy needs me, it aches for the width of my nine-inch 3/4, thick veiny dick, thrusting in and out of her pussy. It would long, for my deep strokes of my thick tongue caressing her clit and its lower lips. She's held out for so many men. She hasn't been handled by a man ever, and she hasn't been fucked properly in such a long time. But, she had held out; denied any other man the privilege and the pleasure of fucking her sweet, and wet pussy hole. She was frightened. Giving me more time with her, would have her hooked on me, and my dick like it was crack. More potent than cocaine. She would be insane. In ways more than she was now. Most she has been doing was sucking and fucking dildos. But, nothing compares to the touch of another being. She was fucking horny, and she went home dressed in my stuff, and went to masturbate. She held my dress shirt in her hand, and put it to her face, so she can inhale my scent off of the shirt. While she laid on her back, shut her eyes, and filled her wet, tight begging pussy hole with her large thick black dildo into herself. Slowly thrusting it with her hands, back and forth into and out of her wet pussy hole. Imagining it was my thick long cock. Shutting her eyes, biting her bottom lip. She was screaming and cumin, "oh Discipline, yes, yes, just like that." She was imagining it was me touching her flesh once again. My ears were ringing, and I was hearing my name. But, I ignored it. I had to get back to business. She was a dripping mess, with my shirt in her hand, and I was heading back to the meeting, like nothing happened.

Chapter 14- Are You Going To Invite Me In?

I arrived back to the club, and Susan didn't notice a fucking thing out of place. And she waited to resume for when I arrived. "Shall we continue, shall we proceed? Excuse me for taking so long, I have so many prior engagements as I go on for the running of these clubs. I'm like a high commodity." I said with a reassuring smile. She added her input, she laughed, "yes, Discipline, we all crave your attention. But seriously, Look, Discipline, you really do not need to be here or there, at all these clubs. You own them, that is why you have people in place to run them. Some of these clubs, you own the property. Like you are really the boss of the boss."

I smirked and said, "I am used to being a workhorse, besides, I like to be here, I love being aware of everything. When it's going on, how it's going, where it's going." She nodded her head, as if she was impressed with me. I continued...

"I know I'm not like most owners, however, that's one of the things that separates me from everyone else. I'm different, therefore, I engage, and I perform different things. Work sometimes, for some people become an escape. Most of our time is spent commuting to work. Most of our day is spent at work, most of the week is spent being productive at work. Work becomes, or starts to become like a second home. You then begin to realize, that you spend more time there than you do at your actual home. With even your actual family. Work becomes like a second home, and now the people you see there and interact with become like your second family. We all get used to that, and it doesn't change. So even if someone told me, I could sit home, and make money, I would never want to just sit home. My physical motor and my mental motor are in sync. Work is just too familiar, and when there's no work, that becomes to seem very unfamiliar."

She looked at me and was like, "my goodness Discipline, I never looked at it like that, but you are right. You're so deep, you should really consider *writing a book one day.*"

Susan and I took a couple days and we went out of town. We went to Miami and Los Angeles. We went to look at these clubs she had there, and I was impressed. The crowd, the buildup, the revenue that those establishments were ranking up. The hustle was exhilarating, the lucrative journey we were embarking, turned me on a little bit.

The meeting went very well, and Cleopatra was still texting my phone, she wanted to meet up with me, and talk. Susan and I then came back to New York. So now Cleopatra, was calling and I then responded. She crossed the chamber, nervously aware that she felt a little weaker, a little more earthbound, than she had felt even when she awoke. It was nothing more than a certain increase of definition where her feet pressed against the soles of her shoes, but it was a signal that she was dealing with one of the rarest things that she knew—limited time.

'We can meet up in the park,' is what I texted back to her. 'Meet me there in a couple of hours, don't be late.' She replied, 'yes, and I won't be late Discipline.' She arrived there before me, I was in the trees just watching, stalking and waiting. The whisper of her heart became noticeable, rising to a whir of uneasy noise.

"Where are you?" Her voice had a flat echo to it. "Hello? You told me to meet you here, don't be late. Mr. who is never late, is now late?" I then appeared in front of her like the wind, and I came as a form of a man. She gasped, "ugh, you scared me." I stared at her flatly, "did I?"

See, I had a difficult time trusting people, even people I allowed in my circle, so, when she asked me to meet, I was not certain what it would entail, therefore, I was waiting in the wind. You could never trust a woman whom was angry and emotional, unless you could check her, or she could get that shit in check herself. Meaning, she could check her own emotions. It was difficult to trust women with a short temper, then all of a sudden, were on some nice shit with you. They were unpredictable. Perhaps, planning your own death, or something, all I could think about was, this bitch was a viper with lipstick, and I had to watch my fucking back until she proved to me, she was other than what I thought she was. Stalking in the skies. Prowling on the ground. For I am an eagle in the sky, a lion and gorilla on the ground, and a shark in the damn water. I could oversee everything, and now I asked her….

"Why did you want to see me? What couldn't wait?" I asked her. She was trying to find her words. "Well, I……. I……. wanted to see if we can have dinner but, in a more comfortable atmosphere. Like my place." She said. I laughed in her face, "ha, are you fucking loca? Have dinner at your place, so you can have better access to fuck me up? Better access to attempt to take my life, huh?"

She shook her head, "you don't trust me by now? I don't want you dead, I kind of like you, asshole! I was on my knees for you."

I then spoke forcefully, "who gives a fuck? That does not mean you wouldn't stab me in the back if you had the damn chance." There she goes with the, 'asshole,' remarks again. "You're so disrespectful, I would take you over my knee and spank your ass bright red, but you might like that, and I wouldn't want to give you what you want or like."

She raised an eyebrow with a smirk on her face, "oooh, yes, don't threaten me with a good fucking time." I shook my head at her... "Anyways, text me the address...." I demand to her, and as she started to protest, "but, wait I...." I vanished, creating a pile of smoke and wind, and then I disappeared from her presence. "Ugh, I hate when he does that," she said, with a grimace. "He is such a character."

So, the following night came, and it was a full moon. I was feeling good, strong and ready. I could've sent my presence into her home, but I wanted to use the front door, because I wanted her to 'invite me in,' that way I'll have the green light, and no matter what happens tonight, she allowed it. I was going in there with the mindset of, she was going to attempt to take me out, food poisoning, with something that was anti-vampire, where when I ate it, it made me sick for like a week, or worse, killed me. So, I was ready, nothing else mattered, not the past or future, if she was going to even attempt to take me out, I was going to literally rip her head off, or snap her neck. I wouldn't even feast on her flesh. She might like that shit. I might fuck around, and not feed enough on her, and turn her into one of me. Man, that would be worse. The way she is, but now into a vampire, and having my blood into her? She would be so powerful. But, fuck that, it was not about to happen. I had to remain focused.

I walked to the door, I knocked three times. *Knock *Knock *Knock, I heard, "who is it?" I answered, "fuck you mean, who is it? I just texted you I was here. Were you expecting someone else?" She answered the door, "good evening, asshole!! No, I wasn't expecting someone else, I figured you would teleport into my home." I then replied, "no, I wanted to do the traditional thing tonight." She looked at me confused, "bullshit, nothing about you is traditional." I changed the subject, "and cut the, 'asshole,' shit already." She gave me a fake smile, "when you stop acting like one, I'll stop calling you one." I shook my head, "Well? Are You Going To Invite Me In?" She stared at me for a few seconds then said, "yes, you may come in."

Perfect, I could feel her blood pumping, I licked my lips. It was like I could taste the blood from her, it was powerful. It felt, delicious. Her mind was racing. Her heart as well. I was thinking in my head, how her blood must taste. I pondered on this for a bit. I then licked my lips once again. "So, what is for dinner?" I asked her. She then said to me, "tonight, dinner is steak."

It was lovely, she didn't have it cooked all the way, so you can still cut and see the blood. I looked at her confused and said, "you couldn't have killed a deer or a human, and brought it here for me? I'm a damn vampire, is this a fucking joke? I am not going to eat human food!"

I was so adamant about not eating what she made. "I am not about to eat that shit, even though I do love steak." She laughed, "well, you do not need to eat human food, this is steak. An animal had to die for this. You ever heard the expression, 'I'm so hungry, I could eat a whole cow?'

I didn't answer her, I wasn't going to entertain her smart-ass remarks, and shit. She then had a change of plan, "listen, no need to get all uptight, no need to eat, you can just watch me eat, and we can chat." She said. She chose a dress of fine linen and her traveling cloak of human leather, made from a species that she had extinguished. She looked like an Egyptian Goddess with her outfit and make up tonight.

The Egyptians were a docile people who respected their rulers, and she would appear to them to be a great lady, and they would drop their eyes and let her pass. She would find a dark corner, make quick work of one of them to regain her strength, then go on and locate her own kind. She was like a Darkness rose. Now, high above, hung the glowing outer arm of the galaxy, the border of the known world. Her eyes focused, then focused again, until the firmament revealed its wonders to her. The reefs of stars became a jeweled host as she began to perceive each individual strand of light. As the rays entered her eyes, each sent its own message to her heart.

Chapter 15- Patiently Waits To Ravage Her Body

I watched her speak. I watched everything; her lips, her eyes, I read her words as I can make them out before they came out of her mouth. I observed her body language. She was still, she didn't move too much. Her stillness was as precise as her movement. Indeed, she was so still that a cruising owl used her as a perch, hooted twice, then swept back into the sky, its wings trembling the silent air. She walked steadily and precisely, a shadow in the shadows of the night. her eyes gleaming with a tiger's shine, she revealed nothing of herself to the world around her. Not the world, but me. I could finally read her, and that just meant one thing, she was breaking those walls down for me. She was releasing. I could read everything about her so easily.

I spread my nostrils and drew in the scent of blood, cooked meat and dates, and the scintillating odor of human skin. I lived as much by scent as sight, and it was one of my favorite smells. Women liked to be kissed, which was a matter of indifference to me. But I would kiss them to smell them. I knew the different ways each part of the female human body smelled and enjoyed it all. Women were and still are the most emotional creatures on earth. Men, you can snap their neck, or go for the throat and feed instantly. However, women, you can play with them. Seduce them. Like you're playing with your food, before you devour it.

I didn't know what was going on with me, 'snap out of it Discipline.' I thought to myself. 'You're a predator. A cold-blooded killer. Known for your ferocity and iron control.' But still, I couldn't kill her, I wanted more. I wanted her soul, her body, her mind, not just her blood. She wasn't a regular kill. She wasn't a regular feast. She wasn't even a feast.

"I want to know more of you. I want to know more about you." I demanded this. She then told me about her childhood. I told her about mine. We had similar things in common. Tormented souls find comfort in each other by how our demons play well with each other.

"Power is exhilarating," I said to her. I am powerful in the streets, the business world and the bedroom. I'm not a fortunate man, I learn to create my own luck. If I'm not in control, I am off balance. I thrive in pressure situations and I excel in fast pace environments. I used to be a guy that had a difficult time dealing with his emotions. My anger, my short temper. As I grew older, I realized I was just afraid of them. I learned how to control them and not the other way around. I'm not good. I'm not innocent, but I'm corrupted."

She whispered to me, "I was raised to be good, but I fell in the darkest cracks." I gazed into her eyes, "parts of you are innocent," I said firmly, and I pointed then grabbed her pussy. I leaned in, and I pressed my lips against her luscious lips. Our lips parted, and our tongues wrestled with each other's. Our clothes were taken off quickly and found their way onto the floor. I made her feel absolutely reckless. Vulnerable. Exposed. She was in need of the most dangerous creature in New York, which was me. I ran my fingers through her hair. I kissed her body all over. I placed my massive hands on her throat. We were back at her place, and so I tossed her onto the bed. I forced her legs apart. I ate her pussy like it was my last meal, like she was my last meal for the night. She moaned to the top of her lungs. Then I put her on her knees. I was going to make her a champ at sucking me. I will show her, she can swallow my big length and width without gagging, or puking.

"Fucking relax, breathe through your nose, extend your tongue all the way out, and then swallow one inch at a time until you have this big chocolate Discipline dick all the way down in your fucking throat. Relax your damn throat for me."

Then she started swallowing while she gave me a nice, slow balls massage with her fingers. She did everything I commanded. I was determined to make her throat please me. Her eyes watered, and the big head of my dick hit the back of her throat. I reach from behind her, and grab that juicy plump ass. I then slap each ass cheek viciously. You could see my red hand print on her ass. It looked beautiful, I reached over her again. Sticking my finger in her pussy hole. She was soaking wet. Yes, soaking wet from all this meat in her mouth. All this length touching the back of her damn throat. I see it excites her. It entices her. No matter if she never knelt for a man prior to me before. She loved it. Correction, she loved to kneel for me.

I grasp a fist full of her hair, utilizing her hair as a handle. I also grab the front of her neck, as my other hand is then placed on her throat. Now, I begin to fuck her face. I then, shove my big cock back and forth inside her mouth. Between her begging lips. Her eyes become wider. Her mouth creating slobbering sounds and gagging noises. Spit streaming down my balls, and onto the ground. Her throat throbbing. She's out of breath. Her eyes water. Yes, tonight, I am throat fucking a greedy, dick-sucking bitch like her. Fucking her mouth, as if I was fucking her pussy. Deep-stroking that pipe down into her gullet until her eyes start to water. Until her eyes start to beg. That was my style. Spit ran from her mouth to her tits.

Cleopatra was full, she had luscious lips; perky, C-cup tits; small, tight waist; firm, plump ass; and smooth, shapely legs... this face and throat fucking session is over. I don't want to nut in her mouth or face yet. I want to feel that wet pussy first. I want to be inside it. My cock and I wanted to feel and know why it was so drenched for me. I then shoved my big, fat, long, chocolate cock into her tight drenched begging pussy hole. Her pussy lips wrapped snug around my girth. She used her witch powers and she shut the lights. She loved doing that shit, huh? I spoke to her softly, but forceful...

"Do you believe that darkness is your ally?" I was starting to reiterate to her what I said to her in the park, but she started to finish my sentence... "I know, I know," she said to me. "let me guess, let's see if I remember what you told me.... I was simply molded into it for so long, light has become blinding. These shadows will always betray you, because they belong to me."

I then added, "not only these shadows, but you. Yes, just like the entirety of you, they fucking belong to me. Your orgasms belong to me, and you will beg for permission to release. And you may only release when I allow It. I want to own you."

She whispered and asked, "all of me?" And I replied, "always." I put her on her back. Naked, vulnerable, and exposed. Completely exposed to my will. Yielding to my confident measured authority. Complete submission to my Dominance. Tantalized by my darkest desires. Wet from the anticipation of Discipline.

I shove my thick, long chocolate dick inside her after I took it out to tease her. Then I placed it back inside her. Between her drenched begging lips. Inside her yielding, yet tight hole. I commanded sharply, "look at it!" I placed my massive hands on the top of her head, I then curled with my muscular fingers inward, grasping a fist full of her hair just to anchor her head toward me. Her eyes rolled back, she stared at it, then shut her eyes and moaned loudly in pleasure.

I slapped her face, "open those eyes, look me in my eyes when I take you. Look me in my damn eyes, when I fuck you over and over. Rub your clit for me, while my chocolate dick thrusts inside and outside of your drenched begging hole."

She created a 'v' with her index and middle finger. I could feel them as they rubbed against my girth. Then she brought those same fingers together, and she rubbed her clitoris as I ordered her to as well. She rubbed her clit clockwise. She has those two fingers down, like as if it were 6:30 on a clock. Good girl, but her mouth dirty. "Oh fuck, Daddy, oh shit. You feel so good!" She gasped out.

I guess I graduated from asshole. I guess when you fuck her great, she changes her tone. In about ten seconds or less, she was already begging... "Daddy, may I!?" I already knew what she wanted to ask, but I wanted to hear those words.

"May you what?" I asked, awaiting an immediate response. "May I please, pretty please, cum?" I pulled out and flipped her over, "not yet, I want you just a little bit longer. Face south, and your ass north."

I pushed her head to the mattress of the bed. I slid into her gaping hole. She gasped for air. Her body no longer her own, she moves how I want. Her words no longer her own, she speaks when I want, how I want. Her thoughts in another world. I slapped her ass, and she spreads a little bit more for me. A raging river becomes of her. I place my massive fingers on her waist, and I move her back and forth on me. Strong pelvis pounding on her cheeks. Slapping of flesh, sounds as though it is now back ground music, as her moans take over the room. I press down with my muscular thumbs on her lower back, and my other fingers hold onto her waist. I thrust deeper, I thrust harder. Now I want her to give it all to me.

"Now I want you to cum for me." She took a deep breath and a major gasp for air, and she breathes out and came. She dripped all over me and onto the mattress sheets. I didn't stop, and she just kept cuming. I cuffed her wrists, while her hands were behind her lower back. Her palms were facing me. I gave her a dose of my Henny big dick. Strong and dark had her fucked up and love drunk real quick. Pistol for a dick, back shots murdered her pussy. Pounding her, left her a dripping mess for me. Walls closed in around me like a vice grip pliers. She was drenched like Niagara Falls. Squirting everywhere like a busted fire hydrant. She used to run from me and held back, but now she loves and is used to the pain.

I exposed her to realness and my world, and now she's disgusted by anything that's lame. Ever since I ran through her mind, body and soul, she has never been the same. I never said I was such a great influence, therefore I will take the blame. Once I gave her a taste of this world of Discipline, the rest of the world pales in comparison. I've changed her emotionally and physically. And now I've left her mentally bound to me. One man's tool is another man's weapon. And I utilize mine to destroy her when I take her over and over again. I choked her, and my grip got tighter, ironic, the tighter my grip, the more she let go.

"Relax, my dear, relax! Or it will be harder for you." My voice was deeper, almost guttural and somewhat monstrously hungry. She struggled against my grip and then she relaxed, she found peace in my chaos, her desire became her surrender.

I took myself out of her, I put her on her knees and I grasped her head. I grasp a fistful of her hair, I shoved my massive cock into her mouth and then I pulled it out and stroked my big cock towards her face....

"Swallow my darkness," I commanded. "Swallow my darkness," I commanded once again. She swallowed every drop.

We cuddled the night away. Something I didn't do in the past. Except with Precious. I haven't felt like this in a long time. It was weird, but it felt right. This was not just a fuck. I was not just here to get a nut off. I then said to her, "get dressed, I must get dressed myself as well. I must be at the club, tonight is the big night."

The sultry night had begun, another great night for the club. It was packed, the music was live, the crowd was wild. I did my rounds, I walked around, greeted everyone. From celebrities, to the regular customers attempting to get close to the celebrities. To the younger generation of early twenty-year-old individuals, that would get club money from the parents. Or worked Monday to Friday, and could not wait until the weekend arrived, just so they could spend their hard-earned money here. Buying bottles, to impress the bitches. It was the power of the bottle. The exclusivity. The fact that, this alone, made you someone that was not regular there. VIP, stamped a declaration, it screamed, 'we are here!' Why? Well, not everyone could get into VIP. Not everyone could afford to get in VIP. And they were placed in prominent areas in the facility, they were taken care of.

I mean, you would always want to take care of the customers that were willing to spend more money on your establishment, or your product. VIP, was huge here, I would see the same young guys in VIP. You know, it was a younger generation, a younger mentality. I mean you think about it, if you would ask one of them if you could give them a million dollars today, or ten million dollars and they would need to wait a year from now. Most of them would choose, the little million today. Why? Their priorities are different. Most people with business minds, would choose the ten million, and they would wait a year for it. Why? They are thinking long term, most likely. Think about it, the ones choosing the little million now, they would most likely blow that shit in a couple of minutes. Probably here in the club, probably on a jet they don't even need.

Money comes, and money goes. A million dollars is not a lot of money when you think about it. The concept is to make as much money as possible, invest, therefore you can make more money in the long run. Something residual. Everything we did in life was an investment. Our time, our energy, our presence, our words, our conversations. A house, a vehicle, a building like a fitness club or a night club. All these people here are investing their time and money, and if they were willing to do that, they would want something out of it.

All I could do was smile, to look at how full it was in the facility, and to see how far I've come. From the streets to corporate offices. From Brooklyn to owning establishments in other states. Heading to now expand internationally. From the slums to the Bahamas. It felt great, and I had a big grin on my face, just reminiscing to myself.

Then suddenly, I felt this strong energy, that shit hit me, like it was a punch to my chest, I then began to look around. I asked myself, 'where was this potent energy coming from?' I felt as if I was being tailed. And I *was* being tailed. I wasn't certain but then I observed, and I turned and saw a woman. I knew immediately why she was here. She showed up at my club. She saw me all over the place; billboards, newspapers, magazines, social media. This is what I was afraid of, people coming to me treating me different because they see me somewhere prominent. Or, attempting to try and take over or pull one over on me, for their personal gain.

Susan Wilts wanted me out there more, therefore, I listened. She made sense, but I had this in the back of my mind constantly, about if this was a possibility of that. I mean my clubs were one of the most popular and prestigious clubs in the New York strip.

The woman spoke to me, "hey there, hello. You must be Mr. Discipline? She stuck her hand out for me to shake it. I observed her clothes, stared her up and down. I watched her close. I didn't answer, then I said to her...

"First of all, don't 'hey,' me, I am not a horse. Secondly, who is asking? Are you the police? Are you a friend? A stock holder? A potential investor? Are you a fan? Stalker? A displeased customer?" She laughed, "perhaps a friend." I smirked, "perhaps?" I questioned her. "You are definitely not an old friend, even if I was not too good at remembering names, I have a great photographic memory. Perhaps, you are attempting to make me a new friend." She smiled, then she asked, "can we go someplace quieter to speak?" I then said, "sure, why not? Look, let's go to my office."

I walked in front of her and guided her to my office. She then said, "it's a lovely office." I ignored the compliment, my mindset was, 'cut the small talk, there is a reason why you have approached me.' I then said to her...

"What was it that you wanted to discuss with me so privately?" She then pulled out a gun, aimed at my back, it was a .50 AE desert eagle. I gazed and scanned it with my eyes really quickly, as I turned around and she said to me, "this is what I wanted to discuss motherfucker!" Now that was a big pistol for a woman to have. It's pretty heavy as well. About 3.5 to 4 pounds. If she would not hold it properly, the blow back would be vicious. For her that is.

I didn't ask the question, 'what she was doing here?' I just said, "my goodness, you women these days do have a way with men. You all are becoming the aggressors now." I had both my hands up, "well that escalated quickly, and so did your whole demeanor." I said sarcastically. She was very aggressive, "shut up!" She shouted.

I then said to her, "I don't mean to interrupt you, but look, I don't take orders very well, perhaps you don't want to make that choice? Maybe you should suggest, not tell me what to do." She cocks the fucking pistol, ready to pull the trigger. She then said to me, "what the fuck did I say?"

Now normally, I could take the gun out of her hands with my eyes, and mind control the shit out of it, with my telekinesis ability, which was the ability to move object with mental power. But, before I could do that, I wanted to know why, where, when and most importantly, who? So, I was patient, I inquired, and I was compliant to her demands. Why? Well, because I knew she was going to tell me why she was here.

"Look, I'm James' sister!" She blurted out. I looked confused. I was waiting patiently to ravage her body. She looked at me, then she said, "yeah go ahead look stupid, I am James' sister, Precious' ex boyfriend's sister."

I raised an eyebrow, but I didn't make any sudden movements. I wanted her to feel in control, and not be afraid, rattled or anything. Why? Two reasons, one I didn't want to expose myself, until I knew what I was working with, and the second and most important reason, if she felt in control, she would just talk, and talk, and talk. And that is what I wanted. She then did exactly what I wanted, she talked, and she then began to continue to bring me up to speed about what has been going on, these past years back....

"James has been missing for several years and the last place he was headed was to Precious' house. He was telling me, he was all crazy for her. He had gotten out of jail and when him and I spoke, that's all this dude was talking about. Getting to Precious. Perhaps starting over with her, building a brand-new life, etc."

I didn't speak, I let her. I just listened. I mean, I had two ears and one mouth for a reason, right? Therefore, I would listen and observe more than I spoke, until the time was right. She then continued...

"You and Precious are or were lovers." I didn't answer her, I had no idea if she was telling me or asking me, so I kept my mouth shut. And she continued, now she was asking me the question...

"So, where the fuck is she? And where is my brother? It's not like him to not call me, there is no sign of him. Nothing within the news, and if he skipped town, I would know about it. If he did something that placed him back in jail, I would know about it."

I looked closer at her, "is that a trick question or do you want an answer today? Uh, would you like me to speak now?" I asked her. She nodded her head, indicating to me 'yes.' I then started to speak...

"First of all, I don't know where he is." And honestly, when I was telling her this, it was not a lie. When Precious killed James, because he had a gun on me, I got rid of the body because I made calls. I ordered to rid the body. And I had my people take care of it, so I was not lying. I really didn't know where he was. He could have gone to a chop shop, could have been in a river somewhere, who knows? The fact of the matter was, I didn't know. And even if I did, do I look like a man, that would tell this strange, crazy bitch holding a pistol to me? Whom wasn't even holding it firmly at me, that if I wanted, any slight movement I could fucking take it out of her fucking hands and show her who really had some fucking authority around here. I would show her who was the one with the balls. Because, the only thing that commanded in this world was balls. So, let me show her, who is the cerebral assassin here. Let me show her, how I can get her to give me the gun using my brain and my mouth, rather than my physical Dominance.

I then said to her, "second, did you come here with an adequate plan? I don't see that you have a change of clothes." She looked at herself as her head went downward. And I then continued, "so, let's see, do you plan to shoot me at close range? Now if you did that, blood will splatter all over you. What will you do when you leave and walk out of my office? Everyone saw you come up with me. I have cameras all over this place, therefore, your face is also plastered all over here. Do you know of any other escapes out of here? No? Like I said, everyone saw you leave with me that is in the club."

I was making that last part up, I don't believe everyone saw us come here. Everyone was way into themselves, the music, friends, and the alcohol to be paying attention to anything else in the facility. I then continued to tell her, "do you know that you would be the first suspect? Oh, you don't think the police, would investigate this? I pay a lot of taxes out here, miss. And I am quite sure, you've seen me on billboards, perhaps magazines, in newspapers, etc. Do you have kids, family, a husband? And what would happen to them? Are they dependent upon you? What happens if you kill me? Will they be safe? Are they safe as of right now? What would they do, if you went to jail. Are you their sole provider? Like I said miss, I have cameras all over my office, that's how weird and psycho I am, yes, I am paranoid. I have cameras outside the office doors, and I have cameras inside here. I know the bouncers scanned your ID as well. They can check the check in list and see all your info. Height, full name, address? Although, you definitely were slick, getting pass the metal detectors, how did you do that?"

She did not answer me, "no need to answer that, that was probably a rhetorical question. You probably slipped by, with someone else, or when the bouncer was not looking. First thing the cops are going to do is check these cameras in here first. Like I said, did you come here with an adequate plan?"

She didn't speak, she didn't answer my questions. She knew I was right. She slowly lowered the gun, and I put my hands down slowly as well. I then spoke to her softly with a calm tone of voice to her...

"Look, I'll forget you were even here and I'll completely erase the cameras and I will pardon you for today. Sorry for your loss. Look myself, I am a black man, where society grants you two sides of the coin. Death or jail, however I am the exception not the rule. I am the epitome of opportunity, and started from the bottom. If I can help you in any way possible...."

She then interjected, "I don't need your fucking help!" She barked at me. I then put my hands up, to display, 'chill, I am no threat to you whatsoever.' I then continued to talk...

"I am a successful businessman, nothing more, and nothing less. Get yourself a drink, calm down, and then you can get the fuck out of my club." She walked out frustrated. Good thing I didn't kill her, because I had no change of clothing myself, and what would it look like if we left or better yet, just me coming back myself? The bartenders saw me go in there with her, and I don't know who this woman could be friends with in here or who she knew. Therefore, some people did see us walk away from the dance floor, and we parted together. So, she went back to the dance floor, and then she left.

I walked back to the bartenders and the VIPs, saying hello to everybody. I was mingling, and just making sure everyone was having a good time. I needed a shot after that exchange. That was intense back there, and hopefully I will not see that bitch ever again. The bartender gave me a shot of henny. But I fucking spoke too soon. James' sister, she didn't leave after all, she came back to me one last time prior to her departure. She taps me on my shoulder, then she whispered... "You are very good Mr. Discipline, but you fucked up." What did she mean that I fucked up? I whispered back to her...

"What do you mean, I fucked up?" She then continued to explain, "you said, 'sorry for your loss?' I never mentioned anything about a death or a loss with my brother. I said he was missing, where is he? However, you were not assuming, you know, or you were involved in his departure, one way or another I know it. Mr. Discipline, we will meet again! You can bet your bottom dollar on that shit, matter fact, you can bet that shit on this nice club."

Fuck, she was right on the money, she didn't say any of that, I did fuck up. I stared at her firmly and said, "indeed we will miss, indeed we will." I thought to myself, 'the next time I will not give you a pass whatsoever. I will take you out indeed. By any means necessary.' These were the thought in my head. She walked out of my club. The woman could not fuck with me on her best fucking day. She cannot fuck with my power. Not even on her best fucking day. I was leaving and headed to my place. Going into my home. I could smell human beings and I knew I could taste them, I knew I could feel their presence. It felt like a couple of them. One was lurking in the bushes and the other was behind my door. With my x-ray vision, I was able to see them, and pinpoint their exact location and shit. They were waiting for me to arrive, so they could ambush me. I smelled it and one was in the bush.

I put my key into the keyhole, and I shoved the door forcefully forward to open. I opened and knocked the man on the floor that was standing behind it. I then hit the other man whom was running up from behind me to come after me. I saw him and sensed him coming for me. As he was jumping out of the bushes, I said forcefully, "you fellows have no idea, I mean no fucking idea who you are fucking with! And I am not in the fucking mood tonight!" I roared. Then I warned them....

"This is not a problem you both want, nor need." I was multitasking, while I was fighting both of them at the same time. One of them ran at me and I kicked him in his shin, and he fell to his knees, and was then laid out on the floor. Then I grabbed him and threw him into the wall. The other one attempted to come at me and I grabbed him by the throat. I lifted him off the ground, and his feet were dangling off the floor like four inches. The other one that I threw towards the wall, rose up and he then reached for a knife from his pocket, he charged at me and the knife was then shoved into my back by him.

I dropped the one guy I had dangling from the ground. Then I said to that guy behind me, that stabbed me, "so, I must have a target on my back tonight or something, that you feel the need to put your pathetic tool there?"

I had my massive hand on his throat and lifted him off the ground. "Ugh!!" I then yelled. The fucking sting from the knife. I reached from behind me, and grabbed the knife from out of my back, and I slashed the guy in the throat that put it in my back with it. I then began to drink his blood, as it was dripping and spilling out of him. His other associate or friend, questioned me...

"What the fuck are you? You freak! You monster!" I looked at him with my changed eyes that were now red and my fangs were out, "I've been called far worse." I hissed at him. I then flew and charged towards him like a speeding bullet. I did not kill him instantly, because I wanted him to tell me whom sent him and the other one.

"Who the fuck sent you here? You both are definitely not professionals, because you both are so fucking sloppy as fuck. So, who sent you?"

He didn't answer me and that was the fucking last time he would breathe another breath. I sank my teeth into his neck and my fangs dug into his flesh, sucking the blood right out of him. "I needed that," I said to myself, and it was like a sport at this point. But I really wanted to know who or what sent them. Was this random? I need to pay attention and protect everyone around me. 'Cleopatra.' I then began to think about her, where she was? And did people see us together? Could they target her? I then texted her, 'we need to see each other, asap.' She was in complete agreement with me. I need to make sure everyone closest to me, were safe and protected. I must get in contact with Cleopatra. I reached for my phone......

Chapter 16- Love Her To Death

'Meet me at my place, right now!' I texted her. She found her way here to my place immediately. She saw the two men that I had destroyed. "Ugh, ohh, oooh, what the fuck? You were that hungry? Two, huh? With your greedy ass," she shook her head.

"It's not even like that," I said to her. "You see, these men were sent by someone whom has been watching me, and tailing me to either rattle me up or kill me." She was shocked, and she gasped for air, "oh shit," she was astonished, then she asked me, "well, do you know who sent them?" I shook my head, "no, I was trying to get answers from this one here, before I killed him, but he would not say a word. Normally, people will display their true colors when their life is on the line. When you have a knife, a gun or threaten a loved one, they'll do anything. Say anything. Especially a knife. The gun is not as effective as when you hold a knife to someone. But, these men were willing to die to keep the identity of their boss a secret. These men were not saying a word. They weren't professionals, they were just too sloppy. They knew where I lived, this was not a random attempt. Someone out there knows me, but they have no idea what I am. If that was the case, they would've came with more firepower. You need to remain close to me, so I can protect you."

She then cut me off, "look, there's something I must tell you." I cut her off back, "we can't talk about this or anything yet, we must plan and remain alert."

She didn't say a word, not another word, she just remained quiet. "As a matter of fact, I am going to get rid of these bodies, and you are going to stay here tonight with me." I told her. She then stared at me, and said, "well, I must make a phone call then, let my child know I am not coming home."

She went outside and made a call, I thought nothing of it, but it felt weird, it felt completely off. I made arrangements to get rid of these bodies that were in my damn place, and I kept feeling something was off, so I told her when she came back in...

"We aren't staying here tonight. Listen to me carefully, I will be having my place cleaned, who knows who these men are, and who would be coming to look for them, or to check to make sure the job was done? Plus, I don't need cops heat or attention on me. Therefore, we will not be spending the night here tonight, we will be in a hotel for the night or two nights if need be."

She grabbed her phone, then I grabbed it from her, "no, you won't need this for the night either, turn it off," she looked at me with a confused look. "You want to control my phone as well? Oh, hell no!" She protested. I gave it back to her. "Turn it off, don't text or call on it, electromagnetic waves can be traced, and if you have your location on, you have no idea who followed you here, do you?"

She agreed with me, "you are right, okay, I will leave it off." She and I then got ourselves ready to be out for the night. We arrived at the hotel, "make yourself comfortable, go shower, do what you must and then come to bed." I told her this. She did as I instructed her to do. She came out of the shower, and she was completely naked, she held between her thighs a moment of ecstasy and sin. She squeezed her legs and thighs together to hold it in. A memory of last night causing tension. Creating this desire to her over and over and over and over once again. Pleasure dripping from within her. Secrets revealed by her fucking devilish grin. She knows what she is doing, she's still a witch as well.

"You know what you are doing, you are evil, and after all you are still a witch, Cleopatra." I said to her. She grinned at me, "you keep draining me of my powers every time we make love, every time we fuck, every time you take me and control me over and over once again."

She revealed to me her gift of flesh sculpted to capture my devilish ways. Momentarily, I will satisfy her with my wickedness, but right now, I wanted to watch her. I inspired her to be free, to be completely free. She loved me unconditionally, she didn't need to tell me this, I knew, and I'm sure she did as well. I gave her freedom.

My gaze followed the curves of her legs to the point of no return. Looking into the center of her rainbow. Pink images were bliss into the deepest parts of my desires. The strength of my lust blending into the softness of her surrender. Love in its physical form. I could not read her when we first started to interact, but now, so much has changed, she has opened up to me fully and let go behind her own imagination. I read her easier now, I stimulated her mind, and her body spoke to me. I wrote her beautifully of many words with my big tongue, refilling my pen with the leaks between her thighs. I read her orgasms, and she strokes my words for more and more. I hear the echoes of her moans, she laid flat on her back, and my tongue kissed those pussy lips, those pretty pussy lips. Every time she shut her eyes, I can feel her seeking the touch. My touch, and seducing her every thought.

She feeds my addiction. My addiction, for her screams, my addiction for her flesh, my addiction for her mind, for her soul, for her powers, for her energy, for her words, for her thoughts, for her love, for her sex. She carried the light of the stars in the curves of her hips. Moving forward through the darkness of midnight. Seducing the moon and daring me to fucking follow. She called for the destruction of beauty. Craving a savage in me so passionate to disrupt the order of things. She could wear silk and lace, but those would only be sacrificed and torn apart in a quest to quench the thirst of her flesh. Every part of her body was calling for me, mercilessly.

I approached as a predator, I saw her as prey. I risk the danger of the flames, for the passion of the heat. She is so addictive. I spoke to her whispering in her ear so softly but forceful...

"Submit to this ravenous love, always. Lose yourself in my sin, in my passion, in my devilish tendencies. Fall victim to the grip of my massive hands upon your flesh, and feel the fire burning beneath the surface of your skin. Let me kiss you, lick you, bite you, into submission. Dance with our desires in this storm, as the warm rain cascades down the walls of your shallow moans, and beg for me to enter you. Fucking beg!!" I growled, and she begged me, "please, please, Discipline." She submits to me now and she allows me inside her. She serves me, at will.

I took my massive chocolate dick out of her and placed it inside her mouth, between her begging lips. Her lips wrapped around me and the warmth of her mouth took hold of my immaculate strength. Perfectly stroking me to a beautiful end. With her lips she enhanced my darkest desires, with her body it cultivated my greatest power. With her pussy, I create her greatest release, but her mind is always the key.

I took myself out of her mouth, and back into her soaking Niagara Falls pussy, wrapping my girth snug. My lips go to reach her lips, and she playfully turns her head away from me, I slap her face, she smiles, I then turn her over, "you denied my dangerously addictive kiss, however my hand on the small of your back you could not," I said.

The force between us is anticipation, and I aim to penetrate it completely. Pushing us both into a realm of passion which neither of us has control of. I tell her all these things, while I am pounding her pussy into a dripping mess. Talk about talking dirty during sex, I take that shit to another level. A gentle push, and down she goes, on the bed with her legs spread wide, she is on her knees. Ass cheeks spread, her gaping wet pussy, and an open invitation for me to fit in, daring me to slide inside. The smirk she had is gone now, replaced with hunger in her eyes and I intend on feeding her. The first thrust set the fucking tone, I could hear her gasp for air, and then moan so loudly. She unleashed the beast within me, and now upon her. I assault her body. I take control of her. Thrusting so deep and rough.

"I have you when you submit to me, I will always have you when you submit to me. There is no height high enough, no fall fast enough, no depth deep enough to keep my powerful hands from getting to you. Bloom peacefully in my hands, safely in my grasp. Live life in my hands, and die in my hands. Trust that these hands will bring you back to life, back to me. Always. Because, you are mine, and there is no distance far enough. And no ocean wide enough, to keep this powerful hand from getting to you. The kind of immortal that makes you bleed, bruise, blush, I am the power you crave, need and want. These are the soft yet rough reminders why you are here; to be controlled, to feel helpless, for strength, for peace, for love, for hate, for phenomenal sex, for fucking, for making love, for violence, for stress, for a stress reliever, for calmness, to cum, to choke, all the sweet sounds, and sweet thoughts. Culminating in this moment where you are lost in me. Lost to the chaos I provide. Now it's your turn, to be used so devilishly. To be teased so deviously. By whom? Me! Leave your inhibitions outside and be lost in here. Feel this type of love where you can't breathe, the type that gives it all to me and feels. Be lost, perfectly, hopelessly, deliciously lost. Now tell me how you feel, my love?"

She's begging to cum, "can I cum please???" I smirk, "yessss, give it all to me," she released and gushed all over. "How do you feel, my love? I asked once again, grasping her as I wanted an answer. "Used, slutted, filthy, appreciative, free?" I asked her. I then stared into her eyes, and I saw the answer. She then replied to me, "yes."

I see what she screams for; to be punished, to make her feel something, to make her forget something, to make her regret nothing, to take and to do so without asking her. To hurt her.

The following day had arrived, and I told her to get dressed. I had to be at one of the fitness clubs later that afternoon. There was a major event. No matter how strong she is and no matter her Dominant character, she moved here when I commanded. And she listened when I spoke, my voice vibrated so loudly and put fear in her body. She did it as I instructed, I got ready as well to get on with my day.

I showed up for the big event at one of the fitness clubs I owned. It was amazing, then I had to show up at one of the night clubs later that evening. The night came in, and it was phenomenal. Everyone looked great, we had politicians from sports athletes to reality television superstars and movie celebrities here. Cleopatra showed up, I saw her from the skybox. I went over to her...

"What are you doing here?" I asked her. She said, "do I need to ask your permission to come here? I said, "well, I mean yes you do." She let out a loud laugh, "ha ha. I mean, we met here at the club. I didn't think I needed to ask for your permission to come here." I then said to her, "I want to make arrangements when I know you're coming. I don't want you waiting on line, I want you to cut the line, I want the VIPs to know you. I want the bouncers to know you. Therefore, you have no issues. Come with me to the skybox, we can see the dance floor and the entire night club from up there." I instructed her. She said, "there is something I need to tell you." I cut her off, "listen, tonight is the big night, what you need to tell me could just wait. You can tell me another time, there's so much to do tonight."

She was frustrated, so she stormed out of the club. Tonight, was lit, it was spectacular. One of our biggest events of the club. Shit feels phenomenal. The atmosphere was phenomenal as well. I was observing everything, I was observing the environment, the atmosphere, the energy to the vibes. So, I left a bit early, Cleopatra came right back to me. She said...

"I'm sorry I stormed out, can we take a stroll? Can we take a stroll in the park?" I said, "sure, why not? And as we started taking a stroll in the park, I felt something completely wrong. The air changed, it was a slight breeze. And my instincts didn't fail me.

Appearing before us was the woman. She stood in front of us, Precious ex-boyfriend's sister. Damn, how many times do I have to fucking tell this bitch? I told her the next time we meet, it would not be good.

"I told you we would meet again, Mr. Discipline!" She said to me, as she shouted out. I held Cleopatra's hand tighter in my grasp. She then continued…

"This time you don't make it out of here alive." She said to me. Before she ran the chamber, and the bullet came out the barrel, I could smell something. I smelled garlic for some reason, it was weird. I was thinking fast, I was looking around to see if there was anything I could utilize.

Thought to myself 'how did she find us here? Why do I smell garlic?' Soon as the bullet was going to shoot out of the pistol she had, Cleopatra jumped right in front of the bullet. 'What the fuck is she doing?' I then thought to myself. She was hit with the bullet; the woman then ran away. I held Cleo in my arms. I placed her body gently on the ground, I then ran after the shooter.

Everything was in slow motion, but I was moving normal, it was as if it looked like I was slowing time for a little bit. She was slow in motion and running, and I grabbed her purse and I saw her ID. And I scanned her ID with my eyes. I wanted a name with the face. An address. Something I can follow up on and I got what I wanted. I kept mental documentations of everything that was on her damn ID.

Once I left from the shooter's side, everything went back to normal. She was faster. It was weird, it's like I slowed down time. That was probably the second time I ever did that. I was still learning my new powers after all these years, because, I really had no one to teach me. I had to pretty much learn as I went along. And I felt when I needed it most, it came to me. Or when I was angry or something. I had no idea how I did this. I guess desperation and adrenaline will make you do things, we have never done. If I didn't need to check on Cleo, I would have killed this woman shooter.

I went back to where Cleo was, but the bullet was made out of garlic. This woman had to have known what I was or what I am. And what this was. Therefore, I then began to think to myself, 'why was the bullet made out of garlic?' Knowing damn well, that can do some harm to me. A regular bullet wouldn't hurt me. It would itch, it would sting, but it would not kill me. It would tickle, but it wouldn't hurt me. But, a garlic bullet? That would do plenty of damage. At least I think it would. Shit, I didn't want to experiment. Someone was meticulous with this attack. Perhaps they didn't act alone. There had to be more to this, but I'll figure this out later.

I took the bullet out of Cleo with my telekinesis ability, I tossed it into a tree with my mind control. The bullet came out of her, and flew through the tree. I then held her in my arms. 'What the fuck was she doing? Jumping in that fucking bullet like that to save my life once again? Fuck, I cannot allow her to die.' I thought to myself.

I started looking around. I started thinking, I had to think quickly, she was losing too much blood. She was dying. She doesn't want this, to be what I am, but at this point, it's about her life. I panicked, its either her life, or she doesn't get what she wants, and I obey her wishes and she dies. I'm going to grant her immortality. There is no other choice for this.

I then sank my teeth into her. I was changing her life forever. She would say good bye to this normal world, she would come into my world. What I did was not enough, in order for her transformation to be complete, she needed real blood. She was still dying. 'What about mine? My blood is powerful.' I thought to myself, 'just as I could take life, I could give life? Right?'

My claws came out, and I slashed my wrist. I kept pumping my fist, so more blood could come out of my wrist. I grasped her by her hair and anchored her head towards my wrist. She fed. She fed some more. She was coming into consciousness. A man that gives his blood to or for a woman, is a man that 'Loves Her To Death.' Irony is, when we met, we started out hating each other. In all of my years of life on earth, I haven't met a woman that hated me for too long. She's a witch, with extraordinary powers, that does extraordinary things. I don't know why she just didn't alter the bullet, so it would've just missed her? Something else is going on here, and I'm going to get to the fucking bottom of this shit.

Chapter 17- A Twist Of Fates

Cleopatra came into consciousness, and I guided her up to her feet. "You saved my life," I said to her thankfully. "There was garlic in that bullet though, and I didn't even know it until it was inside you, and I smelled it. But I smelled garlic, and I just didn't know where it was coming from. A regular bullet would not hurt me, and you knew this, that is why I thought it was odd that you jumped in front of the bullet to help me."

She was in and out of it, still a little weak. But, my blood sustained her. "What really happened?" She asked me. I stared at her, "I just fucking told you. This woman, whom was a shooter, whom is random. She shot at the both of us, but you caught the bullet. The bullet was made from garlic, the woman must know now who I am, and what I am."

I knew who the woman was, but Cleopatra didn't need to know of this danger from the past. This Precious' ex boyfriend's sister, coming to the club and now she was here. It was too much to explain. And too much for her to take right now. She would know, just not right now.

"Who is she?" Cleo asked me... I then said to her, "I don't know. I mean, I know her, but I don't really know her, but now I know more of her and more." Cleo, touched my shoulder, as she was feeling a little faint. "Can't we just go somewhere else, and discuss this, I have a lot of things to tell you."

I took her to my place, and as we get there, my place is trashed. There were things thrown all over the place. Tables flipped over. Broken glass. So, it didn't look like a robbery, because whomever did it did not take shit.

"What the fuck is this?!" I then shouted out, as I was fucking furious. I called my men, and they respectfully said, they had nothing to do with it, nor did they know what was going on. And I didn't feel like having security watch my home, and have shit looking suspicious for me. However, I was going to add in cameras from now on. We were not going to stay there tonight. So, I took her back to the hotel, I was not about to leave her here, and I stay at my place, where it was trashed like that. Someone or people were in my place and they were looking for something or looking for someone, and that someone must have been me.

As we get to the hotel, she then begins to speak, "look, there is so much I need to tell you, and I have been trying to tell you this shit for the longest time. Every time I tried, you brushed me off with some type of business you had to speak of, or a major event and just could not attend to my attention. But tonight, I will not allow you to interrupt me. And what I was trying to tell you."

She exhaled out a deep breath, "tonight is all my fault, I was shot, or we were shot at, because of me!" I gazed at her firmly, "keep, fucking talking, and do not leave shit out! I am going to calm my temper down, and allow you to explain first, before I rip your tongue out, and heart out and kill you. Perhaps, or perhaps not. Let's hear it all!"

Tears were coming out of her eyes, but her tears had no effect on me. She then continued to tell me the next thing she was trying to explain...

"So, listen, it was Precious ex boyfriend's sister that shot at us." I was even more angry, "what! So, you knew this?" I then continued to tell her, "yes, I know it was her before you told me here." I then shut my eyes, and it brought me back in time of the shooting, when I was chasing her down, and I scanned her ID with my eyes, keeping mental documentation in my head.

"Is that woman, whom is Precious ex boyfriend's name Jessica Louis?" I asked her. Cleo nodded her head at me, "yes, that is her name."

The table that was in the hotel, I smashed it out of anger, and I frightened her.

"Look, I am so sorry, but there is much more." Cleo continued. "The night at the club when I was acting like I didn't see you, then I came to the bar where you were, that was a ploy. I already knew who you were, I had the info on you prior to my arrival there. I was briefed on you, so I knew how to approach you. I was forced to do all this, against my will. I was supposed to set you up, and all the information you were giving me, I was feeding to her, that is why she knows you are a vampire, and your weaknesses."

I opened my eyes wide, "are you fucking kidding me right now! She came to my club, and pulled a gun on me. That gun could have had garlic in there, and I was playing around with that woman. But, then again, I didn't smell it, if it had garlic in the bullet, as I smelled it tonight." I shook my head in anger.

She then continued, "honestly, I don't know of any of that. As far as how she knew what things to utilize against you, she learned from me. From me, as you told me the things you told me. I was supposed to take you out, kill you, but I couldn't do it, I started falling in love with you. It would have been so fucking easy, if I still hated you. I then stopped reporting to her with information about you, your whereabouts and your steps. I could not do it anymore, I put everything on the line to betray her for you. I was missing in action from Jessica for days, and she showed up at the club looking for me, and looking to see what was going on. But, I wasn't there."

I shut my eyes, and then said, "yeah, she was there, I guess that's when she showed at my night club with the pistol she pulled on me, as we went into my office." I said, "yup and that night she showed up and we went to my office, and she pulled a gun on me, and she then introduced herself vaguely. I managed to outsmart her and get her to put the gun away, and suddenly, she mentioned to me, that we would eventually see each other again, prior to her leaving and walking out my club, so it makes sense. The set up you indicate, because no one is that certain they were going to find me, or that certain they will meet someone again in general. How did she know if I would be at the club again? I'm an owner, who knows if that's my only club? Who knew if I even show up at my clubs? Nor would they be coming to the club like this constantly. But it all makes sense, because, you were feeding her information. I saw her ID, she lives in Queens, and most of my clubs and my time is in Manhattan. So, she knew that perhaps you would get her that chance."

She put her head down in disgust with herself. "Yes, she found me, she knows how powerful I am, but the one thing that weakens me besides you Discipline, is my son, and she knew how to get to him at will, so I had to make a decision." I gazed at her firmly, "you always have a choice and you made one." She then continued…

"She came to me yesterday and gave me an ultimatum. And I came to you and asked you if we can go for a stroll in the park. That's where she wanted you to be, but alone. But, I couldn't let that happen. I knew she was going to kill you, she feels you killed her brother and she wanted revenge. If I would have told you to go there alone, and meet me there, and not wait for you at your club and not go there together, we would not be standing here right now speaking."

I grabbed her by her throat, "is that suppose to make shit right? So, you're like, 'oh hey, I set you up to get murdered but, I made sure I interfered, so you would not be killed.' Get the fuck out of here, bitch!"

She was gasping for air, "I know what I did was wrong, and you have every right to kill me, or cast me out of your life totally." My grip was tighter, and I could see it in her eyes, but after a few more seconds, I let go. And I gave her my back. She held her hands on her throat, and she was coughing nonstop. I then spoke softly, but forceful…

"I will not kill you, listen, you did tell me the truth after all. I owe you my life twice." She stopped coughing, and said, "I know I owe you for my life as well, even though I would not want this or to become this vampire, in order to live. You saved me, and no matter how you feel about me right now, I will always be grateful to you."

I gazed into her eyes, and my voice raised, "I had no choice, and neither did you, I was not going to let you fucking just die! Therefore, I made a choice. We all have a choice to make, I made the best one to put you in a position to still be here and for your son. Well, all is good now, and I have a plan. Since you got us into this mess, you are going to get us out of it. I owe you for my life, I paid that. Now, you owe me, and this is how you will repay me. This is how you will gain my trust back. I will find a way into her. I will find a way to get to her, and you are going to be the one to take her out. You are going to be the one to kill her. Plus, you need to feed on human flesh, energy and blood. This will make your transition complete. Forming you into a true vampire. Every feast is making you stronger, and you have some of my blood in you, but your transformation is not complete.

I am going to train you to be the most unstoppable, unheralded, cold blooded killing machine. You will not be stronger than I, but you will be stronger than you ever were beyond your wildest dreams. The feel of hunger and the power you are granted by the silver full moon. The senses enhanced, the fragrance of human body, the sight, the voice. The calm and exhilaration of the fucking night life. When danger is near, raising some deep inner string to uneasy vibration. You would now enter the land of tall grass, you will be able to be underestimated, where danger concealed itself in innocence." She was trying to get a word in, "but…."

I raised my own hand in a gesture of dismissal, I gave her a dismissive wave. And yet the gesture inspired silence towards her. Then I said to her, as I gazed into her brown eyes, "so here is the fucking plan……………."

Chapter 18- Hunt Or Be Hunted

I knew she has never killed or hunted before, but she was going to learn today. She was a bomb incarnate, ready to explode at any given time. But, she would not need to feed again for another day or two.

"I don't know about this! I don't know if I can feed. I don't know if I can hunt!" She said, totally unsure of herself. I grasped her by her hair, and anchored her head toward me, "I want you to listen to me, and listen to me good, which is why I pulled you close to me, so you can listen to me a little better. You will either hunt, or you will be fucking hunted. Our bite is venomous, turning every living thing from the inside out to stone, save our eyes and brain."

I'm really not sure what keeps us alive. It wasn't a heart, oxygen or the sun. Maybe it was pure ambition and without it, we'd grow faint then cease to exist. Her eyes were brown, though per her normal vampiric trait, could go blood red in anger or thirst and feast. I then said to her, "now, moving forward, you will require blood to survive, there is no way around this shit, this is life. This is the life of an immortal. This is how we live now. Like I was saying, here is the fucking plan. I am going to find a way to her, and once I do, I will report back to you. I will get you into her home, she is going to invite us in, and once that happens, you, and only you will take her out. I don't want you to hit her, I don't want you to snap her fucking neck, I don't want you using any object to rid her of her existence from this planet. I fucking want you to bite her, I want you to sink your fucking fangs into her neck and I want you to suck the blood and drain the energy out of her, until she can no longer stand! Until her body goes slack. Until her eyes roll back. Until she is motionless. Lifeless in your fucking hands! Do you fucking understand me? Now, I want you to nod your head and say, 'yes Sir,' if you are in compliant to my damn instructions."

She nodded her head, and she then said to me, "yes Sir. I will follow your instructions just as you wish." She felt helpless, and she knew it was all her fault. She had known this wasn't the best decision, being with me. But, she had just wanted so much to be with me, any way she could. That was the thing, she always wanted too much, she always wanted things that were just no good for her. She was never meant to be 'normal.' She dances upon beams of light from rainbow colored unicorns in a world of standard and ordinary. The rules of society are not her rules. And those rules of society she doesn't recognize them. In order to live in this world, one must live without rules. In order to live without rules for yourself, one must be willing to look at the world differently. Not everything that appears, is really meant to be interpreted. Not everything you see or hear, is meant to be truth. There is no other like her, and she stands to be judged by a world that doesn't really fucking understand her. She exists against her wishes. And she does it, and she will do it with a damn smile. She just needs a little getting used to.

Madness is like gravity. It just requires a little push. A little push, and guidance from someone, and that someone is me! She glows, and her beauty is undeniable. She is

everything that ordinary is not, she is amazing. I continued
to brainstorm with her….

"I cannot just be fucking casual, and just walk up to the
woman. I need to know where she is, and how we can set it
up, so she doesn't feel we are coming after her at all. She
can't know it's me, and she can't know you're still alive. If
she sees me right away, she is going to run. And I will
fucking tell you right now, she is not getting away with
this shit. We need to fucking know where she is going to
be!"

I slammed my palms on a desk, really hard. Cleopatra
out of nowhere had a premonition, she gasped and exhaled
for air, "I know where she will be tomorrow!" Cleopatra
then shouted out to me. I stared at her with my darkest
stare. I was intrigued, and I was staring at her, like I
wanted an immediate response. Why? Well, because I
fucking did. And I then began to say...

"This is part of your new power I see, this will come
into use in the future, perfect, good girl. Well? So, where
will she be tomorrow? You didn't mention anything, you
just like left a cliff hanger or something."

She shut her eyes, and concentrated once again, and then
she had an accurate answer for me… "she will be at this
café tomorrow, and she will be meeting a friend, this
friend is a female, she has known this female for years."
She took a pen and paper, and she began to write down the
address. "Good girl," I said. "Now, what I want you to do
is stay put, I want you to stay here, yes, you can check on
your family, but stay out of sight. I want her to think you

are dead, you must remember that. I want to hit her when she least expects it. Rest and get your full strength, and we will reload and energize tomorrow."

Every gesture, every consideration, every thought and every action dripping with lust, love and devotion for me, a man she has chosen to follow. My word, her gospel. My look, smoldering. My ownership, worshipped. My efforts, appreciated. My Dominance, divine. Her only desire now, to thank with her devotion, her dedication, her hard work to inspire with her loyalty. Her loyalty to be great for me.

The following day arrived, and I had one thing on my mind, 'pay back.' I took the note of the address that Cleo wrote down, where Jessica was meeting her best friend for brunch. I showed up at the café address that Cleo wrote down on the piece of paper, but I could only hear so much, I figured, man if I could be a fly on the wall. Suddenly, a damn bee was bothering me, it would not leave me alone. It kept attempting to come by my ear. I swatted at it and missed, and I thought to myself, 'why is this stupid bee bothering me once again? Can't it see I'm fucking busy?' Then I got an idea, I grabbed the bee, and I scanned it with my eyes, after I scanned it adequately, I crushed the bee with my massive hands. Now I shape shifted into the insect, and I waited until someone opened the door of the café, and I then entered through the door cracks.

Damn, that door swung back so quickly, I was lucky to get in there when I could. I could shape shift into anyone, anything or any animal. Just needed some mastery, focus and concentration and I could be anything I wanted to be.

Going into the café as the bee, I kept myself discreet, and out of sight, so I wouldn't scare anyone, or be swatted by anyone. Being something so tiny, did put me at a bit of a risk of being severely hurt. But, it was the risk I was willing to take, to obtain what I wanted to obtain. I was on the side of the table curtain. Listening to everything I could use. I wanted answers. I wanted information, I wanted pay back. Now I had so much access to them. The best friend was asking Jessica, how everything was with her....

"So, girl, how are things? What time do you want me to come over tonight, again?" And then Jessica confirmed, "I want you there like around 8pm girl, we haven't been able to catch up in a little while, and it would be so good to catch up with you. So much craziness has been going on here, so much craziness has been going on in general," the best friend asked, "really? Tell me, tell me? Ooooh, please? Can you just tell me?"

Her friend just loved gossip. Whatever was going on, Jessica's friend knew about it, or she found a way to know about it. She was persistent, as she kept on asking Jessica...

"What has been going on girl?" Jessica shook her head, "no, I can't tell you here, its so much to tell girl, tonight we can catch up, and I'll tell you the entire story." I flew out of the café, and I waited outside, because I wanted to follow the best friend and get more information. They parted ways, Jessica went south, and her friend went north. I followed her friend, and I made sure I remained high in the air. I wanted to make sure I was out of sight of Jessica. I had plans to turn back into myself and work my magic on her friend. But, I didn't want to take the risk of being seen. But, wait, what if she knows all about me? What if she has seen me in the club? No worries, I could use that as my cover up.

She went into a Victoria Secret store. I went into the bushes as the bee, and then I came out, as 'Discipline.' I checked to see, and no one saw me walk right out of the bushes. I fixed my blazer suit, and I adjusted my tie a little bit more. I went into the Victoria Secret store, and I walked by her friend, and all of a sudden, I made believe I wasn't looking where I was going, and we bumped into each other. After I bumped into her, I apologized…

"I'm sorry miss, it's my fault, I wasn't looking. Clumsy me." She accepted my apology, "no, it's okay, don't worry about it." I gazed into her eyes, and I had her stuck. It's like I had her strung already with just one look, one firm gaze. My energy began to Dominate hers. I then just kept talking, as her gaze met my gaze…

"This store is exhilarating, don't you think?" I didn't wait for her to reply, I just kept talking, and talking, and talked some more…

"Female wear is so special; the female body is so sacred. Nothing is more real, and precious than the human body. It's like art. The things that women can do, the changes they go through. They can hold a child inside them for months, and their body changes. You can witness a woman in lingerie. In a gown. In a business suit. In all leather. In heels. I'm scrubs. In a robe. In a dress. Us men cannot do that." She then began to smile, and then a snicker laugh followed, "ha-ha, yes, you are on point with that one, you men would not look good in dresses and heels." I then began to smirk. I agreed, "yes, that would not be a pretty sight there. You women have us beat with that. You queens can move in ways on the chess board, us kings just cannot." She nodded her head, with a smile upon her face. I then continued to tell her…

"If there's a species on earth whom can shape shift, it would be women. They are so transformative. Not to mention attitude, and feelings. They can alter their mood," she then cut me off, "yes, yes, you're absolutely right. Tell me about it." My gaze was firm, and she didn't blink, nor did she look away from me. She put out her hand, "Hello, I'm Melissa, lovely to meet you sir." I accepted her friendly handshake, "nice to meet you as well, the pleasure is all mine."

Never volunteer your name to a woman, if she's interested, if she displays a little interest even, she will ask for your name. "So, what is your name?" She asked, yup, she was interested. I thought to give her a fake name, but I could give her 'Discipline.' But, what if Jessica briefed her on me, she could run away or dismiss herself right away. And I could not afford this, I needed this woman. She was the key to Jessica. And you know I was going to utilize her and this situation as much as I could. I was milking this shit, no expiration. Clearly, she hasn't seen my pictures anywhere, so she doesn't know what I am. Who I am either. Better to just lie....

"Well, my name is Pierre." She was intrigued, "ooooh, very nice, that's French?" I then replied, "yes, it is French.

I am Haitian and Dominican. Je parle le francais, hablo poquito espanol tambien." She entertained me a little, "bueno, es una buena mezcla." She said, it is a good mix. "Je parle un peu Francais aussi bien." She said, she spoke a little French as well. "Wow, I am impressed," my eyes lit up, as I said to her. Then I asked her, "where are you from? What is your nationality?" I asked her as I was to await an immediate response. She then said to me. "My mother is Colombian and Italian; and my father was Canadian. I picked up a little bit of both. But, my parents are not alive anymore."

It's a shame I must kill this woman, we connected a little bit. Perhaps, I could get her to turn on her friend, put her under a spell, that way she does the work for me? No, fuck that, I'm not sure, she would, or the spell would follow through.

"Sorry to hear about your parents." I gave my condolences. She smiled at me, "thank you." I handed her a business card, it was a card of one of the clubs I had out there in Queens. It had the clubs information on it, not mine. Address, telephone, etc. "Look, I have a club out here in Queens, perhaps you want to check it out? It's called, 'Midnights.' And you should bring a friend or two, come check it out." I did that just, so she could open up her purse or bag, I knew she had her ID in there, and when she opened her purse to place my card in there, my eyes looked at the ID. I used my X-ray vision and scanned it, to keep adequate mental documentation. Bingo, I got the fucking address of her home, and I took her ID. I took that shit with such quickness, even if it fell out of her purse, she would have never been the wiser. I mean, come on, I will need an excuse to show up at her house. I could not just fucking show up there. Duh! She would think I was a creep, even though, I was able to show up at her house soon, like a creep. But I needed an excuse to be there, or she would wonder how I got her address. And when I bring her back her ID, acting as if I found it, she will be so relived that I found it, that she will invite me in, to show her gratitude. Can't small talk with this woman anymore, no more time to waste, therefore I cut it short…

"Well, Melissa it was a pleasure meeting and speaking with you," I said to her with an inviting smile on my face, showing teeth. Her eyes, displayed to me, how she loved my smile. She then shook my hand, before I walked away she said, "the pleasure was all mine, Pierre."

I walked away. I made myself discreet, but, I wanted to make sure she wasn't going to tell Jessica, she changed her mind about meeting her. Melissa arrived at her home, and I followed her there without being seen. Now, you know women talk, they can't help it. Even if she said she wasn't going to talk in the street, most likely, she would. Well, most women, not all. But, who cares if she talked, I thought, it's a good thing, and after all, I didn't give my real name. Because, as soon as she got home, she called Jessica, but Jessica didn't answer. So, it went to voicemail, and she left her a voice message...

"Hey, girl, I know it's Wednesday, but this weekend, let's go out to this new club out here in Queens. I googled it and it looks dope, it's called, 'Midnights.' I met the owner, you wouldn't believe it, he was in the Victoria Secret store. Anyways, hit me back girl, when you get this.

Muah!" And she blew a kiss over the phone. How do you blow a kiss over the phone? How is the person on the other end going to receive it? Anyways, fuck it, fuck that thought, I had to stay focused...

I waited to hear what was going on in the home, and Melissa went to take a shower. Soon as she was heading out of the shower, her phone rang. It was Jessica on the phone, Melissa then fucking power walked to her phone to answer it. She was so excited about the things that transpired today, she had to tell someone. Who better than one of her best friends? "Hey, Girl, what's going on? Yeah, so let's go to the club this weekend, not just any club. This club called, 'Midnights,' did you listen to my voicemail?" Jessica on the other side of the phone now said to Melissa, "yes, I did." Melissa then continued, why both her and Jessica, and possibly some more friends should go to the club.

"So, listen, I met the owner there, at the Victoria Secret store. You know what that means? Those free drinks, VIP, etc. bitch! Hahah."

I shook my head as I smirked, man this bitch no doubt needed to die, I thought to myself. She acted like the type of woman whom would use her looks to get whatever she wanted from a man. I mean nowadays, men are pussy whipped, and well, the women do little to none to get and keep their attention. She then continued on...

"He was so handsome, I thought he was a little fruity coming into Victoria Secret, but, he had some swag. He was smooth with his words as well, he dressed so nicely, and he smelled so good, and his eyes were like hypnotic. It looked like they were changing a different color in the sunlight, every time I stared into his eyes. Nah, I'm buggin' girl. But, he probably was there looking for lingerie or something for his girlfriend, wife or mistress. What type of handsome man comes into a Victoria Secret store, to look around? The nice-looking ones, and the ones that got their shit together are always taken. Or they have a few women. And if they're married, they're usually ugly, or fat."

Jessica was laughing on the other side of the phone, as she said to Melissa, "girl, you are assuming, you know none of this, obviously, the way you speak of him now, you sound interested in him, why didn't you just ask him straight up? Shit!" Melissa, then said, "I know I'm assuming, I'm sorry, you're right. But, I was not about to ask him, he would think I was some type of creep or stalker type. Or he would think I was into him. But these men out here in New York, I don't know what to tell you. I'm so sick of all of them. I don't know if I'm coming later, I'm a little exhausted."

Once I heard that from outside, I shut my eyes, and I focused on her heavily, and whispered, "you will be going tonight, you are making coffee as we speak, and you got a second wind. You'll be there at 8pm sharp." She repeated, "you know what girl? I'm making coffee now as we speak, we haven't seen each other in weeks, I got a second wind. I'll see you later, 8pm sharp." Jessica then said on her side of the phone… "Good, good. See you then, love ya! Muah!" And Melissa reciprocated, with a "muah!" I don't get this kiss over the phone thing again, someone would need to explain this to me, maybe I will ask Cleopatra when I see her. Melissa then hung up the phone, and she started to make coffee. I waited until she was dressed, and then I knocked on her door. *Knock *knock *knock, I don't know, I had this weird habit where I just loved to knock on someone's door like three times. Shit, perhaps they didn't hear that shit the first time, or the second time. She then answered the door to me...

"Ooh, you startled me!" I put my hand to my chest, like I was in shock myself..."Well, damn, I hope I am not that ugly." She laughed, "Pierre from the Victoria Secret store, correct?" I pointed my index finger at her, "that is correct, you have a good memory. A memory like an elephant. Anyways, you're probably wondering what and how I got here? Anywho, also wondering, what I am doing here?" She gasped, "oh yes, how do you know where I live? What the hell!" I put both my hands up, as my palms were then facing her, indicating I was no threat. "I then reached for my pocket, and looked at her ID, "Melissa, right? Here is your ID, it has your address here. You must be careful, any psycho could have came here, and just stalked you." She then said, jokingly, "maybe you're a stalker, huh?" I'm just joking. We both laughed. She probably wasn't joking, if she was into me as I suspected, she probably wished I was her stalker. She looked a little crazy. She looked like she would be into a little danger. It was exhilarating to have this thought. I had to remain focused, back to fucking business!!

"Well, you dropped it as you were putting my card inside of your purse." If she was paying attention and very meticulous, she would have known and remembered, I left before her. If she dropped something, why wouldn't I bring it to her attention then? But she was not that attentive. She was focused on the card and the club. Her eyes lit up, "yes, your card, the club, I can't wait to go, I was telling my best friend about it. She's coming along with me, like this weekend." I smiled and then said, "perfect, and I will have VIP and drinks set up for you ladies." She was so grateful, "thank you for my ID back, Pierre." As I was thinking she was about to shut the door, I asked her… "are you making coffee or something?" She looked back, "yes, would you like some?" I put my hand out, "well, I wouldn't want to impose." She shook her head, "no, you are not. I made plenty, and it's the least I can do for your thoughtful gesture." My eye brows raised, "are you inviting me in Melissa?" I gazed into her eyes firmly. She nodded her head at me, "yes, come on in, make yourself feel at home."

I got her, hook, line and sinker, bitch! I then walked inside her place, and she shut the door behind me. "Go ahead, relax, you may sit on the sofa, I'll bring you a cup. Do you like it just black? Or would you like it light and sweet?" I said to her, "well, I love my coffee, like me, dark and sweet. I like it real strong."

She giggled like a little school girl. Then she said she would bring it right out. "I'll be right back with it for you." She said to me. She took longer than what a normal person would take to get another person some coffee. I looked at all her pictures, in her home. I did not sit down. I explored my surroundings. She had childhood photos, photos of her and her parents. She then walked out and said, "you like the pictures you see?" I turned around quickly, "yes of course, they are very cute."

She came out in this sexy gown, but she was hiding some lingerie underneath. Then she started to open the gown a little bit, so I could get a peek. What would possess this woman to do this? A man can't come into a woman's home, talk about the stars, the universe, perhaps some books, sports, global warming, business, have some coffee, kill her and get on his way? He has to murder that pussy as well? Shit! Well, I guess we won't just be drinking coffee tonight, as I see she may have other plans at hand. Maybe she's attempting to seduce me, because of who I am, and the clubs I own. I mean, she will, but maybe she won't. If it's not for the money, it could be for the fame. If not for the fame, she would for the power.

If we did it, would she remember me tomorrow? Who was I kidding? Of course she would remember me tomorrow, if I slang that big dick of mine, on, in and around her. Put it on her like no other. Thug style, pulling her hair, slapping her ass cheeks, and fucking her all wild. She would never forget this big dick, this sharp mind, and this tornado tongue. She might as well, call me 'King Kong,' when I was done. Not even he had anything on me. Forget me? Let me slide up in her, within a few seconds of me being inside her, she would forget her own name. She was not ready for the animal she was about to encounter in 'Discipline.'

We sat down together on the sofa. We drank some coffee, "so, tell me about yourself." She was demanding. "What you see is what you get," I replied. "No, no, no, there's more to you than this exterior. You have this powerful aura." She insisted. I gaze into her eyes, "oh, you don't say? How powerful? What does my aura do to you?" I asked. "I am just drawn to you. It's so strong, it is like so electric. These eyes of yours, are some soulful pools of magnetism. It's like your energy, Dominates me alone. I felt it today in the store. I couldn't take my eyes off of you. I haven't felt that towards a man in such a long time. It's like you have this spell on me. Who are you, really?" I started laughing. And she continued. "You have this mysterious glow to you." I smirk, "do you have trouble, believing a man? You have trust issues, don't you? You're so sick and tired of these men out here in the city? Aren't you? You want authenticity? You want realness? You want something solid?"

She nodded her head. "Yes, yes and yes, it's like you could read my mind. Oh my god! Yes!" I told her, "no, not really, I heard you. I can hear your mind. I can hear your busy thoughts, and I quiet those thoughts at will, when you are in my presence."

She did not speak a word, she just stared at me patiently, waiting for me to finish speaking. "I am no better than these men, I am just a little bit more understanding of who and what I am, but I'm not this nice guy." She looked at me, "I don't need a nice guy." I then said to her, "what if I told you, I was a vampire, would you believe me? Would you scream, run, tell others about me?" She laughed at me, "yeah right, are you going to bite me, Mr. Vampire?" I nodded my head, "Well, yes, I am. Before, during and after."

She then stared at me again, so aroused, and then she laughed and gave me a love tap on my shoulder, laughing and putting her head down, "oh you are so funny, Pierre." I had a serious face on, then I said to her, "I am not joking, and my name is not Pierre, it's actually, 'Discipline.' She then laughed again, "you are mistaken, Pierre, you are funny. Then she put her hand on over her mouth, then spoke, "oh, im sorry, I mean, 'Discipline,' Okay, I'll play along, take me, take me. Do what you wish to me."

I stared at her lips, and I grabbed her chin, with a stone grip and I anchored her chin over towards me, and I pressed my lips against hers. We kissed roughly. We kissed passionately. I bite her lower lip. And then, I picked her up, and I took her to her bedroom, I then tossed her on the bed.

"Oh, my goodness, we barely know each other," she said. That's funny she says that, but she was willing to be half naked in front of me? But we barely know each other, right? I then said, "shhhh, but we are wilding out like we are lovers."

I grabbed her ankles with my massive hands, and I pulled her towards me. I ripped her lingerie off and placed kisses meticulously on each curve on her body. "I will show you what your curves were made for. Make those fucking sounds. Scream for it. Beg to cum until it floods out of you. Breathe and hold on. I am in complete control of you. Your job now is to just feel. Feel completely taken. Fucked. Handled. At my mercy. The pounding. The thrusting. My firm grip. Rougher than you've ever known it. Perhaps this has always been your fantasy, but, now I make it a reality. I grant you memories to now, last an eternity. Having the fucking experience play over and over in your mind. The extreme. The moment. The sounds. The moans. The feelings. The taboo. Embrace these urges that will constantly come back. Like an addict needing their next fix. Potent like chocolate. Potent like cocaine, it drives you insane."

I sucked on her erect nipples, and then I shoved my massive chocolate dick inside her drenched hole. Her pussy walls closed in around me, and her lips wrapped around my big dick. I turned her over, into the doggy style position. Her hips were tossed, back and forth. I turned her out. It's ironic, see ,I controlled her, but she gushed uncontrollably. She was cumming all over me and on the sheets.

I pulled her hair, and then I turned her over. She was moaning so loudly. Then she came again. It didn't take her long to cum for me, she just needed to be handled by the right Beast. Moaning so loudly, like she has not been fucked great in years. I could tell. Like she has not had some good dick in her bed in years. She came, again, and again for a third and fourth time, and then I finally released myself. I growled loudly in her ear. I came...

I was then fully dressed afterward, and she was naked, and laying under the covers. "So, you're not going to spend the night?" She asked, and I answered her immediately, "no, I have some business I must take care of tonight." I said. And she then asked me, "oh the club, right?" I nodded my head at her....

"Yes, something like that, it's going to be a killing tonight." I used those words to sound figuratively. But, it was literally. She cheered me on, "yeah, you're going to kill it." Oh yes bitch, I am going to kill it. She then said, "oh shit, that reminds me, I have to go meet my friend tonight." I smirk and then I said to her, "no, you're not going anywhere tonight." She laughed, "you're right, I could barely move, you fucked the shit out of me. The pain is so good, I'm begging for another round." I stared at her, "you might be looking for another round of this good dick, but I'm looking at the entirety of you like you're food, and I want another bite."

My eyes changed gold and my fangs grew, and I growled, "grrrrr." She yelled, "what the fuuuuuck!" I flew towards her swiftly and devoured her whole. I sank my fangs into her neck, and I took her life. I wrapped her body in the sheets, and I got rid of it.

I drove as I got into my vehicle, and I looked at myself into the mirror. I shape shifted into Melissa, I then played her voice to see if I had it down pact.

"Hey, Jessica, girl, I am so sorry I am late, I hit heavy traffic." I was playing into character. I arrived back to the hotel, and I met with Cleopatra, I commanded her, "hey, get dressed, everything is set and ready to go. We will be taking the car, but I will stop it like a couple blocks or a block away. Then I will teleport us there. So, we will be teleporting over there, I am going to be invited into the house, as she will see me as her best friend, this Melissa woman."

Cleo asked, "hold on, Melissa character? What do you mean? Wait, hold on, how will she trust you enough to let you in?" I then slowly shape shifted into Melissa. "Meet Melissa, Jessica's best friend." Cleo smiled, "very nice, that is amazing, do I have these powers? Can I do the same shit?" I got serious, "fucking pay attention, stay focused!"

I changed back into myself. Then instructed her about the plan. "You will then wait outside on my direct call, I will get her to leave the room, I will get her to go make something for the both of us. Something for her and I to eat or drink so we can, 'catch up,' like the two of them say to each other." I put up my index and middle finger from each hand as if I was putting up a peace sign. And I pressed both my index and middle fingers, indicating quoting like I was when I said, 'catch up.'

"Wait there and I will open the door, and you will come in." Then I paused and asked her, because, just witnessing how the two women interacted made me curious, "Cleo, what is up with this phone kiss thing ya'll women do?" She looked at me confused.

"Wait, what? What are you talking about?" I then elaborated, "yes, ya'll go, 'muah!' on the phone, how does the other person receive the kiss, if they are on the other side of the phone?" She laughed, "yes, you are definitely not from this era. It's a thing certain women do, women love to display emotion in every way possible. We are emotional, remember? Anyways, I don't do that, but some women do."

I shook my head, "you women of this generation and this era, are very strange." She said, "hey! Not all of us, and perhaps it is not us, perhaps it is you. You are the one that does not fit in this generation, maybe you are the weird one?" I gazed at her without saying a word, "whatever, anyways, back to business. "So, when she goes to get us something to eat, and I let you in, wait in the living room closet quietly. I want to get as much information out of her as I can. No matter what she says, don't jump out until I fucking say. Understood?" She nodded her head towards me, "yes Sir." I then continued, "once I get her at a weak spot, you will attack." She nodded her head. "Okay, good, let's get going." I commanded.

We were on our way there, and I reiterated, "remember what I said, don't fucking hit her with shit, don't rip her head off, or snap her neck. I want you to feed. Her blood will be taken by you. Let's fucking go!!!"

Chapter 19- Eternal Love Is Powerful

So, then we were on our way to Jessica's house. I stop the car like a block away from the house. "OK Cleopatra, get out. I want you to be on standby, staying in the bushes or something, but make sure you're out of sight. Out of sight, but not out of mind. I want you to stay focused, block out your emotions if need be, I want this shit flawless. I'm going to knock on the door, she's going to invite me in. I will then alert you, when to come in. We won't waste anymore time, I'm going to reveal myself. And then I'm going to give you the OK, and you are going to take her out."

So, we walked up to the house, but Cleo was in the bushes. I ring on the doorbell as I was shape shifted into Melissa already. She answered the door, I got into character.

"Hey, girl, so sorry I'm late. I hit so much traffic, but I'm so glad I made it. We have so much catching up to do, I would love to tell you about this guy I met, at the Victoria Secret store. His name is Pierre, he owns a nightclub here in Queens." Jessica invited me in, "come on in girl, damn I have been waiting for you." I stepped into the house, she asked me if I wanted to sit down on the couch. "Do you want to sit down on the couch?" I said, using Melissa's voice, "yes, I'm flushed and starving." Jessica looked at me. "Are you hungry?" Then I said as Melissa's voice, "duh, bitch!" Jessica began to laugh. I made their interaction, so sweet, as I witnessed how they both communicated already, and I was able to make the adjustments, falling into character. Smooth as butter. Then Jessica said...

"I'll go make us both something to eat and we can talk about all that we've missed. We have so much catching up to do." As she went to go make us something, I got up and I opened the door and went outside. I called for Cleopatra, "Cleopatra, where are you?" I asked, as I let out a forceful whisper. She appeared clear as day to me, well it wasn't day, but it was night. I got her into the house. I told her to get into the closet.

"Hurry the fuck up, get in the fucking closet." So she got into the closet that was closest to the living room. Closest to the couch. Jessica came back with a couple of fine dishes, "we have so much to catch up on," she said to me, as she still saw me as her best friend, Melissa.

"So, what's this club you have been telling me about? And when are we going to check this place out? You were saying this weekend?" Jessica asked me. I shook my head yes. I then asked, "so, a lot has been going on with you, huh?" She answered my question. "Yeah, so you know how close I was with James, my brother. I haven't heard from him in years, and last place he was going to was to see Precious."

I continued to play along as her best friend Melissa, "oh yeah, Precious, I remember you telling me. That fucking bitch!" Jessica nodded her head, "yeah, that bitch. So, I found out that her man, this Discipline guy has a series of fitness and nightclubs around. Figured I asked this guy. I haven't seen Precious, and the things I was hearing from my brother was, this guy was with Precious. I don't know if he was just fucking her or they were exclusive or an item or what not. I go to one of his clubs, he's an owner of clubs, kinda like the same guy you were speaking to me about. This Pierre guy who owns a club? Right?"

I nodded my head, as Melissa. Jessica then continued, "well, I pulled a gun on this fucking cornball."

I was furious, hearing this, but I maintained my composure.

"He fucked up though, he may have not been paying attention, but I was. He fucked up when he said, "sorry for your loss," indicating he probably had something to do with the missing of my bro." I cut her off, "yeah, girl, you're right. You never mentioned he was dead. You just knew he was missing. There was nothing on the news either saying your bro was dead. He had something to do with it girl."

I was instigating and shit. Jessica then said, "yup, just like I thought. So, I had this witch bitch that was tailing him for me. But, I think he fucked her so good, the dick got her on his spell or something. I haven't heard from the bitch. That's when I went to the club and this slight altercation happened with me pulling the gun. But, I left there because, it would not have been a good idea, if I shot him there, and blood was all over me, and I ended up leaving that place with all that. I don't know if I would have made it out there, this guy Discipline had guards at

257

every post. So, I fucking dipped, I bounced. I left. I finally caught up with the witch bitch Cleopatra. I had to get personal, to get her to play ball. So, I threatened her son."

I gasped, "oh my god, Jess, her son? Why?" Jessica then said, "that was the only way to get her to cooperate with me. I had her set him up. Yes, I had her set up Discipline. But, her stupid ass jumped in front of the bullet."

I looked over at the closet, I know cleopatra is on fire right now, ready to bust, but she knew my instructions. Jessica continued, "she wasn't suppose to be there. He was suppose to be at the park alone. He's a creature. Like a vampire or some shit. She was telling me his weakness, I don't know of his powers, but I made these bullets with garlic, and she assisted me with it. But, her stupid ass jumped in front of the bullet like I said, and he caught her as she fell backwards towards him."

I cut her off as Melissa, "So, is he, you know, this vampire dude, Discipline? Is he dead?" Jessica went on with story. "The bullet could have went through her and into him. I could have got a two for one deal. Hahha. Who knows? Anyways, so, what was that guy's name again? The one you met at the store? Oh I remember, his name was Pierre. And when is it you wanted to go to the club again? This weekend?"

I rose up from the sofa, as Melissa and said, "Well, his name was Pierre, no, it was Discipline." Jessica laughed, "girl, you must be confused, huh?" I turned around to her as Melissa and said, "no girl, you're confused, and well you see, you won't be making it this weekend, as a matter fact you won't be around." She smiles, but she gave me a confused look, "what do you mean, I won't be around this weekend?"

I transformed into myself, my claws grew, my fangs grew, and my eyes turned a different, yet ferocious color. She was frightened and she pulled back, she tried to reach for something, but I wouldn't allow her. I lifted her off the ground, with just a hand gesture.

"Cleopatra, now!!" I yelled, and Cleo came out of the closet, but she froze, she couldn't move, she couldn't do anything. I was staring at her confused, "what the fuck is going on here?" she started tearing up, "I don't think I can do this."

Jessica stared over and said, "you bitch, you set me up, huh? I thought I killed you both back in the park!" To shut Jessica up, I moved my hand like I was pushing something away, and I flew her body into the damn wall of her house.

"So, Cleo, you're about to chicken out on me huh? That is fine, but let's see, if we have this lady remain alive, how well will your son fare from that? Because, you know that's who she will target if you don't put your damn human emotions fucking aside and fucking do the job that needs to be done, so we can all move on from this!"

Cleo went from sad, to angry, because she knew I was right, and that's the fucking motivation she needed to do what I need her to do, I then reminded her. "Plus, you started this mess, and you will be ending it! I'm going to help you out." I lifted Jessica up, and I slashed the side of her neck with one of my claws. I then took her by the throat, and I said, "feed, you must feed now!" Jessica looked at Cleo, she was fainting, in and out of consciousness, and then Jessica said...

"I have your son, and I have him held somewhere, and at my command, I will have my person holding him captive, kill him. If anything happens to me now, I will kill that boy."

That put not only Cleo in a bad spot, but myself. We can now say, we have a conundrum. Shit! Fuck, this woman has some leverage on us, and still? No way is she walking away from this.

"She's not fucking walking out of this, she tried to kill me, she has your son. No way is she walking!" I said to Cleopatra. Cleo then stared at me with a pleading gaze in her eyes, "but, it's my son, please, you don't have one of those, therefore you do not know. It's my son!"

Jessica looked at me, "better listen to her, she's making sense. Y'all going to make the smart choice here, or what?" I looked at Jessica, "shut the fuck up, no one is talking to you, bitch. You don't see, Cleo and I are having an A and B conversation, and you need to C, yourself out of it?" Jessica then said to me, "that's so old, what era and time are you from, man?"

Cleo, she hesitated a little bit, and Jessica continued, "that's how you treat the lady, that holds your son's life in her hands, huh?" Cleo then grabs Jessica by the throat, "where is my son?" And now Jessica smiles, as she feels all the power is in her hands now. She was so adamant about not saying shit. But, she didn't know who the fuck I was. And when I want to get to something, or when I wanted something, I either took it, or I made it happen.

She continued, "I'm not telling you shit, bitch," but the entire time, I was reading Jessica's mind, and because she was at such high emotions. Desperation, and her mind was open. And it was easy to read, I figured out where Cleo's son was. I looked at Cleo...

"I read her, I know where he is, I'm going to go save him for you. Don't let her go, you have my word, I will bring him back to you safe and sound, I promise." Cleo, looked at me, "please, Discipline, please!"

I teleported out of there and arrived at the warehouse where Cleopatra's son was being held captive, by two gunmen, ready to kill on command. Damn, this Jessica bitch was really on some gangsta shit. Her son was one person, he was young, why did she need two men to hold him? Her son was blindfolded, and tied to a fucking chair. I made myself discreet. There was another gunman, guarding the door, I flew to him faster than a speeding fucking bullet, and bit his neck. I transformed into him, I also put on his clothing quickly and opened the door, but not before I got rid of his body out of sight.

"Hey, you want to take a break?" I said to the gunman, as the shape of the gunman that was standing guard at the door. He said, "yeah, just watch him close, but who is going to guard the door?" he asked me. I then said, "do not worry, I will." The guy asked, "are you sure?" I then said,

"I'm good, trust me, I got this." So, he walks out, and I untied Cleo's son, quickly. And as I was ready to leave, suddenly the guy comes back, "hey, I forgot my.... yo, what the fuck is going on here?"

He went to shoot a bullet, running the chamber, and I was staring down the barrel, the bullet came at myself and Cleo's son. I then put out my hand, and it was like slow motion began once again. Like the time in the park, when I was getting Jessica's information. Everything moved in slow motion, but me. I stopped the bullet, I ran to the bullet, and I turned the bullet towards the gunman, and then I went back to Cleo's son side, and now everything went back to normal speed, and the bullet charged at the gunman, he was killed instantly.

I had to get his body out of sight as well, good thing Cleo's son was blindfolded, he didn't need to see any of that, it was nasty, so much blood everywhere. I teleported us, out of there. And got back to Jessica's house with Cleo's son in my arms, "see, he's safe, now finish her, no more wasted time, do it now..."

And now Cleo, she feeds upon Jessica's neck, she feeds and feeds and takes all her blood and energy. Then she ripped her fucking heart out of her chest, out of her body, I had to hold her back, damn she was in savage mode suddenly.

"That's for my son, you bitch, you will never touch, nor get near him ever again!" Cleo's son heard that, "mom, is that you, mom?" He whimpered. I took the heart out of Cleo's hand, and gave her my suit, to wipe off before she touched her son. A tear dropped down Cleo's cheek, "yes, baby, it's me." She grabbed him from me, and took his blindfold off, she then hugged and kissed him. I looked at Cleo, and her son, and thought, what if Precious would have lived with our child? What would life have been like? I got into a moment, then I snapped myself out of it.

It then began to rain hard, must have been Cleo's tears. She still had control of the weather. I needed to help her keep her emotions in check or I was going to force her to learn to keep her emotions in check.

"Look, get him out of here, take him to the father, or a safe place, where he is away from all this, then meet me at my place. I will get rid of her." The body of Jessica, I covered, with a blanket I found near by, therefore, the son could not see what or whom I was speaking about. I then said, "look, don't worry about her. Cleo looked at me, "thank you." I yelled, "Go now, take my car!" And she left with him. My goodness, seeing Cleo in action tonight, after I saw how Jessica was left by her, turned me on a little bit. But, scared me a little bit too. Shit, how powerful was Cleopatra? Now, when a woman can scare you a little bit, she must be the one. My goodness the way she ripped Jessica's heart out, was fucking amazing to watch.

I disposed of Jessica's corpse, "help me get rid of a body." I called some men. We did just that, got rid of her body, and I went back to my place.

Cleo then stared into the mirror, her eyes were a different color, and her fangs were out. I walked up from behind her slowly. And she asked me, "what have you done to me? What have you created in me?" I ran bath water, brushed my teeth, barely glancing at my reflection. I still scoff at human's idiocy believing vampires have no reflection, of course, I have a fucking reflection, light reflects off of me the same as anything else.

I then went over to her, to see what she was hollering about, I stared at her reflection in the mirror, gazing into her eyes, she had some of my blood, she has a little of my powers. I then asked her, "what do you mean?" And I stared at her as if I wanted an immediate response, because I damn sure did. She turned around and she and I were now face to face with each other. Body to body.

"I am a fucking monster!" She said sharply. I stroked her hair, and then her beautiful face with the back of my fingers, to her chin, "you're beautiful," I said as I placed my hand upon her face once again, just to have her push it away instantly. "I am not beautiful, I am hideous, you fucking asshole! How can my son ever see me like this? She shoved me right after she said that, forcefully. I grasped her by the throat, and lifted her up from the ground, her feet were dangling about four inches off the floor. That shit escalated quickly, I had her pinned to the wall, with just one massive hand of mine that was placed on her throat. And my strong muscular fingers squeezed the flesh around her throat.

"I fucking gave you a gift plenty of women would die for, a gift plenty of women would dream to obtain. You will never age a day in your fucking life. You will never have a wrinkle in your fucking life, sex will be enhanced, and it will be five times better, way more than when you were a mortal. All your damn senses will heighten. You have been granted, superhuman strength, speed, reflexes. Incredible sight, touch, and hearing. I made you a goddess, I made you a fucking Queen, I made you powerful. I gave you the, 'Immortality Of Discipline.' I gave you fucking life. I made you feel fucking alive again."

A tear rolled down her cheek, "this is how you treat the one who loves you so dear? A woman who would die to save you? A woman who would die and live for you?" She said this to me, while tears rolled down her cheeks. I wiped her tears away from her cheeks with my massive hand.

"Do you not remember, I saved you! If you are able to see your son right now, and him being able to see you, I should be the reason. I am the reason. You were dying, I changed you, then I slit my own wrist, and gave you a part of me. Only a man that loves a woman so dear, would sacrifice, would give his own powerful blood. Only a vampire can love you forever, you should be so lucky. You should be so grateful." I said to her.

She was going through the motions; her human emotions were still intact. My grip became tighter, and I could see it in her eyes. However, I released my grip, I put down my hand from her throat. It's just strange how your heart burns, and burns then suddenly turns ice cold. I gave her a major pass, and I didn't hold it against her. However, I was going to train her, and turn her into the most unstoppable, cold-blooded, killing machine ever. She wouldn't be stronger than I, but she would possess powers beyond her wildest dream, and she would learn how to master and control them. I grabbed her by the hand, "come here, I would like to show you something."

I teleported us both out of there, and I brought us up to a garden. The garden where we arrived, I spoke to her softly, but it was forceful...

"If flowers can teach themselves how to bloom after winter passes, so can you! You just need a little assistance. Just as water and sunlight make them grow and become stronger. You need assistance just like the flowers. But, you're not alone in this, you'll know all I know. Just watch, listen, and fucking learn." I then brought us back to my place...

"Well, now that we can breathe, and now that we are in the clear, we can start to go to our homes, well, your home. I am already at mine, but first, give me these clothes you have on, now!" I said adamantly.

She looked confused, and she didn't know what and why I meant this. "I need to burn your clothes, because of evidence, her DNA is all over you and all over me. I need you to give me your clothes." She gave me all her clothes, down to her socks, and her nylon sheer lace panties. She said to me, "I know why we must do this, but, you got rid of her. She is not about to be found!" I shook my head, "see, it does not matter. We do not know who she knows. We do not know, how many people she told about this. You and I, who I really am, and what I am. We don't know who else was invested in her survival. What if they go looking for her, they will know, whom to go talk to, right? Which is why now, I am beefing up on security even more. On your household, on mine. As a matter of fact, you are not going anywhere tonight. You will remain here with me."

I made her take off everything she had. She was completely naked, and so arousing. "I want you to go and shower, rinse yourself off like three times, I want you to use hydrogen peroxide or alcohol with a tooth brush, and clean underneath your finger nails. I want you to shampoo your hair, like three times as well. And don't come out until you have done all these things, I am demanding this shit of you. Yes, we are vampires, and we could get caught, and we can escape the police, but you and I live regular, everyday lives as well, I have people, and investors I don't want to mess up, dreams and aspirations. And you have family who are not aware of this, nor who you are, that you would love to protect as well. That depend on you. We both cannot afford to be gone for a long period of time, or anything to mess up our brand, or name. So, we can never be careless to not cover ourselves, we can never be careless and blow our cover. Do you understand why now?"

She nodded her head at me, "yes sir." She did what was demanded of her, and the next step was getting her to be fierce and totally unstoppable. I then began to train Cleo, I took her to my fitness clubs, I had her physically training. I used boxing techniques with her.

"You must be physically Dominant. And we as vampires are, by nature, but if you don't know how to utilize your power, and your entire strength, you will always lose. You need to understand the human body, learn it. The more you learn it, the better you will be able to kill it efficiently and adequately. What if the lion or lioness didn't know that he or she was an apex predator? It would be fucking killed or captured, and you do not want to have that for yourself, do you?" She shook her head at me, indicating, 'no.' I then continued…

"Sooo! Just like the rules of the fucking jungle, you will either Hunt Or Be Hunted. Let's fucking go!!!! Plus, we don't know if there are more vampire slayers out there. Damn, remember when we kicked that vampire slayer's ass?"

She looked at me quickly, "we? I remember you hanging, and I did most of the work." I smirked, "who cares? I'm just saying, you and I make a great fucking team." She smiled at me, "yes we do." She said. I pointed my index finger at her, "oooh, I got you to smile, finally!" She looked away, but kept smiling, "oh, shut up." She chuckled. My presence caught the goddess in her. That only peaked her head out. Asking herself questions. Like who really is this man, Discipline? How and why in the hell does he have such power, over me? How does he make me feel this way? Which is a crazy feeling she could not think of. With every encounter, every breath. As time passes, it makes sense to her now. She would then think, only God could do such things. Only a King could make me feel such ways. Only an Immortal could have me loving this way, only a Beast could love me the right way. Only a God could bring out this Goddess in a woman, but only a Queen can uplift the King.

She was a Queen, but only a King could appreciate that. She begged to be broken, she begged with her eyes, she begged with her actions, she begged with her behavior.

Perhaps a cry for attention. When two flames find one another, it is an instantaneous melding of souls. With it comes the realization of just how great a gift the twin flames of love truly is. And, the need to protect it. The sad truth is, so many people are in love and not together really. Then there are so many people together, but they are not really in love. Frequenciosexual; when you are so attracted to people who are vibrating on a high frequency. When you find yourself magnetized by awareness to the point where they've made a connection to the cosmos. And they've realized that they are all that is.

There is something so sexy and amazingly aesthetically beautiful about an unforced bond; the energy is just so real. Time can heal, as well as destroy. The concept of time, is like a double-edged sword. The moment we are born, our hour glass is flipped upside down and the process begins. Grains of the sand trickling down as the years go by. Sure, we can slow down the process, by altering our life through the decisions that we make. But, ultimately, we cannot put a complete and total halt on the inevitable. Time is the one thing in the world that is forever. A continuous ticking that we can only accept, and try our very best to adapt to. That is probably why so many humans fear it, being unable to control something that we conceptualized ourselves. I continued to educate her...

"Two things you cannot cheat; one is taxes, and the other one thing is death. We are the last of our kind, there is not a supernatural around, like us anymore. There is something about the dark that is unsettling. Perhaps it's the fact that we are not one hundred percent sure what lurks just beyond our field of vision. Everything evil takes refuge within the shadows. We are unable to see the threats and we wonder, can it see us? Hearts begin to beat faster, confused minds trying to process the potential of the unknown that awaits them. Humans, they are adequately built, they are perfectly equipped to handle this world that is void of light. While creatures like us, Gods like us, Immortals like us, well, we thrive in the realm of darkness."

We then trained outside a lot, I had a goal for her, "I am going to train you to be the most unstoppable, vicious and the most unheralded killing machine, outside of myself of course, alive! Therefore, we will test your speed, we will test your strength, we will test your emotions. We will test your resiliency and intelligence. We will test your hunger, we will test the way you behave during combat, we will test how you attack. Who better to train you than I?"

She cut me off, "oh no, here we go with your arrogance and shit." I smirked, "well, really, who is better than me? Then think about it, and whom else is going to show you this and how to master it, but me? Be honest!"

She was silent, I mean, she knew. She knew I was totally on point, totally one hundred percent accurate. "That is exactly what I thought, shut up, listen, watch and fucking learn!" I demonstrated a couple of tricks as a vampire, she could incorporate into her new life. "Like I said, there is plenty for you to learn. I cannot just have you going around and damn near freezing up and having people running on you. Running from you, after you have exposed yourself and you don't finish them off. What would that do to our legacy? We cannot, allow me to reiterate, we cannot be exposed. We will set up a race, and I will be timing you."

She and I raced in the woods, "you did very well, very well, I am impressed. Good girl." She smiled at me, then she said, "you finally mentioned and acknowledged I did great work." I put my hand up, and my palm faced her, inspiring her silence. I then said, following my gesture, "silence, you're not there yet to be proud and boasting. Don't get ahead of yourself, the minute you allow your guard to be down, that's when you can get got! Always stay fucking focused. You did good, but not great. Good, but, you are still a little slow. You are faster than the fastest human being in the world, but slow for a vampire. We must make you faster."

I took her to a cabin, and I then whispered to her forcefully, "here is where these couples are having a couple's retreat." We were hidden away from the cabin, no one could see us, we were in the bushes. I then continued...

"We are going to kill every last one of them. One by fucking one, no one fucking walks, understand!" She gasped, "but, these humans are innocent, please can we just find some bad people to kill, ones that deserve it?" She pleaded to me. I shook my head, "first and foremost, the answer to that question is, no. Are you making the rules here? How long have you been a vampire? You know how this works, huh?"

She was silent, she had no response. I then gazed into her eyes firmly and said, "exactly. Like I said, shut up, watch, fucking listen and learn. Second of all, how do you know these people here are innocent? You know them?"

She shook her head, no. "None of these people here are innocent," I said. And I then continued to tell her, "if I look inside each of their minds, they have done something to get themselves ahead in life. Possibly by stepping on someone else's toes, or they've cheated, or they have been in situations. Such as, deceit, lies, malice, stole, cut corners, etc. No one is innocent, not you, not me, not even fucking them. Mortals, they are weak, they are weak by their emotions, their greed, slaves to their own desires. Do you think they appreciate life? Fuck no! They fucking take it for granted! We are going to do this, and we are going to wait until it gets dark out. And by then the moon will be out. We are the best of both, all their strengths, we have. This is me referring to vampires. All their weaknesses, we don't have. Many potent energies, few flaws. These humans are like cattle. Pieces of fucking meat, who gives a fuck how they die? Who gives a fuck how their world really ends? War? Cancer? We are on top of the fucking food chain! We are the Alphas. No matter how you try to escape it, I'm telling you now, the hunger will always win. How do you feel? Is your blood on fire? Your stomach aching?" She didn't answer.

We waited for the time to pass, the night had approached us, the silver moon was bright, and the night was exhilarating. "Okay, Cleopatra, let's go in for the kill, remember, we are leaving the bodies there." I pointed with my index finger towards the cabin when I said this to her. "However, when we leave the bodies there, we will be leaving them completely out of sight. No children to be touched, hopefully there are no children there, now they are innocent."

We wore gloves, because, I didn't want any type of DNA being traced to us, we wore beanie hats. One of the couples were in the bathroom, I came in the bathroom, discreet, while they were in the shower. I was hiding in the closet bathroom, and as soon as she looked at herself in the mirror, I came out and placed my massive hand over her mouth, so she would not scream, and I bit her on her neck, and sucked all her blood, draining her energy until she dropped to the fucking ground. But, I caught her while she was going down. That way, she didn't make a single sound. I watched Cleo take out one of the males, she was a savage, she slashed his throat. His jugular with her claws, before she fed on him, I nodded my head in approval, then whispered to her, "very good. But, what is it with you and slashing them before you bite them? Why don't you just go in for the kill right away?" She shrugged her shoulders at me, indicating she didn't know why. Then she said, "maybe it's because, we women are classier. We like to do things in steps, take shit slow, unlike you men!" I smiled, then I said, "that is not fucking true." She challenged me, "oh yeah, well, the next one I want to see you kill with classiness." I completely disregarded what she said, as I made it seem as if I figured out why she would kill the way she did, "oh, I know, you want to watch them suffer before you go in for the kill!" She shook her head, no. I pointed my index finger at her, "oh yes, you savage. Haha. Good work, now drag his body out of sight." I whispered.

There were so many couples there. At least five couples, so that's about ten people. I took Cleo, in a quiet corner in the cabin, and whispered to her, "there are about five women, and five males here, well, now there are four women and four males, because we fucked the other two

273

up. So, here is the plan, you get the males, and I get the women," She questioned, as she was displeased by my plan, "what the hell! Why the fuck must I get the men, and you, the women?" I then explained to her, "the males are stronger, and that will give you more and assist in your training," now let us move quickly and get the rest of these losers. We are wasting time here!"

I wanted to split this one couple up, they were wherever the other was. So, I tipped over something in the bathroom, so it was heard and one of the women said, "honey, did you hear that? Can you go look to see what that was?" The male, was coming, fuck, I pointed to Cleo, to head to the bathroom, I followed her to watch her back. The man was talking to himself, "what fell in here? I don't even see anything," as soon as he turns around, Cleo, grabbed him by his throat, and she covered his mouth, he went to fight back, and Cleo let him go, I swooped in, and I jumped on him, and he fell to the ground, I turned to her, "come here, Cleo."

I held the man's head, and Cleo fed upon him, drinking all his blood, and then I snapped his neck. I looked at her, and I smiled, then she smiled, with blood dripping from her mouth. "You just turned me on just about now," I said to her, with a big smile upon my face. She playfully hit me, and then said, "oh stop." I then said...

"Okay, let's hide his body, most of them are going to come into this bathroom now, I don't know if they heard the thud, after I pounced on him. But, you know what? Fuck it, let's just give them a treat and plan for the element of surprise. "Why don't we wait until they all fall asleep, and then kill them, my King?" That is what Cleo asked me. I looked at her, and smirked, "you love the easy way out, huh? I like the look in their eyes, when they see a monster in their presence, the look is so exhilarating. The feeling that their life is on the line, and you can see it in their eyes. They beg, they beg for their life." She stared at me, "you are way too into this! You are loving this too much, and, how could you?" I gazed into her eyes, "you will love it as well, you will see.

This is you now as a vampire, but you are still going through it, with your human emotions still intact. But, those emotions will eventually fade. What do you plan to be now? A fucking hero or something? You plan to save people, whom you don't even know, or care about? Ready to pounce at the next signal of distress? You want all that trouble and responsibility as a hero? People depend on you and use you. Then dump you aside when they don't need you, or worse, turn against you. These mortals will never remember what you did in the fucking past, just what you do now. What you have done today. That moment where there is a cry for help, let's say you are a second late. You are now the villain!! You want that type of stress?"

She didn't answer me, "yeah," I said, then I continued, "I guess you didn't think that through, huh? You just like the concept of hero, because it sounds good. Makes you feel good? Nah, the villain is the real hero." She looked at me confused. I then continued, "we are a fucking special breed of super naturals, whom are cut from a different set of fucking cloth, willing to embrace challenges with outstretched arms. You do not appreciate your gifts, you do not care to master your talents?" I asked her. "You want to fight evil? Ready to defy the odds and prove the naysayers and doubters wrong? There is something to be said about their eagerness to walk so confidently into the valley of the shadow of death ready to face the enemy head on. But that shit is in the fucking comic books. That shit is in the fucking movies, this is no fucking happy ending."

I grabbed her firmly, then said, "we create our own happy ending. Saving the fucking day is not always guaranteed. The good guys don't always win." She had nothing to say, but gazes at me, her eyes were captivating. And I held her gaze with my eyes, as I stared squarely at her, penetrating the exterior of her flesh peering into her soul. Unable to break the trance like hypnosis, so she has no choice but to fucking stare back. Fickle emotions, consisting of euphoria and stillness. Hearts intertwine and becoming one as they fall into each other. A moment in time, as if we stop time, where all is right with the world and no outside force can disturb it. Eyes speak, mouths stay shut, it's like eyes are lost at sea with one another.

"You want this, you are in denial. See, what you desire is deliberately placed out of reach, so that you may become the person it takes in order to obtain it. Men go shopping to find what they want, and women go shopping to go find out what they want. You know what you want, but you are indecisive about it. Then again you are window shopping to find out what you want, but we both know, this is what you want, sooner or later you will realize that as well. I froze up just like you, years and years ago, when I first turned. I was feeling just like yourself. This is why I can train you to feed, I won't just say, 'go out there and fend for yourself.' You see me, I was thrown to the wolves, no one helped me, I figured out a lot of my powers through anger, emotion, helplessness. Like I said, I was thrown to the fucking wolves, and guess what?"

She was speechless, and didn't know the answer, "umm, what?" I then answered her, "I came back fucking leading the entire fucking pack."

We then finished off all of the rest of the people in the cabin, I teleported us out of there, and made certain we were not seen, at all. We went back to my place, and I said to her, "the hunt is always better when she is just as hungry." She looked at me, and she said...

"I love you, I will love you until my last breath." I grabbed her head, my hands curled inward into her scalp, I grasped a fist full of her hair, and anchored her head towards my face, and said, "Eternal Love Is So Powerful." Then I kissed her lips so passionate and roughly......

Chapter 20- You Belong To Me Forever

She gave her all to me; her body, mind, heart. Her obedience, devotion, gratitude. She gave her all to me; and I took her in my hand and shaped her into the woman she was meant to be. Kisses made our body feel like flames. I brought out some rope, some handcuffs....I cuffed her wrists, while her hands were behind her lower back. Her palms were facing me. I gave her a dose of my Henny big dick. Strong and dark had her fucked up and love drunk real quick. Pistol in my pants, back shots murdered her pussy. Pounding her, left her a dripping mess for me. Walls closed in around me like a vice grip pliers. She was drenched like Niagara Falls. Squirting everywhere like a busted fire hydrant. Screaming, as her body convulsed. She could not stop shaking, for like ten seconds. She used to run from me, but now she loves and is used to the pain. I exposed her to realness and my world, and now she's disgusted by anything that's so lame.

Ever since I ran through her mind, body and soul, she has never been the same. I never said I was such a great influence, therefore I will take the blame. Once I gave her a taste of this world of Discipline, the rest of the world paled in comparison. Part of seduction is simple, like I've been saying, and I will say it again...you take everything she has, then give her everything she needs. I will corrupt her sensibilities. I will challenge any notion of pleasures she has ever known. I introduce her to my big "choker." Then I choked her. She was my vampire and witch Queen, a woman that submitted to me not just sexually, but psychologically and emotionally.

"I want you to wear one of my favorite color lingerie for me," I showed her. "Yes, this, the blue one." She replied immediately, "yes Daddy, yes Master, yes king."

Later that night, she went into the bathroom, and went to change into the lingerie I got for her. She met me at my feet, then she knelt immediately. She's such a good girl for me. She sat kneeling with her juicy, plump ass cheeks resting on her heels. I walked around her slowly, watching every curve meticulously. I meet her back at the starting position, face to face, looking downward at her, she was looking upward at me. I grasp her by the jaw and kissed her lips passionately. I grab her breasts and pinch her erect nipples. I rip that lingerie right off of her, like the animal in me was loose. The beast was unhinged. She was completely naked, "This Is Exactly How I Want You." I will corrupt her sensibilities. I instruct her to stick her tongue out, and say, "ahh," as if I were her doctor. "Relax your throat, yeah just like that. Don't stop until I say so, or I will pull it out of your mouth." She craved me anyway she could have me inside her. Whether it was her mouth or pussy, it didn't matter the hole.

I made her breathe through her nose. Thrusting into her mouth; fast, slow, deep. She can't take all of it, but I love watching her try. Touching the back of her throat, gagging sounds as though it's like music to my ears. Her eyes water and run down her cheeks. She has a shortness of breath. "Sloppy, nasty, that's right my bitch, my whore get all that spit. Work that neck, so magnificent." I said to her. I love to see her pupils dilate when she looks up at me. "Yes, release that beast that I have created inside you, out." I grasp a fist full of her hair. Just enough to hold onto like a handle. I take out my big dick 'choker' and I slap it on her face real hard. Before I place it back in her mouth, I spoke sharply, "this is your corrector, it will relax you, overwhelm you, elevate you, change you, and shape you. It will heal you and break you. Build your confidence, leave you sore, you will be begging me for more. It will overpower you. It will become your addiction. More potent than cocaine. This shit could make you insane. Now open your mouth and take this protein, it's going to make you strong."

She serves me, and that makes her happy. I would allow her to please me. But first, I make her earn that. How romantic it is, to choose my big muscular chocolate dick over oxygen. That lack of oxygen builds up her blood flow. Ultimately, seeping down into her pussy. "Choke on it, gag, slurp, spit. Suck like you are dying and you require my Dominant juices for your survival. Suck like it's game seven and you want that championship ring. Suck like it's the fourth quarter and you want that touchdown to win the game. Suck like if you don't suck it good, you won't get any of this good dick."

I treat her good, I treat her bad, but I always fuck her better. I didn't even need to touch it, that pussy of hers was wetter that Niagara Falls, from her imagination of me Dominating her walls. Wetter than like a hurricane sandy, I then said forcefully, "walk over to the bed, get on top of the sheets. Now, lay on your back. Take both of your hands, use your fingers and spread that pussy open, and get ready to take all of me in."

Before I slid in, I was ready to eat. Ready to fucking eat and I didn't need a spoon. Big strong muscular chocolate man hands of mine, pinning her down. Nowhere to run, animal instincts takes over. The urges are too strong. Desires are potent. Just so she can take all of my big, long chocolate muscular dick.. I lean over and speak in her ear....

"I'm not a good guy, this big chocolate dick will save your mind, but ruin your life. Lower your stress but make you insane at the same time. I am your alpha and omega. Your first of many things and your last. Your creator and your destroyer. A brand-new woman, as you witness the complete alteration of your entire existence."

I go harder, my thrusts are more brutal and callous. I make her feel every thickness, as it is spreading her pussy open. Deeper, I make her feel every inch.

"Queef, let that pussy queef for me, I said to her. Then I continued, "yes, Daddy loves when what belongs to him speaks to him." I make her remember every slap, spank, I free her busy mind with ferocious impact. I fuck those doubts, shyness, fears, and insecurities right out of her. I go harder...I make that ass shake.

"Twerk on that big chocolate dick, like an ocean wave. Take it, you're not running, I don't care if it's too much, take it. This is what you wanted, now you have it, so fuck that, and take it." I growled at her. She wants to be beaten.

She wants to be taken. She may moan, cry, whimper, but she loves to feel helpless. She wants to be degraded, she wants to be slutted. She wants to be manhandled. She wants to be devoured. She doesn't want hard, she wants brutal. To not be taken kindly, or nice. To not be handled by a soft and weak man. But to be Dominated rough, and to be pounded like you mean it. She wants to be disrespected. She wants to feel sore. She wants to struggle to walk. She wants the thoughts the following day. She wants the mini orgasms to herself when she's lost in thought at her work. She wants pain. She wants pleasure. If not, she would not be here, she knows who I am, she knows I won't change. She knows why she's here. To subject herself to this type of sexual, deviant, masochism, sadism, bondage, Discipline, Dominance, submission she's more insane than I thought, and I like it.

She will come to me, then she will beg to cum for me. "Just don't forget to thank me." I told her. This was that intense love making, where her legs were wrapped around his waist. And he held you so tightly. Cradling your neck and your head. That intense love making where he is buried so deep inside, that the arousing ache feels like you are being reborn. That intense love making shit, where you both are so entangled in each other that you don't know where you end, and he begins. But he knew. I roared softly. Not a moan, but a big growl, "grrrr," in her ear. She didn't do well with rules, however, she let me tell her what to do. She could have loved being in control, but you would never guess, because of the way she loves it when I take it from her. I bring her closer to the moon, and I undo her. Just to reconstruct her into a brand-new woman.

"I'm taking you to another world, don't worry when we're finished, I'll bring you back down to earth." The calm and soft but forceful whisper of my words in her ear. "Sometimes I crave it more than you. The moment you open yourself up to me. Your mind, your soul, your body. The moment you shut your eyes and I take you the fuck away. Bring you into another world. In the eyes of the vanilla(regular) world, you are a strong woman. However, to me you will always be my naughty, meek, dirty little girl and deviant. Your desire to be great at being owned. Owned by not just any man. Not just any Dom. But this powerful vampire Dominant. This King. Your majesty. Your highness. Your royalty. Your Master. A prize worthy of being coveted, perfect for me and not society. Available whenever, however, wherever I want you and need you. You love it when I use you for my pleasures.

You love it when I abuse you. Beg for it, then fucking earn it. Turn your back on normal. Now you're different. Appreciate the hand that beats, takes, slaps, spanks, controls, protects, loves and changes you. You will never meet a man like me, ever in your entire lifetime. I will mark and bruise your flesh, in places only you and I will see, to show you and remind you that you belong to me. I own you. I will mark your soul, so you never forget where you belong. Which is in my zone. In my grasp. Submission because of my confident, measured authority. Appreciative of my Dominance. Unburdened by my leadership. Trusting in my decisions. Kneeling at my feet. I will imprint my essence in your mind and soul, that anyone that attempts to know you, will need to know me well, I mean fucking well, in order to understand you. Used. Slutted. Filthy.

Appreciative and free. I'll break you, before I heal you. I will hurt you, then I tell you I love you."

She was like art. Nothing for amateur hands, a part time adorer or lovers. She was made for art. To be touched in meaningful ways. To be molded like clay in the skilled hands of a sculptor. To be sketched properly and expertly like canvas in the hands of a painter. To be written on a scroll in the hands of a poet. She was made for more, definitely not mediocre. She was made for art. I knew she was mine before she did. The things she needs I've known prior to her own consciousness. She needs her throat throbbing from being face fucked. She needs spit running from her mouth, down to her chin and onto her breasts. She needs to feel shortness of breath. She needs her face red from being slapped. Slapped with big dick and slapped with a big hand. She needs her ass punished and her pussy handled. She needs to walk with a limp from after I've pounded her the fuck out. She needs the memory of me dancing in her head the following day, while she's bored at her regular work. She needs my insanity to keep her sane. She needs my bad to keep her good.

She needs my good to keep her filthy. It can't be clean and proper all the fucking times. She needs slutty, nasty, filthy. She begged for me without a word. I'm her escape from everything that confines her. Whether that's work, duties, family, father of her child, choirs, friends, bills, coworkers and this mundane vanilla (ordinary) world. The only things that are vanilla in her life. They can have her temporarily when I'm finished. But, I want her back, I demand her back just, so I can do it all over again.

I had some anal beads with me, and I told her to place them inside her.

"Get on your knees," I spoke sharply. "Open your mouth, open wider. Stick your tongue out, and make sure you leave it just like that." I said softly but forceful. I pulled out my already erect fat long muscular chocolate cock and slapped it on her tongue a few times. Teasing and tantalizing her.

"Is this what you are craving baby girl?" I asked her. She said, "it's you I crave, and whatever you're willing to offer me. Whatever you are willing to provide."

She wanted me anyway she could have me, and she would have me in her mouth right now. She was salivating at the beautiful sight and at the thought. Her kitty was drenched from anticipation. Waiting for my next command, she needed my guidance like she needed air. I spoke softly but I was forceful.

"You will earn it, you must earn it. Hands behind your back, now!" I growled. I slapped all this enormous meat across her face. Left cheek, then right cheek roughly. "Keep your eyes on me and nothing else, no matter what." I shoved all this chocolate dessert inside her mouth. I placed both my thumbs on the back of her neck, and my four other fingers (eight total) across her throat. I'm going to give her a crazy experience as I fuck her face to a next dimension. Pressing downward with my thumbs and shoving my big dick inside her mouth at the same time. I could feel her throat expanding in my hands. Tears and mascara running down her cheeks. Shortness of breath, pussy vibrating, clit throbbing. I'm her first of everything. I kept going, and I could see her pussy dripping. I ordered her to the bed, "I want you flat on your back. Mouth open."

I brought out my rope, and began to bind her wrists, then I anchored her hands above her head with my left hand using the lead end rope. I then guided my beast in her already opened lustful and begging mouth with my Dominant hand (right handed, but I am ambidextrous). I then began to ride her face with my massive chocolate dick. She told me that she could handle it, I made a liar out of her. I shoved my thick Dominant long chocolate dick between her begging yielding lips, through her drenched tight hole. After ten stokes she was crying, moaning, running, dripping, shaking and begging to cum for me. She talks plenty of shit, she can't back up. No matter what she thinks or thought she could do, she's nothing until I make her something. She's worthless until I make her priceless. She hasn't experienced Discipline, until she has experienced Discipline.

She's no longer from this world, I've taken her to a place of no return. I have taken a piece of her. She is completely changed. And she doesn't follow the rules of the norm. She follows my rules, she's in my fucking world. No safe word will save her, but I don't think she wants to use any. I believe she's too stubborn, and she wants to prove something to me. Her submission is her strength, my control becomes her release. I don't just want to fuck her, I want to ruin her. Ruin her completely for me. And the fact that I love her, won't save her today. She knows why she's here. She's here because she does not crave mediocrity. She craves phenomenal. She craves to feel alive. She needs to be in this world, my world. The space between us, that has been long gone knows it. Grunts and strains and delicious pain. My words escape my mouth with wings on them. Her mind cloudy with thoughts of past, present and future. Whispered gifts, as she begins to transition. Words slicing through the silence. Penetrating her crowded mind. A warm, wet comfortable yielding begins in the back of her neck. She shuts her eyes, and now I force her to feel. Shoulders go slack. She's relaxed and slowly dripping down her thighs. Body is begging, pussy is vibrating. Ass bright red from my vicious, ruthless spankings. She's here to be taken, manhandled, Dominated, Disciplined, degraded, to be vulnerable, to feel helpless. To be slapped. To be spanked. Controlled. For the "need." She needs structure. She needs stability. Strength.

She needs a firm hand. She needs to be exposed. She needs accountability. She needs vulnerability. She needs pain, pleasure, joy, anger, safety, danger, hurt, love, hate, orgasms, sub-space, drop, to be broken and to be healed, freedom. Freedom from choice. From confusion, from questions, from decisions. I am the escape, the only thing that makes sense. I am relief and I am vacation. With me, I take her to a place in her mind, losing herself in my insanity, and she forgets about this vanilla(ordinary) world. I am the most dangerous, mean, loving, savage, kind of precious thing she could ever fucking have. One that knows his true value. And in my fucking hands, I hold the keys to her satisfaction, happiness, pain, pleasure, excitement, fulfillment and peace. Her Alpha and Omega. I am her first of many things, and her last. I am her creator, and I am damn sure her destroyer. A brand new woman, she will never like the same things, nor will she ever be the same again. In this moment, she is truly MINE. Love to pin her legs back, and gaze into her eyes while I take her over and over and over again. The big gasp she gives, when I first slide in. She has never felt anything so intense, so erotic, so primal. The Sadist. The animal. The beast is unhinged. Tasting and destroying what I've created. Quick breaths from her, followed with moans and cries. Her body not her own. Her movements not her own. Complete surrender to my thick, long chocolate muscular relentless dick. My lips, my tongue, my power, my hands. My aggression. My Dominance.

She is placed, and man handled in different positions, as if she was being handled by many different lovers, and she has never experienced prior. Stimulating her erogenous zones. Slapping her face so mercilessly while I thrust. My ruthless aggression strangely turns her on. The pain palpable. Her pussy dripping. Now shit gets fucking real, only to ask me, "Daddy, can I cum now?" I allow it, because, there's more to come. More I will give her. I love watching her suffer. She thanked me for each one, because, that's what good girls do. Orgasms have never tossed her so violently into rapture, into such ecstasy that there is no control, no denial or reality but that of me, and the culmination of my touch. Feeling every thrust from this thick chocolate long muscular relentless dick of mine, the same time as I suck on her toes, and lick on her soles. Hard chocolate muscular dick spits her open, filling her up with every fucking inch. While we both listen to how wet she becomes from every hard, slow, fast yet deep stroke. Her lips part, mouth open wide. Eyes rolls back, serotonin and oxytocin dripping from her pituitary gland, she gazes in deeper love than ever before. My big muscular fingers curl inward to grasp a fist full of her hair. Momentarily, as I transition my hand to her throat, and squeeze the flesh around it. Stone grip, yes now she transforms into my whore. Kissing her lips, as I bite the bottom lip as hard as I could, prior to my vicious slap. I take her breath away, I kill the pussy and bring her back to life a brand new woman. She tells me that it's mine...

"This is your pussy Daddy. All yours." And I say, "of course it's mine, no one will ever do your body like this, they're not this fucking great." She laughs, then I go deeper, and I then begin stabbing her with my big cock. The giggles come to an abrupt halt. "Yeah, laugh now, cry later." I said sharply, flowing a growl in her ear while I'm thrusting inside her, then a sadistic laugh following after. How sore I leave her when we are through, and how much she struggles to walk to the bathroom. I want her to feel me when I'm gone. I want it so that only my next thrust is required, to keep her sane.

Her mind, body and soul, all belong to me. I caused a problem for myself, more importantly, I've ruined her forever. She will control it, because if not, the punishment will be greater. I know it's not fair, but I really do not care. I control her in every way, and she does what I say. You know why? Because, I fucking.....say. You always hurt the one you love, and the one you love, will always hurt for you.

"In this moment I will not hold your hand. I will not guide you. I do what I want. I want what I take, and when I take, I fucking Dominate. I feed you my energy and corrupt your sensibilities. I will challenge every notion of pleasure you've ever known. I will shatter every boundary you thought you would never cross. If you come here to just fuck, I will make you fall in love. If you come here to just love, I will make you a chocolate addict. If you come here to just give, I will leave you giving me everything with no limits.

You will come to me, then you will cum for me. I am your first of many things, last of few. I am the Alpha and Omega, as I have reiterated this. The beginning and end. You are a submissive of mine, you are a full time submissive. Not part time submissive. Not a weekend submissive. Not a holiday submissive. Not a vacation submissive. Your submission for me is not part time either, or half obtainable. I will protect you like you are a piece of fragile glass. Cherish your heart like a gift, but I will destroy, devour, Dominate, gradually dismantle, your body like it is unbreakable. Savagely. The fact that I love you, won't save you tonight. I am going to fuck you up. Every touch, no matter how rough or how tender. It is a reminder of how much you need me. You are appreciative. I show you how I appreciate you....to be stuck. Slapped. Kissed. Fucked. Made love to. Caressed. Used. As I choose to use you. You Are Mine. A man who ruins you perfectly in every way you have ever secretly desired. A powerful MAN. A Chocolate KING. A Dominant BEAST. A Sadistic vampire DADDY. A prominent MASTER. Who shows you love in many forms. Kind and unkind. All for you. All needed. Now smile for me......so I can fucking just slap that smile off your face and grab it. Muscular hands grasp ahold of you. Breathless. But breathe for me one more time. As I make all your dreams come true, I want you to whisper, 'thank you.'

You will always be humble to me, no matter how long it is, whether we are here, there or not there, because you respect what I can do. Which is the best in the world at what I fucking do. You respect how I make you feel, and you now respect what I've done to you. You will always respect me, because of how I Dominate you. How I've Dominated you. You will respect my Dominance for as long as you live. And when you don't, you know I can always take it away, for a short period of time to punish and control you.

The way I leave you in a trance. Put you in subspace. Punish you emotionally, physically, or psychologically. For as long as you live, no other man nor beast will ever love you or fuck you as passionately. Dominantly. Forcefully. Roughly. Powerfully. Properly as I do you.

Two lovers you will always remember. Number one, your first love, and second, myself. And even there it will pale in comparison to me. I will pleasure you with pain. Spoil you with bruises. Those are your gifts. Wear them with pride. I will bite the meatiest parts of your flesh. Meticulously. Methodical. Calculating and taking my time. You are my main course meal. I will savor every bite. As you are momentarily dazed by my Dominant behavior. Enjoying you to the fullest. Your body and my body. My mouth and your mouth. My thick, long chocolate dick, and your tight, drenched delicious pussy get along famously. Stern Dominant. On top of the fucking food chain. Now I show you why I will always be on top of you. With knowledge comes trust automatically. One of the reasons you confide in me. One of the reasons you give yourself to me. An inexperienced man will always leave a level of uncertainty for you. To you I'm everything. Beast incarnate. Daddy. Sadist. King Kong.

You will never forget this sharp mind, big ass morphine, demon dick, and tornado tongue. And I know what to do with all three to you, and I do it extremely well. To be mine, you will be giving up many parts of you. When I take, I take completely. The psychological and physical abuse I give you, will either make or break you forever. Give you a case of algolagnia. Pain without sex and sex without pain will never make sense to you. As you will need both to be fulfilled. You will witness the alteration of your entire being. You will evolve into a strong woman, or deteriorate and become a weak one. You are worthless, until I make you priceless. You are nothing, until I make you something. You know nothing, until I've shown you everything. I'll fuck you to every song, so when you hear them when I'm not around, you will think of me."

I grabbed her by her ankles, as I command her to get on top of me, "get on this horse, and giddy up, now bounce on that shit like you mean it slut!" Staring down at it like that, whispering softly but forcefully in her ear, "oh you're fucking nasty, aren't you? You love bouncing off of Daddy I see."

Maneuvering my muscular, big hands to her waist. Mastering her curves. Controlling all her movements. Her love handles, I handle just to handle. Spreading her ass cheeks hard, just to get in there deeper. Grasp a fist full of her hair, with one hand, other slapping each ass cheek. Love how my hand print looks on her, branding my territory. She screams with every delicious, impactful slap.

"Yes, you whore, get my big chocolate dick rock hard with your pain. With your suffering. With your cries. With your moans. Your whimpering. All that shit belongs to me. I created it." Thumb in her butt. Double the pain. Double the pleasure. She and I both hear and feel every impactful, delicious slap. Hair pulling can be essential. When the endorphins kick in, it can be extremely pleasurable. Women have twice as many nerve receptors than men. Causing them to feel pain more intensely. They have a high tolerance for it as well. When pulling her hair, pull more towards the scalp. It's an intense feeling.

As the few chemicals released from our brains during intercourse that Oxytocin now turns your pain into pleasure. Now it becomes addictive. The endorphins kicking in. What would normally hurt, is soothing. So, I pull it, I pull it harder.

"You now need consistent Discipline. There will be pain involved, but only if you ask nicely. Now beg bitch!" As I whisper softly in her ear, my firm grasp by my powerful hands maintain her. "Lose yourself in my insanity. As you find peace in my chaos. I trigger your fickle emotions. You will never be one thing forever. You will never be one way forever. When the endorphins kick in, and the oxytocin drip from your brain. Penetrating your pituitary gland, dripping of dopamine, as you fall in deeper love than ever before. Causing you to rain down all over me. A monsoon is due, as I witness a raging river of you. Give me everything I fucking own; your screams, your pain, your lust, your breaths, your cries, your body temperature, your begging, your orgasms. As I explore the depths of your body. Go ahead now and beg me to allow you to cum. I'm going to train you on how to take this thick, long chocolate dick like the animal I want you to be. The nymphomaniac I turn you into for me."

Fucking her like the filthy slut she is for me. The whore she wants to be. The bitch she wants, was brought out of her. She needs this 'Discipline therapy.' I crave her flesh. The beast in me yearns to feast upon her. I crave her moans, her screams, her cries. She yearns for my bruises, and my marks, as a reminder of where she belongs, and to whom she belongs to. She needs the pain. But not just any damn pain, my pain. And she needs it from my hand. She yearns for my Dominance, and my strength. I am her balance she's searched for her entire fucking life. I am her potent drug. I provide what she needs, she never realized she needed. I quiet her busy thoughts, she doesn't need to analyze everything all the time. I am her escape. I make her feel like a real woman, I make her feel like a Goddess. I make her feel alive.

"We both drown in your pool of lust. We die together. Reborn as immortals. Where do you belong?" I asked her. She said, "I belong with you." And I then said…."Always, and don't you ever forget it. I want you sore, I want you to hurt. I will leave my mark on you, therefore, when you feel it the following day it is a constant reminder of what we've done. Who you are to me, who the fuck I am, what this is, and where the fuck you belong. Exactly how I want you. Exactly how I need you. Stick to me like scotch tape. I want to eat you alive like an entree. When you are helpless. Vulnerable. Completely bound. It is when you are the most beautiful. You trigger my voracious appetite. Whether you are bound physically or bound psychologically just know it is where your soul craves to be. You will witness the power I possess. As you will experience it as well. My mind will seduce you. My hand will correct you. My thick long chocolate dick will destroy you. My eyes will quiet your noisy soul. My words will hold your mind captive. In my presence I will not even need to say a word. Instincts will take you to your knees. My Dominance will take you deep into the welcoming darkness. You will become brutally, roughly, savagely in love with me. You will be obsessed with me. EXACTLY HOW I WANT YOU. You will be crazy for me. EXACTLY HOW I WANT YOU. I will love you violently, as you are destroyed by the extent of my sadism. EXACTLY HOW I WANT YOU. I'm the kush, you are the blunt. The fire between us will take you to heights you've never been. I am your ecstasy and you can't resist or deny me. You are my peace to my nightmares, as I am your chaos to your wonderful dreams. You are the object of my unbridled lust. To be taken. To be desired. To be hurt. To be Dominated. To be conquered. No matter what, you are obedient, you are a star in my eyes.

You will start to realize that stars cannot shine without the dark. How you are not just expected to wait on your knees, at my feet. But it is the place you feel safest. EXACTLY.......HOW........I........WANT......YOU." I said, "no one would dare to say something or look at your pretty self. They don't want to see that vicious monster shit come out of me. I'm over protective. You will never get the love

I provide to you from another as long as you shall live."
She said, "all these men, but my eyes are on a King. But
not just any king. On you." I asked a rhetorical question
"why?" She said, "because you're a good witch girl's
Sadistic Daddy." I said, "good girl." She said to me...

"Discipline, you're real. You do exist." I chuckled. "You
will always be fond of someone like me. Fuck that, you
will always be fond of me. You will crave Discipline. It
will become a requirement. You will witness power that's
unprecedented. I'm more than breathing to you. I'm
intoxicating. I'm like your most potent drug. Like, even if
you were to walk away, the urge would keep coming back.
Every man you encounter from this day forward, you will
compare me to. Wish they possess the qualities and
attributes I possess. You will experience my all. I will not
be satisfied until you gush. Pop that pussy, like a six-shot
magnum .357 ruger, when you pull the trigger. Gush many
times as I throw this big, chocolate dick like darts. I'm your
guilty pleasure. Your delicious chocolate addiction. Your
favorite sin. We have no secrets. Thus, making our bond
not only unbreakable, but very powerful. I looked inside
your mind, and said to myself, 'I have plans for you.' This
is deeper than sex. Deeper beyond the physical and body,
that when I fuck you, I will blow your mind. I will bind
your soul to mine. Every time I give you a part of me, you
feel as though I've casted a spell or gave you some drugs. I
will get you higher than you've never been. Drunk off my
Dominance. As you take down all this Discipline thug
passion.

You crave me mentally. Your body yearns for my touch
greatly. Your soul seeks my words. You came to me. I

didn't ask, I didn't force you here. You were mine the moment you said, "hello." I knew it, you just didn't know it yet. As you stare into my eyes, looking for a void to be filled. An avid little precious kitten searching to cater, worship, serve and please me. Looking for a man worthy of your greatness. To have him give you immense greatness in return."

Whether she's innocent, a goody two shoes. A delicate flower. A beautiful disaster. Whether she's a damaged individual; mentally, physically, emotionally, it is irrelevant. Im going to give you a lot, but I demand a little bit. I'm not here to change her. I'm here to enhance her life. I'm not here to judge her, or certain things she finds gratification in, punishments she likes, or give her certain pains, etc. I'm here to corrupt her even more. To make her better.

"You follow Queen, and I lead. I set the tone. It is not my big chocolate muscular cock, my Dominance, my looks, etc that keeps you here. It is my words. It is the strength of my character that allows your submission to remain consistent and thrive. To allow you to be the things, you so yearn to be. I am your release. The control you seek. The surrender you've yearned for. The power you crave. The power from my hand. My mind. My body. My soul. I am your light at the end of the tunnel. You find peace in my chaos. As you lose yourself in my insanity. You can be left in a daze, lost in my erotic maze. Skin to skin, I'm your favorite type of sin. The best submissive in the world, is one who willingly come to you and kneels. Whispering of their love. Their pain. Their desires. As I cherish, heal and soothe the entirety of you. To read your body language, when you are not talking. To quiet your busy thoughts. You are truly mine. This is your destiny. The inevitability and now the reality. You will yearn for my touch. My hand. My gaze. My words. My power. My strength. Your surrender. My control. Your release. My Discipline, your need. Right where you are to be. This is where you fucking belong."

Once you have stolen the heart of a witch, the entire world shall be yours. Once a female vampire loves you, she'll always love you. I spoke softly but forceful…

"You were mine, the first night you approached me at my club and said, hello." I said to her as I touched her, "mine." And she looked at me and whispered as she nodded her head at me, "yours."

Powerful bond is, incomparable, and very unbreakable, no need to remind her, she knows where she belongs. And she belongs to me forever.

***

Suddenly, I rose up from the bed, "ughh!" cold sweats, and I was out of breath, and I heard a voice next to me. The voice was soft, it was gentle, it was a most precious voice...

"Daddy, what's wrong?" The woman turned on the light. It was Precious, but wait, what the fuck was Precious doing next to me? "Daddy, why are you staring at me like that? Did I do something wrong? You look like you've seen a ghost?" She said. I was sweating, "Precious? Is that really you? But, you're dead, shit, am I still dreaming now?" She shook her head, "no. I am not dead, I am right here my dear Daddy." I touched her face, her arms, her legs, her thighs, her hair and she was as real as can be. "But...I watched you die." I then said to her. "Wait, but we were attacked in the park by a female vampire, I went to your funeral, you came to me as a spirit to help me kill that same female bitch vampire Alexandria, and then years past, I met this witch. The witch whom was trying to set me up and get me killed, and I was a vampire myself. I had these crazy incredible powers.

The witch then saved me from the sister of your ex-boyfriend, who was trying to kill me, on several occasions, because she thought I killed her brother. I had so many clubs that I owned, one in each of the five boroughs. Two out of state; one in Los Angeles and the other in Miami. And I owned a couple of casinos...."

She cut me off, "looks like Daddy had himself a crazy nightmare, but also a little dream, I know the clubs were always a thing you always wanted to obtain, however Daddy, it was just a dream."

I shook my head, "but Precious it felt so fucking real." She hugged me, "aww, let me massage you Daddy back to sleep, you are stressed out from this nightmare of yours."

I stared at the mirror that was behind Precious, and I was staring into my own reflection. "Daddy, it's okay, it was just a nightmare." She said softly. I then repeated what she was saying. "It was just a nightmare, it was just a nightmare, it was just a nightmare."

I said this over and over and over once again, while I stared into the mirror, as my chin was over Precious' shoulder. And then suddenly, my eyes turned yellow, and fangs in my mouth grew.

Perhaps, it was not a nightmare. I looked at Precious dead in her eyes, and my vampire self just came out, but she didn't budge, nor did she scream……

About the Author

Born and raised in New York, E.L Discipline is educating the masses on the true form of spiritual connections and knowledge. He is the author of The Seduction of Discipline, The Importance of Discipline, and Discipline's World. With his fourth book, The Immortality of Discipline, E.L Discipline has now stepped into the realm of paranormal horror, giving readers a thrilling experience, they would never forget. His reputation for being known as the king of erotica is widely spreading and is changing the way we view relationships forever. His tenacity as an entrepreneur has caused him to develop a number of projects. From an eclectic Model, to marketing and social media advertising. His knowledge has reached towards network marketing and working with small business owners and celebrities, in new and upcoming promotions.

Also, as a certified fitness trainer, he mentors and teaches about endurance not only in the body, but the mind as well. His will to dominate has pushed him to master a variety of enterprises. His books are creating ripples everywhere, and his education speaks volumes. His goal is clear, as he has one main purpose in mind: To change the world, one reader at a time.

Photo by: Tina Vasquez, New Jersey.

www.ingramcontent.com/pod-product-compliance
Lightning Source LLC
Chambersburg PA
CBHW031144050726
47495CB00018B/813